SPOTIFY PLAYLIST

SPOTIFY PLAYLIST

all the good girls go to hell – Billie Ellish

Vigilante Shit – Taylor Swift

Violent – Carolesdaughter

Murder Party – NOT THE MAIN CHARACTER

killing boys – Halsey

I'm So Sick – Flyleaf

Her – Megan Thee Stallion

Montero   Lil Nas X

Play with Fire – Sam Tinnesz, Yacht Money

Chop Suey! – System Of A Down

Hate Me – Ellie Goulding, Juice WRLD

Erase Me – Kid Cudi

Miss YOU! – CORPSE

The Perfect Girl – Mareux

Judas – Lady Gaga

Me and the Devil – Soap&skin

Beggin' – Måneskin

Take Me to Church – Hozier

Love Like Mine – Stela Cole

THE DEATH OF PEACE OF MIND – Bad Omens

Still into You – Paramore

Centuries – Fall Out Boy

Heaven – Julia Michaels

DEDICATION

To the good girls who love to be bad.

P.S. *Justin 1 (Justin 2, you're safe for now). I was too young for you, and you really need to trim your beard, jfc.*

PREVIOUSLY ON THE CHARMING SERIES....

Thank you for picking up Charming the Devil. For a content warning, please visit my website. www.authorsarahblue.com

Charming the Devil starts in the past, before to the events of Charming Your Dad. Eventually, the story meets up to modern day—the same timeline in Charming Your Dad.

If you haven't read Charming Your Dad, it is advised to read first. However, this can be read as a standalone. If daddy isn't your thing, or you have the brain of a goldfish, like me, here is a little refresher of what happened in Charming Your Dad:

Our favorite witch-demon, Blair, was on a mission to make her ex's life miserable and seek revenge against her coven. In the process of her revenge, she falls in love with Dax, one of Lucifer's key demons, who also happens to be her ex-boyfriend's dad. Along the way, they are hunting the same enemy, a demon who is possessing people and leaving a massive body count in their wake. As the mystery unfolds, it comes to life that Blair is the daughter of Lucifer himself and the demon who was possessing people is her half-sister, Mara. It's not a mystery to those who live in the Manor that Lucifer is with his assistant Lilith... but where and how long ago does that love story begin...

PROLOGUE

Lilith
Age 19

Hallowsdeep is basically the taint of the tri-state area. Yet, I find myself here at a ridiculous house party... on Halloween of all days. I can't lie and say I don't have a morbid curiosity about the obscure town, but coming here on Halloween wasn't my idea. It was my sister's—my twin—Diana. I sure as fuck wasn't going to let her come here by herself. It's not safe, and Diana can be so naive sometimes.

Even if it means that I have to sit here and listen to MMMBop while watching her sit on the campus asshole's lap. It's what a good sister should do, and it doesn't hurt that the party is being held at a mansion that I'm growing more and more curious about each time I look around. I stare at an old portrait for a moment before my gaze sweeps back to my sister.

Diana looks pretty tonight, wearing a pink skirt and top with the butterfly wings that she made by hand, sitting gently on her back. We might be twins, but tonight I've dressed like a character from *Men in Black*. It goes above most of the party-goers' heads. I'm just a girl in an awkwardly large suit that I dug out of my dad's old things.

I cross my legs, sitting in an oversized chair in the corner and watch. It's what I do best. Diana is the bubbly one, the one with all the friends and the budding social life. It's not that I don't know how to talk to people or that I dislike people... well, I do dislike *a lot* of people. It's just that something has always felt off. Like I don't belong.

And not in a socially awkward way. In a way that makes my skin itch and has me wanting more than this mediocre life of frat parties and white picket fences. It's not that I think I'm better than most people, I just know there's more to my life than a white picket fence and some stale American dream. I'm not sure what my destiny is, but I know it's got to be more than *this*.

God, I sound like an asshole, and maybe I am. I can live with that.

While my purpose in life hasn't been given to me by some burning bush or written out for me in the stars, I know that I have one. I shake off my nearly narcissistic train of thought as I watch Diana. Right now, my purpose is to make sure she gets home safe and doesn't do anything she'll regret later. She snuggles deeper onto Tyler's lap, and it makes me want to vomit.

He's a known player throughout campus, and my sister seems to think she can change him or that she'll be *the one* to make him settle down. Men like him can't be changed. I think they're born defective. Mix that with a life of privilege, where mommy and daddy get them out of every situation, and it leads to them being an insufferable douche.

He drapes his hand on her hip as he speaks to her, and I do my best to stay put and just watch.

"Wanna dance?" he asks her.

"Sure," she replies, grinning happily while shooting me a look that screams *please stop staring at me and being a freak.*

They dance together, and it's gross to watch her touch him, so I make my way to get a drink. The guy who owns the place, Doug, is standing next to the keg.

He looks me up and down before smiling wide; it's creepy. It looks like he's about to turn around and try talking to me again. So I quickly turn away and make my way down a hallway in the opposite direction of the dance floor.

The mansion is odd, to say the least, like it was built in the early forties and hasn't changed much since. The floors look to be original, but that's not the most interesting thing about the house. It's the items in the home. As I walk through the corridor, the bass of the music quiets while I snoop through dear-old-Doug's house.

Old art lines the walls, easily dating back to the Renaissance era. Every six feet, there is a pedestal with a different artifact. Some are covered by glass, like the book I'm currently standing in front of. The language is one I don't recognize, and the pages are worn, having yellowed over time. I shrug my shoulders, walking to the next piece. It's a decanter of some sort, and it looks ancient. *Who in their right mind would invite all of these people here when they have so much interesting—and very stealable—stuff?* I pass by a few pieces of jewelry in protective glass cases as I reach the door at the end of the hall.

It feels like something behind the door is calling to me. It's unlike anything I've ever felt. Like a dark pull gripping me around my heart, and it tugs at me relentlessly. I can't stop myself from grasping the crystal doorknob, turning the handle, and walking into the room.

The door creaks loudly with my entry, but no alarms go off. As I look around, it's obvious that it's an arms room. Swords, knives, daggers, and other sharp weapons line the walls, along with the trays laid out on the three tables inside this small room.

I glance at all the different weapons. Some of them look so old I wonder how much they're worth and what I could sell them for. I shake the thought out of my head when I calculate the possibility of getting caught. I need to be smart about this.

My hands glide against the wooden edge of the table when the glint of a dagger draws my attention, and I stop dead in my tracks. The hilt is black with roses chiseled into it. The blade doesn't look particularly sharp, but something about it screams 'danger'. When my finger touches the cool metal, it's as if something powerful shoots through me. A dark deep strength I've never felt before touches every nerve, forcing me to wrap my hand around the handle and fully examine the dagger.

The way it feels against my skin is indescribable, like this dagger is meant to be mine. It feels warm under my palm. Weird thoughts creep into my mind about all of the things I've wanted to do but haven't acted on. I attempt to put the dagger down, but it's like my body is acting of its own accord. My fist is unrelenting as my grip unintentionally tightens. I swear it's like I've been reunited with a parted item; that this dagger was always mine, but now we're reconnected. I know I said I was going to be smart about not stealing anything tonight, but... *fuck it!*

I take it, tucking it in the waist of my black slacks as I leave the room.

I walk back to the party, worried that someone will know I stole something. I should get Diana and get the fuck out of here as soon as possible. I have to push people out of the way as *The Sign* by Ace of Base blasts throughout the expensive mansion. It feels poetic in a sense as the dagger warms my hip. It felt like a sign, like a blaring neon sign saying *we've found each other at last.*

"Woah, where's the fire?" a masculine voice asks as a hand cups my shoulder. I hold back a shiver, my instincts immediately firing off that the touch is unwanted. I pull the sunglasses that go along with my costume, which have been sitting on top of my head, down to cover my eyes. I can not get caught stealing what I'm sure is a priceless antique.

I look up at the guy, who gives me another one of those creepy grins. "I'm Doug Cummings, this is my house."

"Oh, hi. Sorry, just looking for my sister."

"Men in Black, right?" he says, ignoring the fact that I said I was looking for my sister.

"Yeah. My sister is dressed like a butterfly," I say sweetly. I'm great at mimicking my sister and how she speaks to people. It makes people underestimate me, and that's how I always want to be seen.

He rubs at his chin in thought. Somehow Doug looks thirty-seven at the ripe age of twenty. I can't imagine what he'll look like thirty years from now. "Haven't seen any butterflies." He invades my space, stepping a little too close. He smells like stale beer and cologne so thick that it should be illegal.

"Excuse me," I reply, trying to duck under his arm. I swear I feel the dagger heat at my hip, but I ignore it. The last thing I need is for this guy to know I stole from him. *What if he touches my hip and feels it?*

He grips my arm, and for a serious moment, I think about chopping it off by the wrist. Literally, a vision of me using the dagger to slice his encroaching hand right off flashes through my mind. I have to hide my smile from Doug, so he doesn't get the impression that his touch is warranted. *What is it with men thinking they have the right to touch a woman without their permission?*

"Don't you want to stay, get to know each other? I've got more fun stuff if that's what you're into."

I really want to punch him in the dick and tell him I hope one day a woman shows him what his worth is. But instead, I smile and shake my head. "Maybe, if I find my sister first."

His sleazy grin widens, and you can just tell that Doug is the subject of generational wealth and privilege. It's written in the way he holds himself. It's even more obvious how he was stupid enough to hold a party in his family home filled to the brim with expensive shit—shit that could turn a profit.

Suddenly a bright pink butterfly runs into me, her cheeks stained pink. She's clearly been crying.

"Diana?" I ask with a slight hint of panic while holding onto her forearms as she falls apart.

"He was dancing with Savannah Bell," she whines as she tries to hold herself together.

"Let's get out of here unless you want me to punch him in the throat for you?"

That garners a slight smile from my sister, but she shakes her head no.

Doug looks pissed. Little does he know, not only did I get out of an encounter where I would have the disprivilege of his company, but I've also stolen one of the Cummings' family treasures. As we walk further and further from the house, I swear I can feel contentment flow through me. The dagger warms my skin like it's excited to be taken away from this place.

I can tell Diana had a drink or two as she stumbles in her shoes.

"You can say it, say you told me so."

"That's not what I want to say, Diana."

"I don't get it; how come I couldn't see what a jerk he was?"

I sigh as I help her get into the car on the passenger's side.

"You like to see the best in people; that's not a bad thing."

"But you don't?"

"No." I keep it simple, knowing that, without a doubt, most people's intentions are based in a selfish nature. As I look over at my innocent and endearing sister, I know that it's my job to take care of her and protect her from the evil in this world, even if it darkens my soul further.

CHAPTER ONE

LILITH

Two years later...

"Remember, your papers on Camus are due next Wednesday. Is finding happiness even in the darkest moments of our life an act of rebellion? Do you think he's blowing smoke up our ass? Are his ideologies actually possible in real life?" Professor Montague recites to the class. Sue me for taking one of his classes all four years of college. He's a silver fox who bends me over and fucks me the way I like—*mostly*.

I probably shouldn't have let him turn me into his dirty, little secret. He keeps promising me that once I graduate, we can go public, and I'm apparently deluded enough to believe him. Because I need something to feel alive—and what I want to do to feel alive is considered a felony—so fucking my professor will have to do. The thoughts that have been consuming me lately have gotten worrisome, but I lock them away. I do my best to fit in and sedate what feels like a beast lurking inside of me.

"Lilith, can I see you after class?" he asks, and I nod. I watch him in his beige slacks and rolled-up white shirt. He has wavey, dark blond hair and thick-rimmed glasses that give him that bangable professor look that I love so much. There's something about an older man that appeals to me. Maybe it's how many drunk college guys I've witnessed acting like complete neanderthals. Or maybe it has to do with wanting a man to be able to take control of me, for once. I'm always in my own head, and I just want the release of not constantly overthinking. Professor Montague almost gets me there.

I stay in my seat, taking longer to pack up as the other students leave the lecture hall. I look good today, more than good if I do say so myself. My thick, long blonde hair is in a high ponytail, and I wear a simple white blouse with a checkered navy skirt. I watch as Mr. Montague licks his finger to flip through a book. I really should start calling him Henry, but something about calling him professor does something for me.

"You wanted to see me, Mr. Montague," I ask, leaning my ass against the edge of his desk and spreading my legs slightly. He clears his throat and smiles at me.

"Sorry, sweetheart, I have to cancel tonight."

"Oh," I say, not letting the rejection show on my face. He was supposed to take me on a real date tonight. We were going to drive to North Point—a little town away from campus. But it was going to be a date with tablecloths and all. Anger bubbles up inside of me, and I force a smile on my face and nod. "We can reschedule?"

"I'd love that. My sister and her husband are coming into town unexpectedly."

Of course, he doesn't want them to meet his girlfriend, who is also his student. "Of course, I understand."

"I knew you would. That's what I like about you, Lilith. You're so mature," he compliments. His hand grazes my skirt and pushes it up as he kisses the side of my head. "You know if I could, I'd make it happen... right, honey?"

"No, I get it. We can go out to dinner another time. But do you have any time right now?" I ask, feeling a little pathetic, searching for his approval and wanting to get laid. Maybe I have some unresolved daddy issues. But I'm definitely not ready to dig into that concept right now.

"Sorry, Lilith. It will need to be next week. I do have these for you, though." He holds out a tin of chocolate chip cookies to me. It's cute that he bakes for me, it makes me feel special. I smile as I take the box. "See you on Monday," he says with a parting kiss to the side of my head.

I nod as he leaves the lecture hall, leaving me in the wake of his rejection. I'm supposed to know better, know when a man is using me. But Mr. Montague is my secret; Diana doesn't even know about him, so I only have myself to wade through the shame with. I have no outlet to work through how manipulated I feel. I stand up straight, clutching my secret cookies against my chest. I'm supposed to be better than this.

Maybe since I have nothing to do tonight, Diana will want to go see a movie or get out of the house. I feel like my relationship with Diana has been on the back-burner lately, with both of us being so busy with our own lives. I suppose it was going to happen eventually. There's a point when you grow up and stop leaning on your sister for everything. We've spent our whole lives together; my role was to protect her, and her role was to make me feel normal. I can't help but feel with this drift between us, those two things are going to fall through the cracks.

I shake off the feeling of not needing to protect Diana like I used to. It's a rough feeling when you feel like you're not doing anything right. I'm clearly not girlfriend material to Henry, and I've been slacking in the sister department. At least my grades in school are decent, which probably has more to do with me wanting to leave this cesspool of a campus than wanting to start a career and being an actual adult.

I think about everything Henry said as I walk through campus to my apartment. This is the first time that he's ever mentioned having a sister, and I guess it's not a huge shock. Looking back at our conversations, they were all pretty superficial. We fuck at school, his car, and sometimes my place. I feel like an idiot as I make my way home. Was I so blinded by a decent dick that I didn't see the warning signs? Was I so desperate for authoritative attention that I've become this sex-crazed moron?

Our apartment isn't anything special, but they allow pets, not that I'm paying that pet deposit. The door creaks as I open it and shut it behind me. Tossing my bag on the floor, I look around the small living space.

Otis greets me by rubbing his small black body against my legs as I enter the foyer. I crouch down to pet along his spine, and he chirps at me as he walks away. Maybe I should get another kitten friend for him.

I sigh, mentally preparing myself to spill my guts to Diana. Maybe she'll have some good advice, or maybe she'll be my partner in crime on a spy mission to see what he's *actually* doing tonight. All my plans crumble when I see Diana curled into a ball on the couch. She has a glazed-over expression on her face, like she's completely zoned out.

"Diana?" I say her name, but she doesn't respond.

When I go and sit next to her, the blue eyes that look exactly like mine bore into me. I can tell she's lying when she sighs and shakes her head, saying, "Just really bad cramps."

"Diana, did something happen? Is something bothering you?"

She fakes a smile and shakes her head again. "No, just not feeling great," she answers, bushing off my concern.

Now is definitely not the time to talk about my drama with fucking my professor or my speculations about what's *really* going on tonight. I push her hair back and smile. "Want to rent a movie and just have a night in, like we used to?"

She grins and nods. "Get Clueless," she instructs as I grab the keys to head to the rental place. I nod my head and glance at her one last time. Something is definitely going on that she isn't telling me.

It seems like my twin and I might both be keeping secrets from one another.

When I get back from the store, it's like Diana is back to her old self; she isn't moping around and actually laughs at the right times during the movie. She falls asleep early, leaving me too much time on my hands to think and plot. My nightstand drawer pulses like a beacon, pulling me towards it, but I try to shake the feeling away.

I don't need it. Why would I need it?

But the pull is too strong, and I open the drawer and withdraw the dagger. It feels like it's been tugging at me incessantly every night when I crawl into bed. Like if I don't take it out of the drawer and touch it, I won't be able to sleep. It wants to be used, I know that much as my hand shakes around the dark hilt.

The pull isn't usually this heavy on my chest, but it feels like I won't be able to leave the house unless I bring it with me.

When I stole it two years ago, I thought maybe I'd sell it and make some money. But instead, I had a sheath made and now carry it around in my purse more often than not. I don't know why the call is so strong lately, but it doesn't hurt to be a protected woman anyways.

Knowing that Diana is content in her bed and that Otis is fed, I grab the keys to the Camry and drive out to Professor Montague's house. Has he ever taken me to his house? No. Do I know where he lives? Absolutely yes.

His home is nice, a two-story mid-century style home with a garden out front. The other times I've been by, I haven't seen another vehicle, which probably isn't surprising since he has a two-car garage. His windows are large, allowing me to see everything in his living room and kitchen. It's like looking into a fishbowl. A woman is bending over, taking out a tray of cookies, when he wraps his arms around her and kisses the side of her face. She places some of the previously baked cookies into a familiar tin and spins around to greet him with a kiss.

Cheating motherfucker.

He gave me cookies this other woman made for him? I feel like I'm going to be sick. I guess deep down, I should have known. Nothing ever good comes from being someone's dirty, little secret.

I suppose we were never official, but I did have expectations of some sort of loyalty to me. His promised words were ones of monogamy or at least of a potential relationship.

He's gentle with her, unlike the way he is with me. He's delicate as he cradles her face while kissing her. He smiles in between their kisses, and I wonder how come I didn't get that too. Instead, I got his rough side. Don't get me wrong, I fucking love the roughness, but as I watch them together, I realize that it wasn't me that he was cheating on, it was her.

Her hand caresses his cheek, and that's when the shimmering of her diamond ring sparkling in the light catches my attention.

He has a wife.

He wasn't meeting his sister, he couldn't go on a date with me because he has *a wife.*

She looks so sweet, a tiny little thing with short brown hair and big brown eyes. My stomach sinks as I think about how she would feel if she found out about our affair. I didn't dedicate myself to this man, but I still feel extremely hurt. If she knew, she would be devastated.

I find it interesting that he teaches philosophy as I ponder the thought of telling her or not. He teaches us all the time about the conundrums between right and wrong, and now he's at the center of my moral struggle. Is it better to live a lie and be happy or to know the truth and be devastated?

I'm not paying attention, and before I know it, I'm looking down to see my hand wrapped around the dark hilt of my dagger. It seems to center me as it heats my palm.

Maybe I can help her, she doesn't have to know everything. She can live in her blissful bubble full of lies while this lying piece of shit gets what he deserves.

With that possibility floating through my mind, I continue watching them enjoy their night in the living room. It's so domestic the way they interact as they watch a show and eat their dinner on the couch. *How can some men be so absolutely fucking foul?*

My anger only gets worse the longer I watch them. I feel nothing but pity and anger for his wife. She's an unknowing party, who deserves vengeance, just like I do. While I have the right to my anger, I also feel used, worthless, and most of all, unlovable. The woman he decided 'till-death-do-us-part with is completely unaware of the asshole she's living with.

That her husband goes off to work, giving younger women sweet promises while making them feel special and smart before he fucks them… and then what? Comes home and acts like a doting husband? Does he use me to get out the dark fantasies that his wife won't act on and then come home to her so he can give her his sweet side?

I always thought he was an attractive man, but as I look at him now, I see him for the hideous person he truly is. And I decide that he needs to pay.

A dark urge, the one I usually tamper down, is bubbling so close to the surface. I know I'll have to act on it. I can only imagine how good it will feel to finally give in to this feeling. To give the dagger what it wants and what I want. So, I wait.

I wait until his wife leaves the living room, and I see the bedroom lamp turn on. I track her movements as she puts lotion on her skin and opens a book, getting comfortable in their bed. In the meantime, professor Montague continues watching TV, his stance relaxed, like he doesn't have a care in the world. *Does the man even have a conscience?*

When his wife finally puts down her book and turns off the lamp, I wait about another fifteen minutes until I get out of the car to go knock on the door. It's ballsy, I know, but I won't be able to leave this house until I confront him, until he's dealt with.

I lightly tap on the door and take a step back on the mat that says 'Home Sweet Home'. When he opens the door, his jaw drops, and he quickly looks behind him before shutting the door and standing on the front step with me.

"Lilith, sweetheart. What are you doing here?"

I don't roll my eyes, I don't scoff, I don't let him know that I know everything. That he's a fucking creep and a user. The more I think about how disgusting of a man he is, the angrier I get. When I think about his unsuspecting wife and how she would feel knowing he cheated on her, I wonder how it compares to how I feel being used as his mistress.

"You're married," I state softly. My calmness has him shifting from foot to foot, telling me just how uncomfortable this makes him.

"Lilith, can we talk about this another time?" He uses his 'professor voice', the one filled with authority, as he tries to manipulate me, and I have to try to keep my temper in check.

"Are you worried your wife will find out now that I'm here?"

That's when his facade drops, and his hand shoots out, his fingers gripping around my chin tightly. I let him hold me there, letting him think that he has the advantage as he squeezes, digging his fingertips into the skin of my cheeks.

It's odd, you would think that at the moment where I'm being threatened, my heart would race and fear would lace every one of my nerve endings, but I'm eerily calm. I want him to think he's the stronger one out of the two of us, that he has complete control, and that I'm not a threat. *But I know better.*

"Listen here, you dumb-little bitch. I'm not about to let some co-ed pussy ruin everything I've worked for. So leave, now."

I can feel the metal of his wedding ring against my jaw, and I can't help the manic smile that takes over my face. He scoffs at me before pushing my face away with malice.

"Knew a bitch who liked it as rough as you was fucked up," he spits, turning around. His hand cups the doorknob, and something about the glint of his wedding ring triggers me.

I've had my hand on the hilt of my dagger the entire time as if it's the source of my courage to not back down; it's like it's driving me. I'm not sure what I plan on doing with the dagger. At least that's what I tell myself as I impulsively slice off his glittering ring finger, the digit separating from his hand. I thought there would be more like a small pop, but the cut is clean and precise.

I expected him to writhe in pain, to clutch his hand against his chest as his hand spurts blood.

That's not what happens, though.

His body instantaneously crumples to the ground, lifeless.

Like I stabbed him directly in the brain instead of just slicing off his finger. He doesn't even look like a *normal* dead body, not that I've seen many. But his veins are all black as his skin shrivels against his bones. He looks like someone who has been dead for months, not just moments.

"Holy fucking shit," I gasp, examining him before looking down at my dagger and then glancing back at the body. "What the actual fuck?" I nudge his body with the toe of my shoe, and that part of him starts to fall apart from the small touch alone. My eyes widen, but I don't panic. How... how did I do this by just trying to slice off his finger?

The obsidian hilt of my dagger glows, and I stare back down at Professor Montague's body. It's not fear that fills me or regret, it's satisfaction. While I didn't mean to kill him, and I have no fucking clue how I made this happen, I don't regret my actions. As I look down at him and think about his wife, I realize the world is a better place without people like him in it.

I glance at his severed finger one last time, a sick part of me wanting to grab it and put it in my pocket, but I'm not that fucking stupid. Instead, I turn on my heel and leisurely take my time walking back to my piece-of-shit Camry. I drive off quietly, wondering if you get an automatic A in a class if a professor dies.

LILITH

I wash the blood off of the dagger, and I guess I should be feel-ing... shocked, guilt, remorse? I just killed my boyfriend—the man I was sleeping with—my professor. His wife will probably open the front door to see his shriveled-up body lying on their front step.

I should feel bad, right?

But I feel calm, the most content I think I've ever felt. It felt good to use the dagger, to let that anger out, to give him what he deserves. I didn't mean to kill him; it's clear that this dagger is more than I thought it was. I swear the blade winks at me as soon as it's shiny and clean again. Its appetite sated—for now.

But am I?

I replay every moment of tonight in my mind. The way he looked at me with disgust, like I was beneath him, that he could use and speak to women any way he wanted to. And then he was nothing; he's a wrinkled gray prune on a welcome mat. I laugh at my own joke and shake my head. Maybe this was the *more* that I always thought I was capable of. This is my purpose, ridding the world of evil men who think they are above others.

I've had thoughts like that before. Thoughts of what it would be like to take someone's life, to have that power, to be the one who chooses. Of course, a moral code needs to be in place—mostly to keep the bloodlust in check. And maybe death wasn't an appropriate punishment for Professor Montague. But it doesn't matter when I think about how good it felt.

When I look down at the dagger, I realize that all this time, we were meant for each other. It's clearly something *other*, far more than a standard dagger. I've heard rumors of supernatural beings and objects. It's not a surprise that I found this dagger in Hallowsdeep, the place where things go bump in the night.

I know I'm crazy when I start speaking to the blade. "We're meant for each other, aren't we?"

The handle warms, which is clearly a yes. I smile at the gift in front of me; maybe the dagger only does what it did to Professor Montague if the person truly deserves it. But to test that theory would be fucked up and involves possibly killing someone who doesn't deserve it.

I hear a retching noise and put the blade back in the nightstand drawer. When I get to our shared bathroom, I find my sister throwing up into the toilet. She's on her knees, crying, so I gather her hair in my hand and rub her back.

"Diana, are you sick? What do you need?"

She just cries harder, throwing up again. She's inconsolable as I continue to rub her back. This is so unlike her that my concern skyrockets when she looks at me. Her expression lacks the usual warmth that it normally holds. My afterglow from the evening fades as worry for Diana takes over.

"What do you need?"

"I just need to go back to sleep," she says softly.

"Okay." I gently hoist her by the waist and take her back to her room, tucking her in before pulling her pink pastel blanket up to her chin. "You know you can tell me if something is wrong, right?"

She nods, her eyes collecting with tears.

"I'm okay, Lilith, really." She turns on her side, but I don't let her get away with it as I crawl behind her and throw my arm around her waist.

"Somethings bothering you, Diana. You know I'll always be on your side. I'll always help you with whatever you need." She sighs heavily and shakes her head.

"I just want to forget about it."

"Forget about what?" I ask, pushing some hair off her sweaty face.

"It's nothing, Lilith. I promise."

"Since when did we start keeping secrets from one another?" I ask.

She scoffs and shakes her head. "Good question," she retorts, and I sigh. "Just go to bed, Lilith." Tonight's events seem irrelevant as I wonder why Diana is pushing me away. I do as she requests and leave her room, even if I just want to stay and push more, to figure out what's bothering her and how I can help her fix it. Diana is the most important person to me. We might not have freaky telepathic twin abilities, but our bond is strong. At least, I thought it was.

When I get to my bed, I struggle to fall asleep. A combination of the dagger in my drawer making demands and a lingering fear of Diana no longer needing me keeps me awake.

The entire campus is talking about Professor Montague. The news isn't giving much information, but it's obvious that detectives are baffled. Rightfully so, the man looks like he's been dead for months, and he has no fatal wounds, just a missing finger. I read the news article further, where they interview his wife. Her name is Debra, and her quote is what makes me feel a small morsel of guilt. *"My husband didn't deserve this. He's a good man, I have no idea who would ever want to harm him."*

I sigh and fold the paper as I look around at the other students reading the same article, speculating about what happened to our dear professor. When I look to my left, I'm greeted by a woman who is observing me in a way that leans towards uncomfortable.

She's just as tall as me, black hair pinned back into a ponytail. She's impeccably dressed and has eyeliner sharply drawn over her eyes. Her brown gaze looks me up and down before she smiles.

"What do you think of all of this professor drama?" she asks as she takes a seat next to me, her skirt rising, showing off her long legs and expensive boots.

"Wondering if I'm going to get an A in his class now," I reply back, and the woman grins at me. She holds out her hand.

"Kas," she says with a smirk on her lips. When our hands touch, I tilt my head, wondering if I've ever met her before. But surely I would remember anyone who looked like this woman. She looks like a runway model, who just strolled into campus. Surely, if she went to school here, I would have noticed her before.

"Lilith." She hums in approval as she crosses her legs and taps her thigh. "You know, I saw the detectives there this morning."

My interest was already piqued, and I can't stop myself as I look at her and raise an eyebrow. "And?"

"Strangest fucking thing I've ever seen. Man looked like a dried-up ball sack." She clicks her tongue. "My money's on the wife. She didn't even shed a tear—well, not a *real* tear—not while I was there."

"How can you tell?" I ask.

"She was crying with no tears, she didn't give a fuck that the man was dead."

"Makes sense," I respond, my guilt from earlier ebbing away, glad that I could do Debra a solid by taking her husband out. Maybe she can find someone new and faithful to live in that big house they shared together.

"I'm sure he deserved it."

"Hmm," I say, acting like I'm reading through my notes for my political science class.

Kas takes out a lollipop and licks it in a ridiculously seductive way. I watch as multiple men on campus almost trip over themselves to watch her.

"Whoever did it, the work was inspired." I stare over at the beautiful woman as she stands up, lollipop still in her mouth as she smirks. "See you around, Lilith."

"Yeah, see ya."

Well, that was fucking weird. Kas walks away, people parting for her like she's royalty as she makes her way through campus, and I tilt my head, wondering what the hell just happened. There's no way she knows who I am or what I did. But to hear that my work is inspired... no, *we* will not get a big ego over our first kill.

Great, now I'm talking about me and the dagger as if we're two people sharing one body.

I grab my book bag and leave the fountain. As I walk to class, I spot my sister, her head downcast, and Tyler's arm is on the wall boxing her in. I hide myself behind a corner as I listen.

"Come on, Diana, you wanted it."

"No, Tyler, I didn't. I told you no."

"You know how it is, yes means no, no means yes. It can be very confusing."

I hear my sister sniffle, and my hand clenches around the strap of my bag.

"No. It meant no, and you didn't listen. It hurt Tyler, it didn't feel good."

"That's because you're so tight. It won't hurt so bad next time."

"There won't be a next time. Stay away from me."

She turns to walk away, but he grabs my sister's arm, looks around, and yanks her back to him roughly. "Listen to me, you tell anyone what happened, and I'll destroy you, Diana. It's all recorded." He holds up a small cassette and then puts it in his pocket. I can see the tears my sister is holding back.

"I won't tell anyone. Please just leave me alone."

He grabs her chin, and it reminds me so much of last night. It's like my nerve endings have been rewired, making the only thing I can think about is how I'm going to kill Tyler, and if there is any way the dagger will enable me to make it as painful as possible.

Tyler steps away from my sister, grinning at her as he turns away. Every ounce of me wants to go to Diana right now, hold her tight and tell her everything will be alright. But she can't know that I heard. Sometimes I feel like I'm Diana's guardian angel, but maybe more of a reaper. Because after what I heard, I'm ready to collect the soul that dared to hurt the person who means the most to me.

Tyler lives at the Sigma Phi Epsilon house, which is extremely inconvenient, considering that it's nestled in the heart of campus living. It's not exactly the best place to carry out a murder. Things have certainly escalated for me this past week, but there's a job to do, so I'm not really trying to ponder my moral compass at the moment.

I walked here, deciding that having my car would probably be a bad idea when it comes to carrying out a murder. The dagger is safely pressed against my hip as I wait. For what—I'm not even sure. But I know there's no way I can walk into that frat house without getting caught.

I look down at my outfit and scoff. I dressed like my sister, thinking that Tyler is such an idiot that he won't be able to tell the difference. Even so, I can't just waltz in there, stab him, and leave with no witnesses.

So I wait. It appears that I've gotten really patient lately, and I'm proud of myself for developing this new trait. Then there's the whole new-taste-for-murder, but right now, we're just thinking about the positives.

It's then that Tyler leaves the building with another frat member, I don't know his name, but they bump fists, and Tyler walks down this way. The street lights are on, but it's still dark enough that I'm not easily noticeable. He lights up a cigarette and smokes as he walks down the street. The rosy ember of the cigarette lights his face as he puffs out a cloud of smoke into the air. I straighten my skirt and follow him down the street.

"Tyler," I say, keeping my voice peppy like Diana's.

He looks to his left, a menacing smile taking over his face, and I have to hold back a gag. Most people would find Tyler attractive; he's tall, has curly brown hair, and sharp cheekbones. But the way the butt of his cigarette lights up his face, shows me the demon that he truly is.

"Diana, I knew you'd be back."

"You were right. I thought maybe we could go somewhere private."

He wraps his hand in my ponytail, and I do my best not to stab him right away. His breath is ashy and harsh as he speaks to me.

"Frat house is back that way."

"Or maybe somewhere that's private but not really?" I say sweetly.

"Never thought you'd be an exhibitionist. But yeah." He drags me down the first alleyway we pass, between the two frat houses, and it's dark and ominous. Tyler's grip is firm on my hip as he trails kisses up and down my throat. I feel repulsed by his touch, and all I can think about is how Diana must have felt. I heard a fraction of their conversation, but it's clear Diana didn't want him to do what he did. He needs to pay.

"Knew you'd be back for more," he mutters cockily. My dagger is nearly blazing on the other side of my hip as he kisses me again. It's become clear that this weapon and I are connected in a way I still haven't wrapped my mind around.

"Maybe we can slow down," I suggest as his teeth drag along my throat.

"Oh, come on, Diana. You can't come to me dressed like this." He tugs on the hem of the pink skirt. "And tell me you aren't asking for it. You said you wanted to go somewhere private."

"Did I say no last time?" I ask, just wanting confirmation.

"These lips," he pauses to drag a thumb across my bottom lip, and it takes every ounce of restraint I have not to bite his finger off. "Might have said no, but..." He trails off, his hand grabbing my pussy and cupping it before he taunts me with, "These ones were begging for it."

Faster than either of us could blink, my hand grips the handle, and I pull the dagger from my waistband, testing a theory. I slash his forearm, causing him to wince.

"Diana, what the fuck?!"

I watch as crimson pools down his arm, flowing wildly as it drips against the dirty, dark pavement.

"Huh." *Not dead, interesting.*

He shoves me with his non-sliced hand. "Bitch, what are you doing?"

I grin at him, and that must be when recognition hits. Of course, he knows Diana has a twin sister.

I slash his skin again, fascinated with the blood speckling his skin. I'm riveted by how cleanly the blade slices him. He growls and pushes me so hard that my head bounces against the brick of the house. I wince, and my fury rises as his hands grip around my throat in a not-fun way. I wanted to toy with him more, slash his skin up and make him bleed, but it seems like I don't have a choice.

"Are you fucking crazy? Why are you doing this?" he shouts in my face.

Tyler focuses too much on trying to choke me. If he weren't closing my air supply completely, I would roll my eyes and call him an idiot. I spent a lot of time at my dad's self-defense studio growing up, I know how to protect myself. His body is close enough to mine that when I lift my right hand, I stab him right in the kidney.

This time I get to watch his face. His expression falls flat as his skin grays, and he crumples to the ground. He nearly takes me with him since his hands were still on my throat, but they lose their grip, shriveling as he falls.

I scoff as I look at how pathetic he looks now. "Dead men don't rape," I say, responding to his question, though he can't hear me. I fix my skirt and make sure to stick to the shadows as I walk home, knowing that there are specks of Tyler's blood on my skin. I grin the whole way home, a sense of pride flowing through me.

Another man meets his maker at the hands of a vengeful woman. It's so poetic and perfect that I can't stop grinning, knowing that Tyler won't be the last.

CHAPTER THREE

LUCIFER

I'm sitting in yet another meeting featuring yet another incompetent demon. It seems this cycle never ends. I'm selective of whom I turn into a full-fledged demon, ones who are allowed to leave our realm and have the benefits of corporeal bodies. It seems that no matter how I try, finding loyal, competent demons is nearly impossible.

I only have a handful of demons that I trust, who have earned their own space at my manor and are provided more luxuries than others. But it takes decades, centuries, and sometimes longer to earn those positions. My most trusted right-hand man is Toth, who is sitting next to me, looking just as fucking bored as we both stare at Autumn. She's a very bland-looking demon. She isn't ugly, but she isn't someone you would do a double take of. Her hair is slightly frizzy like no one told her she's a demon and could put more work into her appearance. Her clothes are plain and meet the trend of the human world, but not in a good way.

She fucked up such an easy task that in my irritation, I'd rather just destroy her soul. But the fact of the matter is that I need as many demons as possible right now. Heaven, as always, is looking for a reason to start shit.

"We told you to collect the souls, not bring them here," Toth says plainly. Toth was a commander of the Battle of Chach. His bloodlust, command, and ability to keep his cool are some things that spoke to me, and I made him a demon only a month after his arrival in Hell. His loyalty is fierce, and he takes a lot of this bullshit off my plate.

"I thought it would be helpful. I know we're low on reapers."

I stand, not liking this demon, who has only been a demon for a few decades, pointing out the faults of my operation. I can't even remember why I turned her when I look back at her. She's not particularly smart or gifted. Then I think back to the sixties and how desperately I was in need of demons, and it all makes sense.

When I speak, Autumn trembles. I lean over the desk, knowing that my height and appearance are menacing as I stare her down. "It is none of your concern how many reapers we have; it is their job to bring the souls to Hell, not yours. Did you know you fractured two of the souls when you portaled here?"

"Fr—fractured?" she shudders.

"They were important souls to me, bargained for souls. Ones that had potential to be demons instead of just living a life of despair in this realm."

"I'm sorry, my lord," she says, bowing her head. I roll my eyes, done with this meeting and all the bullshit I have to deal with on a daily basis. I don't mind being in charge, I quite like people fearing me and listening to what I tell them to do. It's just gotten so mundane. I nearly wish the angels would start a war with me just to switch up the routine.

Suddenly there's a soft knocking from the doorway, looking up, I see Kas. When Autumn swings her gaze to her, I see the hatred she has for Kas, and it makes me smile. I look back at Kas, one of the few demons I find truly competent. I gifted her and others with apartments that aren't complete shitholes. Maybe they can work their way up to living in the manor, but most live on Earth for the majority of the time anyway.

"Sir," she says, and I look up at her incredulously.

"Kasdeya?" I reply, using her full name, knowing she hates it. She has great control of her facial expressions and hides her irritation as she responds.

"I think I have something you'd like to see."

Toth nods, glaring back at Autumn. "A day with Elvor," I command, and Autumn shivers. Toth grins as he grabs her by the upper arm and portals them to the portion of Hell no one wants to see. The place where you're gifted with an endless lifetime of torture.

"How benevolent of you," Kas comments as we leave the meeting room and walk through the gardens.

"Where are we going?" I ask, not in the mood for games.

"To see the new arrivals, of course."

Kasdeya is nearly as old as me and has been in Hell forever. I always keep her at an arm's length, mostly because of her sarcasm and her connections to other realms. I never truly know if I can trust her, even if after a millenia she hasn't let me down.

"Because?"

"Fuck's sake, can't a demon just surprise the devil for once?"

"Anytime a demon surprises me, it's usually done by being a fucking disappointment."

"Not this time," she replies, opening the gate to new arrivals. This is where the souls get sorted. They go straight to the pit if their lives deemed them worthy of torture, or they go to general population where life goes on; it's not physical torture, but it's not great either. The dead who prove their worth to me in Hell are the ones that I bestow the blessing of becoming a demon.

"There's actually a new one today," she grins as she leads me to a side room. A man in his forties looks around, clutching his hand. He looks to be missing his ring finger.

"Where am I?" he asks. I'm sure it's confusing since I made the admittance area stark white. I get a little thrill when people think they've made it to Heaven and not Hell.

"Hell, silly," Kas answers, conjuring two chairs for us to sit. "Mind telling the big boss how you got here?" She points her thumb in my direction, and I remember why I can only take her in small doses.

"My student," he says, looking between us, and I can taste the lie coming from his lips. "She came to my home and chopped off my finger. I'm not sure how that killed me."

I glance at Kas, surely it can't be.

"Thank you for your time; you should be sorted shortly."

Kas stands without touching me. I fucking hate being touched, and I appreciate her giving me space as she escorts me down the white corridor to the next door. She grins up at me, but I keep my face stoic.

"Kas, what is the meaning of this?"

Without saying a word, she swings open the door to reveal a college-aged man blinking questionably at us. His arms are cut, and I assume that he's killed himself until I see the stab wound on his side. I tilt my head and wonder if he bled out.

"What the fuck did she do to me?" he asks Kas, who has a feral grin on her face.

"Would you mind raising your shirt so we can see your wound?"

"The fuck?"

I arch my eyebrow at him, taking multiple steps forward. My height is always menacing, and I know even new souls can sense my power. As I approach him, he swallows, lifting his shirt and showing me the wound. When I see the gray and black veins protruding from the wound, my mouth opens.

"Who did this to you?"

"Her fucking sister... I can't remember her name. It's like an old lady's name."

"Thank you for your time; you will be sorted shortly," Kas informs him as she shuts the door behind us, and we walk back into the hallway.

I go to open my mouth, but Kas shakes her head. "Not here, somewhere private."

I groan as I touch her sleeve and portal us to the study in my mansion. I'm impatient as I round the desk and sit in my high back chair, pouring whiskey into a glass and taking a sip.

"It can't be," I state, and Kas shakes her head.

"I saw the first one's body in the human realm. It definitely is."

"But it can only be used by—" I stop my train of thought and glance over at Kas. "How much do you know?"

"You forget how old I am," she says. I nod my head, remembering when the dagger was forged at my expense. I was being toyed with, I never imagined that the prophecy would come true.

"Her name?" I ask softly, knowing that this is a secret I need Kas to keep. The idea of history repeating itself makes my stomach sink. *What if she doesn't make it to Hell, what if I'm being tricked?*

"Her name is Lilith. She's very pretty in a psychopathic way," she says, grinning.

I rub my temples. She's on earth, alive. She could be there for decades, and I'll just be here waiting.

"Is she young?" I ask, thinking about the college student she murdered.

"Senior in college."

"You've been following her?" I ask, arching an eyebrow.

"You think I'd show you what I found without all the facts?"

"Do you know why she chose them? And so close together?" I shake my head, thinking about the recklessness of it, of getting caught. She can't come here until she dies; it's part of the power of the dagger. Even if I wanted to go to Earth and collect her, I couldn't.

"Definitely think she was fucking the professor." A growl rumbles low in my throat over this woman I haven't seen. I can't help but smirk while I think of the vicious little creature she must be. She killed two men in two days. *She's come back to me stronger*, is all I can think.

"Any chance of her getting caught?"

"She's pretty unsuspecting. Plus, you know how humans love to refuse the idea of anything supernatural. They probably don't know where to start."

I groan when I think about what else is possibly on Earth. The dagger has been activated; the person destined to be mine is out there, and I've possibly ruined it with my recent actions.

"And anything else to report from Earth?" I ask.

"No Devil spawns as far as I can tell." I let out a breath. I was hoping that I could create halflings on earth and make demons who were loyal. While I wanted that program to succeed previously, now all I can hope is that it didn't. There's something far more precious waiting for me in the human realm currently.

"Good," I tell her. "Keep an eye on her, on Lilith," I instruct, and it's the first time I've spoken her name. It tastes sweet on my tongue, and for the first time in a long time, I feel excitement.

Kas clears her throat. "Any word on Michael?" she throws in, always so nervous when it comes to him. I've known Kas for far too long, and the one person she fears above all, even me, is Michael.

"No sign of him since he escaped."

She nods, though I can tell she's tense.

"I'll keep an eye on her, make sure she doesn't get too out of hand."

"Seems she has a taste for killing." I can't help the small smile that takes over my face, and Kas looks at me like I've grown five heads.

"Don't worry, I'll take care of your—"

"Thank you, you're dismissed."

Kas scoffs but leaves nonetheless. My head falls back against my chair, and everything that Kas has said sinks in. *How didn't I feel it?* Perhaps I did, but time and self-loathing hardened me to the point that I didn't feel her touching the dagger for the first time.

I dream of a tall blonde goddess that night, and all I can think about is how I wish time and fate would bring us together sooner.

CHAPTER FOUR

LILITH

D iana has the news blasting on the TV as I make breakfast and
listen to the broadcast. The news reporter is an older man
who looks to be in his fifties, and he's walking around our campus
as he interviews students.

"This is sophomore, Jessie Klem." He looks over at a student I
don't recognize. "In a span of two days, both a beloved professor
and a student in a popular fraternity have been found dead in the
most peculiar way. Is there fear or any speculation floating around
campus?"

Jessie looks like she has two hundred plants hiding in her dorm
room and has definitely smoked copious amounts of weed today.
She shakes her head as she grabs the microphone. "Tyler was popular
for taking advantage of girls, and Professor Montague slept with
multiple students. As a woman, honestly, this is the safest I've felt
on campus."

The reporter clears his throat, and I attempt to hide my smile
behind my coffee cup. Maybe I should reach out to her and see if
there are any other men who have done her wrong recently. Diana

is completely fascinated by the news story, and I don't want to force her to tell me what happened; that's up to her.

The reporter turns to address a different student. I recognize him as the guy that left the frat house with Tyler. "I'm with Dirk Samuels," the reporter says, and I snap my fingers, now remembering his name. My sister turns around and gives me a puzzled look before turning back to the TV. "Dirk, is it true you were the last person to see Tyler alive?"

"Yeah, man. He was just going out for a smoke and maybe to hit up a party, and now he's dead."

"Do you fear for your life, for your safety on this campus?"

"How can I not? Tyler was a good guy, just smoking a cigarette, and he was murdered. This isn't a safe place. That's like the exact opposite of safe, man."

My grin is huge as his words sink in. I love hearing the differences between the two interviews. How Jessie feels safer and how a man like Dirk is now scared.

They should be.

The power trip I'm spiraling down is steep. I know my ego is huge, and this vigilante shit can only end with me dying or behind bars. But fuck, if the thrill isn't worth it.

Diana points the clicker at the TV and turns it off with a deep sigh. I'm not sure what her reaction is going to be, but when I circle the couch and see a blank stare on her face, I start to worry. Otis jumps on my lap, and I stroke his fur as he purs.

"I can't believe it," she says softly, pulling the pink pillow against her chest. "I can't believe he's dead."

"Did you still like him?" I ask softly, petting Otis and looking down at him.

"No, but he didn't deserve to die." I swallow thickly but don't say anything. Diana shakes her head back and forth, getting some idea out of her head. "I could use a drink, do you want to go out tonight?" The request is odd, but however Diana needs to handle this, I'll be right alongside her.

"What did you have in mind?"

"There's some cool bars on Main Street. We've hardly gone out since we turned twenty-one. Plus, I'd rather it just be us." She gives me a small smile, and I hope that this is the start of her feeling like herself again. Tyler is gone; she can feel safe now, live her life how she wants because I'll always be there to protect her. And with Professor Montague out of the way, it's time for us to reconnect. No more distractions, just some simple twin bonding.

"Let's do it," I agree, giving her hand a squeeze. She squeezes back and gives me a look that I can't decipher. Under any other circumstance, I would have assumed she knows what I've done. But if she truly knew, she'd never be able to look at me again.

"You're the best," she says, leaning over the cushions to give me a huge hug. I wrap my arms around her and let out a content sigh. At this moment, I feel more whole than I ever have in my entire life. More me than I ever could have imagined.

"Two shots of tequila, please!" Diana yells over the bar while leaning over to wave down the bartender. We're both wearing jeans, and I'm thankful as she leans as far over as possible. The bartender smiles at her and acknowledges we need a refill. It's our third of the night, and I can definitely feel it already. I know Diana is feeling it as well, with the glazed-over look in her eyes.

The bar is... eclectic. The tabletop, along with the floor is sticky, and I'm shocked that Diana picked this place. The people are... interesting. The bartender is extremely attractive; honestly, most everyone in the place is beautiful. Men who are taller than I'm used to seeing and women who could be cover models. I can't help but feel like I'm being watched. As I look around at the patrons, it doesn't seem like anyone in particular is looking at me. I shake off the feeling and look over at Diana.

"What made you want to come here?" I ask as the bartender pours our shots and slides over the salt and limes. We both take our shots and wince as the sharp liquor slides down our throats.

"I heard about it from Shannon, a girl from my women's studies class. She said she met a really hot guy here once." I arch my eyebrow at my sister.

"So what, you're on the prowl?" I joke with a laugh.

"No, but it would be nice to flirt with someone." I nod my head in understanding, sometimes it's nice to have someone tell you that you're interesting and attractive.

"Anyone look appealing to you?"

She grins and points with her head to the corner of the room. To a man in his mid-twenties, pale, dark hair; he's attractive, and he's basically staring at Diana.

I'm leery, though, and I grab Diana's arm softly. "You just need to be careful. You don't know him."

She squints her eyes at me, the tequila hitting her more than it's hitting me. "You always think you know everything," she snarls.

I'm taken aback and look at her skeptically. "I just wouldn't want anything to happen to you, Diana."

She glares at me and waves down the bartender to pour us another shot. "What do you know?"

I shake my head without answering her. She's acting completely out of character, and I just wish she would tell me everything. What happened with Tyler, and how she's feeling. All I want to do is make it better.

"Nothing, don't worry about it."

She grips my arm hard, nearly stumbling off her stool. "You know what he did?"

I could deny it, but at this moment, all I want to do is prove to Diana how much I look out for her, how I would do anything for her, and how she's always so unappreciative.

"Yeah, I know."

The bartender hands us our shots, and with the way Diana's looking at me right now, I sling back the shot. She's looking at me like she doesn't know me.

"Well, I know you were fucking Professor Montague. I also know about the dagger you hide in your nightstand," she says softly before downing her shot and looking at me like she's disgusted with me. "It was you, wasn't it?" I turn so I'm not facing her, but she grabs my arm and spins me on the stool. "You killed them, didn't you?"

"Fuck, Diana. Why don't you scream it and let everyone hear you?"

Her hand drops my arm like I've burned her like my skin is dirty, and if she touches me, it will rub off on her. I was so sure of myself, I felt so good after I did what I did. But when I see the way Diana looks at me now, I feel lower than low.

"Lilith, how could you?"

"He raped you," I respond quietly.

"It was a misunderstanding, you shouldn't have killed him."

I rear back and stare at her like she's lost her mind. "I was protecting you!"

"I don't even know you," she sneers, grabbing her purse and stumbling off of the stool. I make a grab for her arm, but she snatches it out of reach. "Get off me."

"Diana, you're drunk. Let me take you home."

"How can I trust anything you say?" Her words are slurred, and I have to take a few deep breaths before I yell at her for being an ungrateful bitch. So I do, I breathe and keep my tone calm.

"Let's call a cab and go home. There we can talk some more."

"I don't want to go home with you. I can barely look at you."

"I was protecting you," I argue, wanting to show her how unreasonable and ungrateful she's being. I protected her, I took care of her, and she's acting like I'm a deplorable person.

"No, you've just made me feel like this is my fault. You've made me as bad as you, Lilith. How could you do something like this so easily? You don't even seem to feel guilty. You're a monster. You're evil, Lilith."

"Yeah, and you're an ungrateful bitch," I throw back at her. She shoves past me, and I stand there, watching her walk out of the club. Some of the bar-goers watch her leave as well after witnessing the altercation.

"The tab?" the bartender asks from behind me. I nod and push some cash across the bartop.

I never meant for Diana to find out, but hearing her say those things has me feeling conflicted. I can't deny the gratification I felt when taking the two men out, but what if she's right? What if I am a monster? Evil? I scratch my arm and let her words sink in. If it was anyone else, I could probably let this feeling go without a second thought. But the person I shared a womb with, who I share the same DNA strands with, thinks I'm a horrible person.

My gut sinks when I think about the fact that she might turn me in. Maybe it's what I deserve, no one should have the power that I hold. I brought my blade with me; obviously, I've become codependent on the bloodthirsty piece of metal.

I feel like a fucking idiot. Thinking I was doing other women a favor, being their champion. But when they find out my misdeeds, they'll think I'm sick, evil, a fucking freak.

As badly as I'd love to sit here in self-pity and drink myself stupid, I have to make sure Diana gets home okay. I exit the bar, realizing it's late as I look left and right. The streets are lined with glowing lights, and there are only a few people walking down the cobblestone streets. Again, it feels like a looming presence is following me, but I ignore it. I decide to go left, the same direction we walked from, and that's when I hear a gasp.

It came from a dark alleyway on my left. It's wide enough for a car, and there's a big trash can in the middle of the dark pathway. I hear something solid hit the metal of the trash can and then a whimper.

Fear hits me in the gut as I take my dagger in my hand, and as quietly as possible, I walk closer, my footsteps quiet on the dark pavement. The stench of the trash is strong, but there's also a metallic tang in the air. When I finally round the dumpster. That's when I see it.

The man from the bar has my sister pushed against the wall, his hand wrapped in her hair as... *he bites her neck?*

A trail of blood leaks down her pink top, and her eyes widen as she sees me. I can see her mouth my name as I raise my dagger in the air, ready to stab him in the back. But he's exceptionally fast—inhumanly fast—as he spins, grabbing my throat while pushing me against the opposite wall from my sister.

"Well, fuck me, two-for-one special. I wonder if you taste the same."

I raise my dagger again, but I'm too slow. His teeth meet my neck, and it's not like a simple puncture, it's more like he's ripping my throat out. I want to scream, but nothing comes out. Blood runs down my neck from where the immeasurable pain radiates from. All I can see is my sister slumped against the wall, the life leaving her eyes like I imagine it's about to leave mine. Her head slumps, her chin hitting her collarbone.

With every ounce of strength I have, I stab him in the thigh with the dagger. It's not deep, but it punctures him slightly.

He laughs as he pulls back from me. A mixture of my and my sister's blood smeared across his lips as he stares at me. "Already dead, sweetheart. Mmm. I think you taste better than the other one. She was sweet, you've got a little more tang to ya."

He goes back to my brutalized neck, and I'm starting to feel light-headed. The pain in my throat is merciless and all-consuming. I feel like I'm going to black out when his presence is taken away from me. I hear a crash as I slump to the ground, my back dragging along the brick wall as I stare across from me.

"D—" I try to speak, but it's too painful. Tears prick my eyes as I look across from me. It wasn't supposed to be like this. The last words we said to each other were terrible. My eyes are heavy, and I blink a few times, the world going dark.

I hear other voices but can't make them out. It sounds like multiple men. The last thing I hear before I go is a deep voice. A voice that would probably make others tremble, but it fills me with warmth.

"It's alright, love. You're coming home now."

That sounds nice. With the voice and a sense of gentle warmth around me, I let go, and it feels more peaceful than I ever imagined.

CHAPTER FIVE

LUCIFER

K as alerted me that my presence was needed in Hallowsdeep, a place I'm far too familiar with. The demon I've known far too long has me on edge. This is a secret that needs to be protected at all costs, and I'm not sure that I can trust the cunning brunette.

I portaled here immediately, and as soon as I saw her, it was like everything clicked. She might be a twin, but I know immediately which one she is—which one is mine. She has a delicious arrogance to her, one that I can say I also possess. Lilith is stunning; her blonde hair is pulled back away from her face but hangs loosely down her back. It's long, thick, and beautiful. I can't help but want to touch it and see what it smells like. It could be decades before I know, and watching her from afar is a slow torture.

The deal with the dagger is that I can't interfere with her life on earth, can't bring her to her true home, Hell, until it's her time. She might not be exactly like the person I remember, but all that matters is she's here, making her way back to me.

It will be torture, but I'm patient. If all I can do is watch from afar, then that's what I'll do. Her jeans fit the curve of her ass and showcase her long legs nicely. I like that she's taller than most human women. It will be an advantage to not break my neck every time I touch her. Her blue eyes are soft as she looks at her sister but harden whenever she looks away from her. It's clear she cares deeply for her, and I know I'm being ridiculous, honestly pathetic, as I hope that one day she will look at me the same way.

I've been alone for a long time.

Sure, I've held the company of other demons, but it was always the physical. This is so much more, and she has no fucking clue.

I stay in my corner, unseen, as I watch them take shot after shot. It's clear her sister is getting more on edge as they start to argue. I watch the altercation, and Lilith's face falls as her sister tells her what a horrible person she is.

Her twin storms out of the disturbingly disgusting bar as Lilith pays their tab, and she looks contemplative as she stares at the exit. She looks down at the floor, and I swear I can feel her sister's words burrowing into her skin.

She believes them, that's clear. But my Lilith doesn't let that deter her as she collects herself and leaves the bar, following after her sister.

I have to give her a wide berth as I follow her while she searches for her ungrateful twin. I can sense the presence of death before she even turns the corner. Keeping my distance as I hear her cry out for her sister and listening to her in pain is the sickest torture I've ever endured.

She dies before my eyes, from a vampire of all things. It's horrific to watch, but at the same time, there's the sick satisfaction that she'll be mine now. Far earlier than I ever imagined, I get to bring her with me.

The vampire is about to take another bite out of her when she's nearly gone. So I rip him off of her, and his eyes widen as I grip him by the throat.

His mouth is covered in blood, and he shrieks as I hold him in the air.

"What do you want, demon?" I forgot that he doesn't have to breathe to live, so crushing his windpipe doesn't affect him the same way it would a mortal.

I give him an evil grin. "Wrong, you can call me Devil if you'd like to address me."

I squeeze his throat, and if he had a pulse, I'm sure it would be racing right now. Without further ado, I extend my fingers into claws and reach into his chest with brutal force, puncturing his flesh and breaking his ribs with ease. I rip out his heart and squash it between my fingers.

The being may have given me Lilith far sooner than I ever dreamed possible, but he hurt her, and that's unacceptable.

As I approach Lilith, I look to the side, and as I imagined, her sister is dead. I know her soul is likely to be collected, and I groan thinking of how this might be an obstacle. I approach Lilith, her eyes glazing over as she stares across the alleyway at her dead twin.

There are two cracks of thunder, and I groan.

"Always a displeasure seeing you, Ronan," the angel says to my reaper.

"One day, I'm going to crack those ugly little rat wings off your back, Ezekiel," Ronan replies.

It takes a moment, but then the reaper and angel turn to look at me. I can tell Ezekiel is taken off guard, it's been centuries since I've seen him. I barely give him a once over, grimacing when I think about him knowing this information. I've never come to Earth to collect a soul before. It would be suspicious for me to come just to collect this female.

"Lucifer, what are you doing here?" my once brother asks me as he walks over to Lilith's twin. I sigh, thinking of the effects of one twin in heaven and one in hell. I might be a selfish bastard, but I'm not completely unfeeling.

"I don't answer to you, Ezekiel. Take your soul and leave. Ronan," I snap the reaper's name, and he walks over to me. Ronan is easily one of the best reapers I have. He does his job well, never causing problems, and he never asks questions.

"Michael sends his regards," Ezekiel says with a smirk before collecting the soul and portalling back to heaven.

"Fucking prick," I sneer. When I find out who helped him escape Hell, I'm going to destroy their soul.

"Fucking Archangels," Ronan growls in agreement, and I grunt.

"Can I count on your discretion on this manner?" I ask Ronan.

"Of course, my lord," he says.

"Wonderful. When you stay in Hell, you will have a room at the manor," I tell him, and he grins.

"I usually stick to Lust when I go to Hell, but I thank you for your generosity." It's no surprise that the sex club is the place he visits the most in Hell. I nod, and he looks down at Lilith before he disappears.

"Great. Now I have two fucking people to worry about," I groan, not trusting anyone with this precious secret.

Lilith's eyes are closed, and her neck is a mess—a nasty fucking way to go. Her body finally succumbs to her wounds.

"It's alright, love. You're coming home now," I tell her as her mortal life ends and our forever begins. *Again.*

I see the death dagger in her lifeless hand, and I take it, putting it in my suit pocket as I reach into her chest, cradling her soul. Her soul is one of the headiest I've been in the presence of as I keep her close to me. Souls are soft, wispy things here on earth. A smoky shell of the once vibrant woman she was. Her soul weighs nothing, and it clings to me, knowing that it belongs to me. I don't waste any time taking us back to Hell. Once we're there, I can make her whole again.

While I watched her tonight, I memorized every piece of her so that I can get it right when I make her corporeal body.

I portal us to my library, and now that we're in Hell, she looks like herself again—but less. Once you die and you're brought to Hell, you have a form. It's similar to your form when you were alive, but not completely. You can touch and feel when you're dead, but everything is less—true vibrance is left behind in your mortal life. I suppose it's part of the reason why the residents of Hell go to extremes to feel anything.

Only my most trusted demons are given fully corporeal bodies and the ability to portal to other realms, leaving Hell. All other beings are trapped here in Hell for eternity unless I deem otherwise.

I lay her form on the couch as I take the dagger from my jacket and slice my wrist. My blood immediately clings to her, recognizing her immediately. I shiver as it attaches to her and creates her anew, into something stronger and more powerful than she was in her mortal life. The magic in my blood and the power of my mind give her form.

Everything about her is nothing like I remember as I watch the magic of my blood and her soul combine. She's naked in front of me, and I feel like I can't breathe as I finally take her in. She's fucking everything.

Not wanting our first encounter to be awkward, I immediately grab a blanket and tuck it around her body. She doesn't stir, and I'm not sure how long it will take her to wake up. I've never turned a soul this fresh into a demon before.

I want to hold her as she makes the transition, but I don't know how she would handle my touch when she comes to. So I sit at my desk and drink. I drink, I stare, and I wait.

Her chest rises and falls under the blanket while every scenario runs through my head. Will she know immediately that she's mine once she wakes up? Will she be thrilled to no longer be held by mortal customs? Will she be grief-stricken over her twin?

I swirl the whiskey in the glass, intermittently looking at the amber liquid and the pools of golden hair lying on my couch. Rubbing my chest from excitement and fear, I haven't felt this alive in—I don't even know how long.

She stirs, and I immediately put the crystal glass on top of the desk as I watch her blink open her beautiful blue eyes. She stares at the ceiling for a few moments before clutching the blanket and sitting upright. The bare skin of her side catches my attention as she sits up, and I try to not stare.

"Who the fuck are you, and where am I?" she asks. I swallow, not having been spoken to like that in—well, ever. I insight fear and loyalty; if someone is out of line, it's not to my face.

"Lilith," I say in a tone that is far more aggressive than I intended. She narrows her eyes at me, and as adorable as it is, I feel frustrated. I don't know if I expected immediate recognition of what I am to her, but it's clear that that's not what I'm getting from her.

"Did you do something to me?"

I stare right back at her. "What do you remember?" I don't even answer her question because where would I even start? I didn't take advantage of her, but I have turned her into something else entirely than what she was a few hours ago. Something I should have done centuries ago, and all I've done is suffer from that choice since. When I look at her and see how confused she is, I realize that my idea of her remembering anything is all for naught. Of course, they are. I sigh in frustration and look at her, waiting for her to speak.

She glares at me, and I can see the gears in her head turning. It must hit her then. "My sister," she says softly. I pick up the whiskey glass and down the rest of the liquid. It doesn't even burn anymore when I drink, I miss that feeling. "She's dead?"

"You both are."

She looks around the room. "Where's Diana? I want to see her."

I sigh and stand. Lilith's gaze tracks me, and when I stand to my full height, her eyes widen. I know that my presence can be intimidating, and I considered altering my appearance, but I wanted her to see the true me during our first meeting.

"Diana is in Heaven," I try to say gently, but she winces at my deep tenor.

"So that means I'm..."

"In Hell," I finish her sentence.

"I'm in Hell, and you're what?" she scoffs. "The Devil?"

I keep my eyes fixated on hers. "I believe that's one of the terms mortals use for me. I'd prefer for you to call me Lucifer, however." Or sir, or any number of delicious things.

She laughs, full-out laughs so hard that she can barely hold onto the blanket covering her chest. "This is great. Great joke. Where's Diana, and can I go home now?" She looks around the room, and my patience grows thin. It's like she doesn't feel the same bond that I do.

"Lilith, you're dead. You're in Hell, and you're—"

"I'm not," she denies as she stands up, the red material pooling around her body as she stands. Her head reaches my chest, and she looks up at me defiantly. "Take me to Diana, now."

I look down at her in frustration, this was not the initial meeting I had planned. "I'm sorry, but you can't see her."

She holds onto the blanket with one hand and shoves at my chest with the other. "Listen here, you big motherfucker. Take me to see my sister right now." Her blue eyes look glossy as she pushes her small little hand against me. No doubt she's stronger now as a demon than she ever was as a human. She must notice her strength at some point as she pulls away her hand and inspects it.

"Where... where's my scar?" she asks, looking at her hand and then back up at me. She pulls her leg out and looks at her ankle. "And my tattoo."

"I didn't know about those, I tried to make you look the same," I say, but she just blinks owlishly at me.

"This... this can't be real. You die, and that's it. There's no Heaven or Hell."

"There is, and you're here with me in Hell."

She blinks at me a few more times. "Am I going to be tortured for all eternity?" she asks.

"No." I would never hurt her, but I guess she wouldn't automatically know that.

"Why not?" she asks, as if she believes that's what she deserves.

"Do you want to be tortured, Lilith?" I see goosebumps spread across her flesh when I say her name, and she shakes her head, sitting back down on the couch.

"My sister's in Heaven, and I'm here?"

"Yes."

"I'll never see her again?"

I sigh and shake my head. "I'm afraid not."

She looks up at me and back down at the blanket. Her eyes fill with moisture, but she doesn't let the tears fall. I realize that the exciting reunion I anticipated isn't going to happen tonight. I groan, looking down at the small, scared, precious demon in front of me.

"Would you like to go to your room?"

"Room?" she parrots. I nod, and she wraps the blanket around herself as I open the door to the library, walking out in front of her.

I wish I could watch her reaction to see if she likes *our* home, but I play it cool as we get to her door. When I open it, I walk in first, holding out my arm.

She looks around the emerald green and gray room. Kas said she didn't seem like a pink and purple type of girl, that was more of her twin. She licks her lips, taking in the opulence of the room before turning to face me.

"This doesn't look like Hell."

I'm not sure where to even start with that, so I just nod.

"We can talk tomorrow."

"Okay," she says softly. It's an intrusive feeling to want to comfort someone, but I'm not sure how to, so I glance at her one last time before exiting her quarters. As soon as the door closes, I hear her sobs leave her and wonder if there was a better way to handle this whole situation. A few things have been made perfectly clear in finally meeting Lilith, she's stubborn and clearly going through a spectrum of emotions I can not handle right now.

Kas passes me in the hallway, and I grab her arm.

"My lord," she says with a slight bow of her head.

"Can you talk to her?"

"And what pray tell would you like me to say to your little—"

I squeeze her arm, glaring down at her. "She would hardly let me get a word in, and she's in there fucking crying like I'm the one who killed her sanctimonious sister. Just do something."

Kas eyes me cautiously. "I want something in return."

"Fine," I bark back, just wanting Lilith to stop hurting.

"Wonderful," Kas replies with a smile on her face as she turns to Lilith's door and knocks. I exhale and walk away, hoping that Kas can speak to her in a way I obviously wasn't capable of.

CHAPTER SIX

LILITH

My sobs wreck my body. It's not that I'm in Hell or that I was in the presence of fucking Satan himself. *It's Diana.*

Our last words together.

The fact that she was right.

Clearly, she was right. Only evil people go to Hell, meanwhile, my sister is in Heaven, and I'm never going to be able to see her again. Never be able to talk to her again, never make up for our stupid fight.

I don't really care about being dead. If I'm being honest, I'm a little disappointed there's an afterlife. It's probably why I don't care about being a complete bitch to the Devil. He thinks I'll just come here and bow down and listen to him for no reason? I've never been scared of much in real life, I'm certainly not afraid of him. The only thing I feel right now is grief, not fear over my situation.

I cry into the beautiful bedding—it's green—my favorite color. While I might be in Hell, it definitely doesn't seem like it. The room screams expensive and luxurious. Everything is high-end, from the thread counts on these sheets to the gold lighting fixtures hanging from the wall. It's not extravagant in a way that I would see on Earth, at least not in this century. It reminds me of palaces before the Renaissance era. There's a royal quality to the room that I just can't seem to compute is somehow in Hell. I pinch myself, I've got to be dreaming.

My skin feels different, I haven't looked at myself in a mirror yet, but I know when I do, I won't look completely the same.

All I want to do is see Diana one last time, tell her I'm sorry and that I love her. Then I think about Otis and how neither of us went home. My cat probably thinks I fucking abandoned him, so the tears start all over again.

I'm a mess; without looking, I know my cheeks are blotchy, and my eyes are lined in red. There's a knock at the door, and I groan, thinking that it's the Devil—Lucifer. I'm not sure that man is used to actually speaking with people. He was so short and aggressive with me, I want nothing to do with him. I just want to see Diana and then cease to exist.

I don't say anything to the person knocking at the door, but they enter anyway. The woman who enters looks so familiar, and I remember her sitting next to me at the fountain on campus. I search through my brain for her name. The first letter on the tip of my tongue when it hits me.

"Kas?"

"Lilith, I didn't expect to see you here so soon."

She walks over and sits on top of my bed like she owns the place, and I hold the blanket close to my chest. I haven't even looked for clothes yet, just immediately sat down on this ridiculously massive bed and started crying my eyes out.

"Oh, none of that. Demon girls don't cry."

My head swings in her direction. "Demon?"

"For the nine circles of Hell, he didn't tell you he made you into a demon?"

"He just said I was in Hell," I deadpan. I guess I didn't understand that going to Hell automatically made me a demon. The word itself feels evil, I guess it's good to encompass everything that Diana thought I was—what I am.

"You have to help me, I have to see my sister."

Kas sighs. "Listen, having angel siblings sucks ass. I would not recommend it. If you thought they were little goody two-shoes on earth, they only act like bigger assholes once they get to Heaven."

"But... we left on bad terms. She's my twin."

Kas looks at me like she feels sorry for me, but I can't tell if it's genuine or not. "I'm sure all of this is hard for you. It's probably the reason why demons aren't turned right away. You didn't get to go through sorting and get the whole spiel about Hell or how it works."

"What do you mean?" I ask her, furrowing my brows.

"You're a special case."

"Why?"

She shrugs her shoulders. "Listen, why don't you finish having this little sad-girl-party tonight, and first thing tomorrow, I'll show you around and explain a few things about Hell."

"There really is no leaving?" I ask her.

She gives me a grin, and when Kas smiles, I feel like she could devour someone whole. "Not right now, but once you figure out how to portal and how to manage your abilities, you should be able to go to any dimension you want."

"Even Heaven?"

She laughs, a barking sarcastic laugh. "Sweetheart, if you were to portal into Heaven, they would kill you on sight. Listen, Hell isn't as bad as it seems, especially as a demon. Let me show you around tomorrow and explain some things."

"Alright," I reply, sitting up straight and trying to compose myself.

"Make sure you wear some actual clothes," Kas comments, looking me up and down. "Not that it's a bad look. I just don't want to have to deal with any eyeballs being gouged out tomorrow."

I open my mouth to ask another question because half of what Kas said makes no sense to me, but I shut my mouth instead. I'm going to do what she said, use the rest of the night to grieve, and tomorrow I can ask all the questions I need.

"Okay," I say softly, and Kas nods her head.

"I'll be back bright and early—well, as bright as it gets in Hell. Bye!" She shuts the door, and I hear her retreating footsteps down the hall.

With a heavy plop, I fall back into the bed and look at the ceiling, coming to terms with my new life. Diana, Otis, finishing school, Dad, and the killing spree I was on, are all clearly in my past. Apparently, I'm a demon now, and I don't even know the first thing about who I'm supposed to be or how I'm supposed to act.

Why did he turn me immediately upon arrival, and why am I in such a nice room? I feel completely drained and out of place. I just wish I could go back in time and not argue with Diana. If we had just stuck together, if we never went to Hallowsdeep that night... maybe it wouldn't have ended this way. I just want to take it all back.

I'd even take back killing Tyler... *well, maybe not that.*

I focus on breathing in and out, calming my nerves, and not wanting to cry another tear. I sealed my fate with my own actions, and I have to live with it. Diana is in Heaven, which I'm assuming isn't a bad gig, and I suppose she'll be happy there. Janice in the apartment next to us will notice we didn't come home, and hopefully, she'll adopt Otis.

The fact that my presence on Earth is so insignificant hits me right in the gut, and I groan, rolling over to lie on my side. I don't know what's worse, not knowing who I am anymore or having no control over my situation.

I'm at least able to get some relief from my depressing thoughts as exhaustion takes me. Somehow no dreams plague me during my sleep.

I'm not sure how long I slept for, only that I didn't want to make Kas wait for me to get ready whenever she comes to collect me. The bathroom in this place is even more ridiculously luxurious than the bedroom. There are multiple shower heads, and the water is steaming hot, unlike our apartment, where you were lucky if you could get a lukewarm shower. Emerald tiles line the floor and the walls, while black sconces light up the room. It's really confusing that there's running water, electricity, and modern-day electronics in this place... yet it also feels like I'm in a different time. It seems as though Hell follows its own timeline and trends.

The closet is filled to the brim with different clothes. The interesting thing being that all the clothes look like they come from different time periods. It's just like the confusing nature of the decor. Most of the clothing options are dresses; luxurious and extravagant gowns that I would have never worn on Earth. I wouldn't have even had access to clothes like this, let alone a place to wear them. As tempting as the silky gowns are, I think of what I saw Kas wearing, and decide to wear what I know, bell bottom jeans and a simple black t-shirt. I keep my hair down, and I stare at myself in the mirror.

A few of the freckles on my face aren't in the right place, but for the most part, I look like me. My body shape seems exactly the same, it's just different. I can't deny that I feel stronger, and I hate to say it, but I feel more powerful. Even though my dagger was left behind on Earth, I swear it feels like I absorbed all of its power, and it's a part of me now.

I wonder if there are therapists in Hell, maybe that's something I should seek out.

I'm staring at myself in the mirror, getting acquainted with the new me, when Kas just waltzes into my room, holding two to-go cups of coffee and a bakery bag.

"Yes, yes, you're very pretty. Are you ready to go?"

"I wasn't—"

Kas grins and shakes her head. "Listen, if you're going to survive in Hell, you're going to need to learn how to take a joke and deal with criticism. That's lesson number one."

"Okay," I concede as she hands me the coffee, and I take a sip. She hands me a Boston cream donut, and I tilt my head in wonder, silently asking how she knows it's my favorite. Kas shrugs her shoulders but walks out of the room ahead of me.

"Let's start at sorting and then work our way from there." I nod my head and follow her. Her hand circles my upper arm, and all of a sudden, it's like I'm being gripped by my chest while being spun in fifty directions before I land back on my feet.

I groan, wrapping my other arm around my stomach. "What the fuck was that?"

"Portalling, you'll get used to it." Her tall heels click against the white tile floor as she leads me down a hallway. Everything is white: the doors, the floors, the walls, even the door knobs. "This is sorting. This is where the reapers drop off the souls when they die in their realm."

"Their realm?"

"Fucking Heaven, I'm going to have to start from the beginning. The world as you know it is only a small piece of the universe that exists out there. There are many worlds. Heaven and Hell are a part of those worlds. We are the afterlife. So whether you die as a human on Earth or, let's say, as a fae in the fae realm, once you die, you come here or there."

"Okay." That by itself is a lot to process, but she already looks irritated with me, so I nod my head.

"Reapers are a lot like demons, but they have a special gift that allows them to easily travel with souls and not have any issues with bringing them here." I nod my head, trying to absorb everything she's saying.

"A few demons are in charge of sorting, there are mainly two places you can go. The pit," she says with a smirk. "And general population. If you're lucky and Lucifer, or the demon sorting you, sees that you have potential, you could be one of the chosen few to become a demon by our lord."

I can't help the snort of a laugh that comes out of me. "You all call him your lord?"

Kas doesn't answer, she just grins at me.

"Anyway, the pit is for those who have done the most fucked-up unacceptable shit go to be tortured for their everlasting existence, and general population is a mix, some people are worse than others. Life isn't grand, but it isn't horrible either."

I know I have a confused look on my face as I follow her down the hall. "But my room, it's so nice."

"That is the perk of living at Lucifer's manor."

"And why am I there and not in the general population?"

She shrugs her shoulders. "You'd have to ask him. Grab on, let's go into the city." I grab her arm, and she portals us to a new location. Now that I know what to expect, it doesn't feel so jarring to travel this way.

The city is... well, not great. The sky is gloomy, and there's a slight chill in the air. There are tall buildings everywhere you look.

People—I guess that's a slightly broad term because they mostly look like ghosts—walk the sidewalks and go into different buildings.

"The dead have jobs, homes, and sometimes families. But this is where most people go when they die," Kas informs me in a bored tone as we walk down the street. "I imagine you won't spend much time here, most demons don't."

"No?"

"Most of us spend the majority of our time in other realms, but when we do come to Hell, we're usually closer to the manor than the city."

"So you don't like being here?"

Kas is contemplative as she thinks about her response. "It's not that I hate it here, living beings are just more fun to play with."

I make a humming noise as I follow her. None of the spirits–dead people–ghosts–whatever the hell they are, pay us any attention. It almost seems like most of them are in a trance as they do their daily routines. It looks fairly like a rundown or post-apocalyptic New York City as people go about their business. It's definitely stark, comparing my modern-day outfit and solid figure to the slightly wispy ones before me.

"Do you want to see the pit?" she asks, and I just nod my head. I need to know everything about my surroundings and where I am. Kas doesn't even have to ask as I hold out my arm, and she portals us to the pit. The temperature around us is hotter than fuck, and immediately sweat starts dripping from my brow as she walks us deeper into the building.

I guess I was expecting caves with hellfire, but it's more like a laboratory built underground. There are no windows, and unlike the sorting room or a typical science lab, everything is dark and eerie. I feel like I'm in an abandoned mental asylum as Kas leads me down the halls.

Screams ricochet off the walls, and there's a sickening stench of decay and blood in the air. "The worst of the worst come here, rapists, people who hurt children, specific murderers." My gaze meets hers, and she shrugs. "Senseless murderers, people who kill the innocent or do so with no remorse." I go to open my mouth and explain how I don't have remorse about who I've killed, just how my sister reacted, and Kas shakes her head back and forth at me. "It's different, I don't know how to explain it really, but there are people who seek vengeance and others who kill for sport, those are the people who wind up here."

There's a man begging, shouting, "Please, not again." Kas swings that door open to reveal a massive man, bigger than Lucifer. He's easily over seven feet tall with blood covering his face and his white blonde hair is up in a bun. I notice then that his ears are pointed. He doesn't even look over in our direction, just grunts.

"Elvor, this is Lilith, a new demon. I was just giving her the grand tour." Elvor grunts again as he glares at the man in front of him. He's tied to a chair, three fingers already missing as Elvor takes his knife and cuts off a fourth digit. The finger plops to the ground, and the man in the chair starts wailing again. I notice that the man in the chair seems just like any other human, not like the dead I saw in the city.

"Is he a demon?" I ask Kas, and she shakes her head.

"No, Lucifer just makes them corporeal so the torture hurts more." I nod, that makes sense to me.

"What did he do?" I ask. Elvor wipes the blade clean of the man's blood by rubbing it on the man's cheeks. It's fucked up but also kinda awesome.

"Tell her," Elvor commands, his voice deep and growly and scary as fuck. He squeezes the man's bloody cheeks, forcing his head towards me, so he can look at me. His grip looks punishing as the man tries to shake his head. Elvor grunts and stabs the man in his thigh, making him whimper. "Tell her."

"She wanted it, okay? So what? She came on to me." Elvor shakes his head in disgust, and I know the man is lying, but I don't want to know any more details.

I grimace and look at the man before me, easily in his forties. "Elvor, may I?" I ask, holding my hand out for the knife. The massive man smirks at me as he pulls the knife out from his thigh and hands me the bloody blade. I might be in Hell, but knowing that people like this get this treatment for the rest of their pathetic afterlife gives me some joy.

The man sputters, watching as I test the weight of the blade in my hand. "If I kill him?" I ask.

Kas responds. "He'll regenerate tomorrow."

A grin spreads across my face, and with strength I didn't know I had, I easily glide the knife into his throat. It takes him a minute to die, and I hope that he feels every ounce of the pain. It feels good—until it doesn't.

My sister's words rattle in my brain. I know they're true because I liked it; I liked ending his life, seeing him bleeding, and knowing he will have to suffer again tomorrow. I'm the monster Diana said I was, but I'm not sure if I'm allowed to embrace it here. Or if her thoughts of me will haunt me for the rest of eternity.

Elvor gives us a grunt and leaves the room, leaving the man's lifeless body tied to the chair.

"Well, that's an exciting trip to the pit. Shall we go back to the manor?"

"That's it?" I ask.

"Mostly. That concludes your grand tour of Hell."

I thought that she would take me back to my room, but instead, she transports us to a massive banquet hall of people. Actual real-life people, not the spirit-like people we saw in the city.

"Stay close to me," Kas instructs as we walk down yet another hall.

"Are they all demons?"

"Yes. Most of the demons here are in charge of securing souls for Hell. Others have different jobs."

"Like what?"

Before she can answer, a man approaches us. He's attractive, tall with dark hair, graying around the sides. He might be a demon, but there's a gentle quality to him.

"Any word on Asmodeus?" he asks her.

"Nothing yet," she says softly, looking at the demon in front of her before glancing back at me. "This is Lilith, she's new."

"Hi," he says curtly before looking back at Kas. "If you hear anything, let me know."

CHARMING THE DEVIL 77

"Didn't think you cared that much, Daxaddon."

"Oh, fuck off," he says, waving Kas off and walking down the hall.

"Who's Asmodeus?" I ask.

"You always were a nosy one," she says, and I can't help but think that she's only known me for a few days. I realize then, that she just doesn't want to answer the question, so I drop it. She groans and looks at me quickly. "Brace yourself," she says as three women approach us.

The one in the front has freakishly white teeth and short blonde hair. She grins as she looks between Kas and me. "Who's this?" she asks in a fake sweet voice.

Kas sighs. "Lilith, this is Lisa, Autumn, and Tina." She points to Lisa first, she's the one with the creepy-looking smile and blonde hair. Autumn is pretty plain, someone I wouldn't look at twice, but she clings to Lisa while twirling her slightly frizzy hair around her finger. Tina looks dazed, her brown eyes unfocused, and her hair is pulled back in a tight bun. Tina is definitely a follower, it's clear that Lisa is the one in charge of this group of women. I can tell that Kas is unimpressed, and I can't say that I am any different.

"Didn't know Lucifer was accepting new souls. You don't look familiar," Lisa sneers, her lackluster eyes looking me over from head to toe. She smiles, and I wonder if her teeth were like that when she died or if Lucifer has a sick sense of humor and gave them to her after he made her a demon.

"Yeah, well, you know how it goes. Was time to upgrade Lilith from gen pop." I hold my tongue and try not to say anything stupid. Kas is lying to these demons, but why?

"Interesting choice," Lisa says spitefully.

I can't hold my tongue anymore. "Maybe he just got tired of seeing the same demons day in and out."

"Mmm. I doubt that," Autumn, the mousey one says.

"Times must be getting rough," Tina says, bored and picking at her nails.

"Well, this has just been riveting. Why don't we head back to your room," Kas says, and that garners all the women's attention. They form a tight circle and start gossiping together as Kas and I walk away. "Don't mind them, I like to call them the cunt gang."

I can't help the genuine laugh that rips out of me. It feels nice to laugh, and when I see Kas' smile, I can tell she's proud of herself as well.

I might not know what I'm doing or who I'm supposed to be, but I'm starting to wonder if life in Hell might not be so bad after all.

CHAPTER SEVEN

LUCIFER

I can't focus.

All I want is to be able to get through this meeting without thinking about her, without worrying about her being in my realm. I trust Kas to a degree—but I'll never trust anyone with Lilith—possibly not even myself.

She seems so fragile, so broken right now. What's worse is it's clear she wants absolutely nothing to do with me. Beelzebub says something I didn't catch, and when I don't answer he repeats himself.

"The angels are getting bolder regarding their position on the offensive, my lord. We should take action."

Toth and Milcom sit at the table as well, and it's just the four of us. Out of the three, I trust Toth the most and Beelzebub the least. There's something about him that just makes him seem... off. Or maybe it's because he's such a kiss-ass, his cowering nature annoys me.

"We don't want a war with the angels if we can help it." Which is true, it's always a cycle of war with them. We end a feud, and another starts. For no apparent reason, the being they follow left them leaderless forever ago, and now they're all on a righteous warpath against anything they don't deem to be holy.

"With Michael being back alongside the angels, he seems to be stirring up some rumors," Beelzebub says.

"And how do you know this?" He sinks back into his seat slightly as he responds.

"Heritis, the recently fallen angel, he told me everything."

I arch my eyebrow at him and nod. "For now, we stay put. We don't engage with the angels, and we don't ruffle any feathers." Toth shakes his head next to me when I mention feathers, but Milcom and Beelzebub don't seem entertained.

"They're still upset that Michael was captured and kept here for so long, my lord. They won't let this stand."

I exhale through my nose and try to keep my anger at bay. "You brought him here, Beelzebub. How did you manage that again?"

"A trap," he says plainly. His story never made sense, this is the second time he's brought Michael up in conversation, and it's made me grow suspicious of Beelzebub's loyalty. I still don't know how Michael got out of Hell, but I'm looking at my number one suspect.

"Very well. Like I said, we will not be the ones who start anything. Understood?"

"Yes," all three demons say in unison.

"Toth, stay. You two are dismissed."

Beelzebub and Milcom leave the room, and I can finally speak freely. "As much as I dislike the little weasel you know I've been preparing us for this," I ask, and Toth nods.

"So far there have only been a few successes of demons procreating, my lord, but offspring are all very human."

I nod my head and sigh. "We need to check from my time on Earth."

"Sir?"

I sigh, hating to admit this, especially now. How the fuck was I supposed to know that Lilith would be coming into my life? I can't just make an heir with another demon. "There's a possibility that I have an heir or two on Earth. They need to be found and protected."

"Sir, if the angels know you have an heir—"

I wave my hand at him, cutting him off. "That's why I said they need to be protected. If they are simply human, then they never need to know."

"Of course, my lord. When should we start searching?"

I can't face this reality just yet, not while Lilith is here and hasn't even spoken to me today.

"Soon, this stays between us for now."

Toth bows, leaving the room, and I groan while rubbing my face. Thank fuck, I don't have to worry about stress-induced heart attacks, or else I'd probably have had more than I could possibly count. The angels, Lilith, the fact that I probably have spawns of Satan roaming earth right now—it's too much.

There's a knock on the door and my anger bubbles. "What?" I demand irritated, hoping that the person knocking will fuck off and leave me to my own little mental breakdown.

"Sorry, I'll come back," her soft voice replies, and I shoot up out of my seat, walking towards the door.

"I thought you were someone else."

She looks up at me, straight in the eye. She doesn't cower, doesn't even look phased by my presence at all.

"I thought we were going to talk today."

"Of course," I say, holding out my arm and indicating the direction we should both walk in, away from the meeting room. I don't even think as I grab her arm and portal us to my study.

She recoils from my touch as soon as our feet are flat on the ground. I try to not let it irritate me, but it does to my core. How can she not feel this? When I'm near her, every fiber of my being knows that she's mine. Yet, Lilith doesn't even seem to be phased by my touch at all, while hers sears deep into my skin. She doesn't even seem curious about my appearance or who I am.

"How was your tour with Kas?"

"Insightful," she says as she sits down on the couch and crosses her legs. I've never really thought about denim jeans before, but I quite like them now as I watch them stretch around her thighs.

I stand in front of my desk and sit slightly on top of the oak as I appraise her. She isn't lying, I'd be able to taste it if she was.

Her blue eyes take in my height, and she can't seem to hold back her opinion on the matter. "Why are you so freakishly tall? Are you fae like Elvor?"

My eyes widen. "You met Elvor?" While he is my best demon in the pit, he has a wickedly nasty temper, and his patience is as thin as a spider web.

"Yeah, he was nice."

"Nice?" I'm pissed that she even noticed Elvor enough to compare our heights. And what's with her calling him nice? *I can be fucking nice.*

"He let me stab a guy," she declares, relaxing further against the couch. "Doesn't answer my question as to why you're so tall."

"This is how tall people were when I died. He let you stab someone?" I question, and Lilith nods her head.

"Yes, is that abnormal?" I don't reply. Elvor hardly speaks, and the list of people he likes is short, so I just shrug off the question. *Does he somehow know something? Does he know who Lilith is to me?*

"Do you have any other pressing questions?"

"No, and I wouldn't want to take up any of your time," she snarks, and I have to check myself. I'm so used to being short and direct with people that I didn't even realize that I was acting that way with her. *It's something that I'll have to stop,* I think as I shake my head.

"No, what other questions do you have?"

"Why did you change me right away?"

"Because I wanted to," I state, not ready to tell her everything. If she doesn't feel it, maybe the prophecy was wrong. Another way for God to torture me after all of these years. I've learned my lesson, if Lilith is to be mine, it will need to be on her own volition, nothing less.

"Well, that's helpful. Why do I have such a nice room?"

"Because I wanted you to have it."

She sighs and rolls her eyes. My palm twitches at her bratty display, but I reign in my urges to touch her as I stare at her. She crosses her arms over her chest and stares right back at me.

"You're being extremely helpful right now," she deadpans, every word dripping with sarcasm.

I stand up from the desk and slowly approach her. She unfolds her arms, placing her palms flat on the couch as she waits for what I will do next.

Placing my hands on the back of the sofa, I lean forward so my face is close to hers.

"Let's get some things clear, Lilith." She shivers at the use of her name falling from my lips, and I realize this is what gets a reaction out of her. "You're in Hell—which I happen to be the king of. When I want something, I have it. When I need something done, I have one of my demons do it. This realm is under my command, and you will do as you're told."

I expect her to cower slightly, nod her head, and be a sweet, obedient little demon. Instead, she laughs in my face and leans in even closer to me.

"Does that little speech work on all the pretty demons?" *Yes, it usually does.* In my moment of shock, she scoffs before continuing, "First, you bring me to Hell, make me a demon right away which, according to what everyone else says, you never do. Then today, I saw how your other residents of Hell live, while I just so happen to have a room made for a queen, and you think I'm not going to ask questions? If you wanted a demon, who was going to follow orders you chose the wrong twin."

"I *did not* choose wrong," I immediately correct.

"So why did you turn me? Why do you turn anyone specifically? Because they're loyal? Willing to do your bidding? Because they're just evil enough but not too far gone to do all the fucked up—"

Before I can even think straight, my hand shoots out, wrapping my fingers around her jaw and forcing her to look at me. This wasn't how things were supposed to go.

"Are you so easily manipulated by lies, little Hellfire? Hmm, do you believe all those stories of me that you've heard in the mortal realm? Well, let me tell you something." I'm so close to her face that it's hard to focus on her eyes. There's still no fear in them, though. She's pissed but not scared. "Some of them may be true. I may be fucking evil, but I embrace who I am. I don't give a fuck what anyone thinks about me—"

"Then why are you in my face trying to convince me otherwise?" she interrupts.

I squeeze her chin harder, but she doesn't break as she glares at me. "Go to your room," I tell her. I'm feeling so fucking volatile right now, I just need her out of my space.

She grins against my hold on her, a shit-eating grin that makes me want to spank her ass and show her who's in charge. But she doesn't waver. "Are you going to let go of me?" she taunts.

I release her jaw a little harder than I meant to, and she glares at me for a moment before standing up and leaving my office. I hear her mutter, "Fucking asshole," as she leaves my study. She slams the door petulantly, and I groan, taking a seat behind my desk, my thumbs kneading my temples.

I'm not sure what my expectations were. I mean, I assumed any woman that was found compatible by the dagger wouldn't be meek, but Lilith is... difficult.

Beautiful, headstrong, and fucking vibrant.

I pour whiskey into a glass and sip it while I contemplate.

Am I so far gone as the person who is always in charge that I don't know how to communicate in a tone that isn't that of a dictator's? I know what it is, but I feel like a pathetic fool for vocalizing it.

She doesn't remember me, she doesn't love me, just like she didn't in her last life. She's so different; honestly, the polar opposite. Lily was soft, demure, and scared of her own shadow—of me. A bond wasn't strong enough to protect her then, and it won't be now. Maybe the dagger is wrong, maybe she isn't Lily reincarnated but someone else. She couldn't be more different, and I hate to admit how much I like it.

Her defiance does something for me because no one else would dare to be so brazen with their life by talking to me that way. Her talking back and not showing an interest is both frustrating and a turn-on.

Unlike other demons, she doesn't want to use me to get what she wants. If anything, she wants nothing to do with me, and it makes me crave her even more. This isn't like before, and I don't plan on making the same mistakes twice. There's already a base instinct telling me that Lilith is mine. Maybe she isn't my soulmate reincarnated, but I need to work harder to convince her that she *is* mine—that I'm hers. I wonder if she'll ever feel it too, because if it's up to me and my personality to convince her, I'm not sure I have a shot in Heaven. I was clearly banking on the idea that she would remember or instinctively know that we're fated. But it's clear, I'm a fool.

CHAPTER EIGHT

LILITH

L ucifer keeps his distance, and that's just how I like it.

I think.

He frustrates me, and I'm not sure what it is, but every time he's around me, I want to get under his skin and annoy him. In return, he doesn't know what to do with me, so he sends me away, or he runs away himself.

It's easier that way. Because coming to terms with the fact that I find the fucking Devil to be the most handsome man I've ever seen is just not going to happen.

I mean, does he have to be six-foot-nine and have thick, dark brown hair with eyes so dark they nearly look black? Every time he holds a glass with his long fingers, I want to scream. Or I have inappropriate thoughts of where he could put his hands on me.

So instead of even considering that Lucifer is attractive in a bad boy kind of way, I spend my days training. Kas has become my Yoda in a sense, teaching me how to portal and what I can expect from my so-called powers alongside additional combat training. Having grown up in my dad's studio, I'm already ahead of the game, but it's different with this newly gifted strength. Having freakish strength seems like a pretty common thing among demons, but other than that, it seems as if there's nothing else special about me. Kas keeps telling me that sometimes it takes decades to harness an additional gift. I'm just being impatient.

Portalling is fun, and I found it easy to acclimate, but that's not what Kas wants to work on today—apparently.

"We're going to Earth today," she tells me.

My face lights up as I take her in; she's dressed like she's ready for fashion week in Paris, and I think I look a little lackluster next to her in my Sailor moon shirt and jeans. Kas looks me up and down and scoffs. "Come on, you can *borrow* something of mine." She accentuates the word borrow very heavily, and it's clear Kas takes her clothes very seriously. It's not like I don't have a massive closet filled with clothes, I'm just not sure how to accept them, knowing that they're from Lucifer.

She quickly portals us to an apartment. It's not what I would expect from Kas, but more from a dwelling in Hell. I look around, and she scoffs at the expression I must have on my face. "Trust me, it's not as bad as some of the others."

I hum, and it clicks in my brain as to why she doesn't spend the majority of her time here. *Again, I wonder exactly why my room is so nice.*

"Where are we going on Earth?"

"You'll see," she teases with a smirk. Grabbing a red, skin-tight dress, she holds it out for me. I quickly undress and put on the garment. It fits like a glove and grips every inch of my body. It's revealing, in the best way, showing just the right amount of cleavage and thigh through the high slit. Kas clicks her tongue and nods appreciatively. I run my hands down the material, and now I understand why Kas dresses like this all the time. Dressing like this has a way of making you feel powerful in a simplistic kind of way.

"Much better. Now, let's test out these skills of yours."

"Uh, what skills?"

She doesn't answer, just grabs my arm and portals us to Earth. We land outside of a massive mansion. The temperature is warm, and I know that we're far away from North Point or Hallowsdeep.

"Where are we?"

"You'll see," she says, linking her elbow with mine. She helps me walk up the marble stairs, our heels clicking with each step we take.

"Name, please?" a man dressed in a suit with a clipboard asks Kas.

She laughs and unlinks our elbows as she clutches her necklace. She looks the man in the eyes, fluttering her lashes, and smiles. "We're on the list," she says softly.

The man smiles and nods. "Of course you are. Enjoy your night, ladies."

Kas turns back to clasp my hand as the heavy wooden doors open for us.

"Uh, what the fuck was that?"

"One of the perks of being a demon and one of the things you're going to work on tonight. You need to convince someone of something that's not true."

I look around the crowd, everyone is dressed in expensive dresses and suits. A woman with a harp is up front playing light music as waiters walk around the space with champagne flutes. The interior of the home is unique but nowhere near as ornate and opulent as Lucifer's manor.

"How exactly am I supposed to do that?"

"With intent. You want them to believe that what you're saying is true, and they will."

"Is this possibly one of my gifts?"

Kas nods. "Most demons have some level of persuasion in them when dealing with humans. Some are better than others."

"What's your main gift?"

Kas laughs like I'm hilarious. "You can't just ask a girl about her gifts, Lilith."

"Uh, okay." Kas is a strange one, but she's helpful. Sometimes I feel like her only setting is cryptic. But she's been kind and has been more forward with information than anyone else I've met in Hell, so I go with it.

Two men approach us, and Kas gives them a kind smile, so I do the same thing. They're above-average looking. And I hate to say it, but they just seem short even though they're not, definitely not by human standards. But standing next to Lucifer, they would look like miniature men. I shake the thought out of my head and smile as the man with no hair and golden skin smiles at me.

"I haven't seen you at one of these parties," he comments, and I'm not sure when I should test out this gift, so I just keep the conversation going.

"This is our first one," I reply.

"I thought so. Your face is one I would have remembered." I give him another smile and follow Kas' lead. "So, are you ladies participating tonight?"

"Participating?" I ask.

Kas smiles and interrupts his answer to my question by saying, "It depends. How much do you think we would go for?"

"Oh, I'd easily start the bidding at twenty thousand."

Kas scoffs. "Too low."

"Indeed, too low," the man in front of me says in agreement. He looks me up and down like I'm a prized animal, and my hand twitches. Kas nudges me, and I realize this is my time to test out my gift. I touch his arm and look into his brown eyes, copying what Kas did with the bouncer at the door.

"What exactly goes on here?"

"Auctions," he replies instantly.

"For what?"

"A night of entertainment, to do what you want. Your deepest fantasies."

"Gross," I say, dropping my hand from his arm. I look around the room at the women to see if any of them need saving from this situation. Kas shakes her head.

"They're all willing," she says softly as the men leave. "Sad, I know. I saw your dagger hand getting twitchy. It's not as seedy as you think."

"They buy them?"

"For the night," she says matter-of-factly.

"And they are okay with that?"

"More than okay; some of these girls pay off a four-year college tuition after one night."

I nod my head and watch as girls flirt with the men, batting their eyelashes, and showing interest in them. Or in their money. I smile then, taking in the reality of the situation. However, I am a little disappointed that no stabbing or other demon way of killing is going to be happening tonight.

Kas talks to people as we walk through the party, and a part of me wonders if she has an ulterior motive for being here. But I drink champagne while watching and observing, spreading my wings with my new ability nearly every time someone asks me a question.

The fact that I can make someone believe anything I say as a fact can be really helpful, and I wonder what my job will be as a demon. Will I come to Earth to find future demons or souls that will reside in Hell? What other demon jobs are there, anyway? My thoughts are interrupted as a hand snakes around my waist and squeezes.

I look over to see the same man I spoke to earlier.

"You're sure you're not for sale tonight."

"I'm sure," I answer, preparing to pry his fingers off my waist when another hand does it for me.

"That's quite enough," the new guy says. My conversations with Lucifer have been short, but his voice is memorable. I glance up at him, and the man beside me swallows thickly. Lucifer is menacing, just in a neutral state, but the way he's looking at him... it's as if he wants to cut his hands off for touching me.

I like it more than I should.

"Didn't realize she was spoken for," the man whose name I never even got says.

"Fuck off," Lucifer tells him, and the man immediately skitters away. "Are you alright?" he asks in what I feel is the most gentle tone he's ever used when speaking to me.

Why does he look so good? He's dressed better than any of the men here, towering over all of them. And now that he's near me, no one even dares to look in my direction. While I can't deny that I like it, I also had everything under control.

"Fine. I could have handled it, you know?"

"Oh, I know, little Hellfire."

I glare at him and stand a little taller. "Don't call me that."

"You don't like little Hellfire, then?" There's a twinkle in his dark eyes when he looks down at me; it's like he's toying with me, and he enjoys it.

"Lilith is fine."

"Lilith," he says with a roll of his tongue, and I know I shouldn't like it as much as I do. When he says my name, when he says anything to me really, I want to melt into a puddle of contentment. But I can't like the fucking Devil. He's the Devil, a monster, and if I like him, then that would make me one too. I don't know why Diana's last words constantly ring through my head or why they bother me so much, but they do.

I know that I killed people, and it's not a good thing—it's apparently bad enough to get sent to Hell for—but I don't think I'm inherently evil or a monster, and I want to prove her wrong. Being a demon doesn't have to be a bad thing. One of the biggest jobs as a demon is to bring souls that deserve it to Hell. How can that be a bad thing?

"What's wrong?" Lucifer asks.

I look down at my nails and pick at the red polish on my thumbnail. "Nothing's wrong," I answer, looking up at him. He has a smirk leaning towards the right side of his face.

He clicks his tongue and takes a step closer to me. "You know, every demon gets their gifts from me?"

I look up into his eyes, and the smirk deepens. "Any gift a demon possesses, it's because I have that gift. Do you want to know what one of my favorite gifts is?" I shake my head no, but in my head, I think about all the gifts Kas has told me about. Astral projection, dream walking, fire, persuasion, shadows, strength, among so many others. And *Lucifer holds all of these gifts?* He leans down to whisper in my ear.

"I can taste lies. And yours taste so fucking sweet."

I push off of him, and he grabs my wrist. "Let go of me," I snarl at him.

"That's no way to treat your boss," he says, his grip on my wrist tightening. I can't really argue with him, and he looks pleased with my submission. "Speaking of which, I think I'm ready to give you your job assignment."

"What's that?" I ask irritatedly, looking around for Kas, who is nowhere to be seen.

"I've been looking for a personal assistant."

"You've got to be fucking kidding me." The reply slips out before I even have a moment to think. Lucifer grins as the words fall out of my mouth, and he lets go of my wrist.

"Something you might want to learn about me, little Hellfire," he starts, cocking an eyebrow at me. "I don't kid. I'll see you in my library first thing tomorrow morning."

He turns his back and disappears, almost like he was never here. I look around as people slowly make their way into another room. Kas is still nowhere to be found, and I scoff at being ditched on top of having to deal with Lucifer's bullshit.

I leave the party, my red dress trailing me as my heels click against the stone path leading outside. I look back and forth to make sure no one is around to see me before I do just as Kas told me; I picture my room in Hell as my destination, and like a one-way mirror, I see the green sheets as I push myself through the portal. I land on my feet and glare at Kas, who is sitting on my bed.

"Where the fuck did you go?

"You passed your first test, yay!"

I roll my eyes at her and walk over to my closet to change out of the dress. "Did you know he's making me his assistant?"

Kas acts nonchalantly as she shrugs her shoulders. "Not surprised."

"What is it that you're not telling me?" I ask her with narrowed eyes.

She looks down at her wrist even though she isn't wearing a watch. "Oh, look at the time. Bye!" She portals out of my room instantly, and I just know something is up.

Something that Kas and Lucifer aren't telling me. And if there's one thing I hate, it's secrets.

CHAPTER NINE

LUCIFER

I haven't been this excited for a day of work in all of eternity. I hardly slept, not that I need much rest, but still. I'm not sure when it hit me to create this role for Lilith, but it's genius. It's a way to force her to be around me all day, every day, and it also ensures that she doesn't spend too much time out of the realm. I need her here, in Hell, where I know she's safe. It's also a part of my plan to woo her, which I'm not feeling extremely confident about. Nor am I feeling confident about her ability to manage her attitude while working for me.

From what little I've seen of her temperament, I know she has the ability to piss people off, and that's not what I need from her. I need for her to lie low, be undetected, and most importantly, safe. I know that I have my fucking work cut out for me before she even walks into my office.

She's wearing shorts so short I can nearly see the indent of her pussy lips, and her red top clings to her chest, showing off her midriff. Her long blonde hair is in a braid that she has flung over her shoulder.

This is going to be fucking torture.

"So, what do you need me to do, boss-man?" she asks, clearly not pleased with the task of being my assistant.

I take a moment before I answer her to admire her long legs and how defiant she looks as she stares at me.

"First things first," I start standing from my desk and collecting the golden box off the shelf. Her interest piques as she tries to stand on her tiptoes to see what's in the box. I turn it towards her, opening it and allowing her to see the golden chain with the obsidian crystal nestled gently against the velvet interior of the box.

"What's that for?"

"You," I reply, and she rolls her eyes.

"Okay, but why?"

"It's a communicative necklace. It allows either of us to portal to the other's current location. All you need to do is squeeze it and say my name. I have its twin," I say, tugging the necklace from beneath my collar and showing her. She flinches at the word twin, but she shakes it off, not wanting to show me any weakness or to hide her own pain, I'm unsure.

"And why do I need this?"

"You're my assistant. It will make it easier for you to get to me this way." She arches an eyebrow at me, and I'm not sure if she knows if I'm full of shit or not. Sure, it will make her job easier, but really it's a way for me to constantly keep tabs on her.

"Fine," she sighs and turns around. Holding her braided hair to the side. I unclasp the necklace and put it around her delicate throat. When she turns around, the crystal lies delicately against her collarbone, and I smile, knowing that I have direct access to wherever she is at any time in any realm.

"Very well, shall we start?"

"Sure," she says as I hand her a pen and paper.

"Your job will be to help me manage my daily tasks, meetings, and schedule."

"The Devil has meetings?"

I glare at her and lean on my desk. "Yes. I—Lucifer—have meetings." I hand her a ledger that communicates with my own. It automatically updates when anything is scheduled so she can keep track and she could add to my tasks as well. "These are the meetings on today's agenda." I hand her a pen that is able to add events and notes to the ledger, and she takes it, tapping it against the notebook.

Her eyes scroll through today's meetings as well as the next months'. She nearly drops the ledger when she reads what's planned at the end of the month. "You... You have a meeting with the angels?"

"I do," I nod, and I can see the irritation take over her face when I don't go into further detail. "Be a good girl, and perhaps you will get to attend." That shuts her up. I'm not sure if it's the use of the term 'good girl' or the idea that she will get to meet with the angels. I don't want to shatter her excitement by telling her the chances of seeing her sister are slim. We will just need to take this win for what it is.

Her finger tracks the meetings for today. "What is this meeting?" She points to the symbols that she can't read, and I sigh.

"The fae realm," I groan.

"Why do you have to meet with them?"

I run my hand through my hair and wonder how much I can trust Lilith. I know she's mine, but she doesn't know that. My loyalty to her isn't the same loyalty she has gifted me with—yet.

"They are currently at war. The king has requested a meeting with me."

"People can just request meetings with you? If you want to cut down your schedule, why don't you just tell them to fuck off?" she asks.

"As much as I would love to do that, it's easier to just keep things cordial with the different realms, trust me."

"Okay." She eyes the schedule one more time and looks at me. "You were supposed to be in the pit ten minutes ago," she says quietly. I smirk at her and grab her arm. She doesn't pull away as we portal to the pit.

As soon as we're there, we hear the argument taking place and the reason behind this meeting.

"You can't just keep cutting their fingers off and sewing them back on," Ponds says to Elvor. The giant fae doesn't even acknowledge the demon as he chastises him. "You need to be more creative, Elvor." That is when Elvor loses it. He picks up Ponds by his neck, suspending him in the air. He doesn't say anything, just roars in his face before putting him back down.

"What seems to be the problem?" I ask in a bored tone.

Ponds straightens his jacket and clears his throat. "Elvor isn't—" Elvor growls in Ponds' direction, "—following torture protocol."

"Torture protocol?" Lilith whispers under her breath.

"Why? Are you unhappy with Elvor's performance?"

"He just does the same thing every time; cuts their fingers off, sews them back on, and then cuts them off again."

"I don't see why you can't mind your own business," Lilith says to Ponds, a demon she hasn't even met before. "Obviously, Elvor elicits fear in those that he tortures. And don't you think the worst torture for his victims is knowing what's going to happen every day. They probably piss themselves thinking about having their fingers chopped off day in and day out."

Elvor grunts in approval. He doesn't smile at Lilith, but there is the slightest tilt at the corner of his lips.

"And you are?" Ponds sneers in a shitty tone.

"This is Lilith, and she works directly with me, and I happen to agree. If Elvor's methods work, there's no reason to argue. You torture how you want to, and Elvor will do the same."

"But my lord," Ponds starts, but I give him a pointed look, annoyed that I have to deal with this bullshit. I swear it's like wrangling children.

"If that's all?" I question, raising an eyebrow and wanting to know how much longer he wants to complain about this.

"Of course, thank you for your time." Ponds gives Lilith a death glare, and she flips him the finger as I grab her forearm, portalling us to the city of the dead.

My grip is slightly rough with her forearm as she tugs it away. "That's some seriously dumb bullshit. Do you need to deal with that every day?" She rubs her forearm, and I wince, thinking that I hurt her. She turns to one of the decrepit buildings where the souls work. "What are we doing here anyway?"

"Looking for a specific soul."

"Why?" she questions, walking next to me and rubbing her arm again.

"Was I too rough with your arm?"

She laughs and shakes her head. "No, but who are we looking for?"

"His name is Kirk, and we just need to ask him some questions."

"You couldn't have a demon do this?"

"When you want something done right, you do it yourself." She nods her head in agreement and stops talking as I open the door for the both of us to walk in. I don't speak to anyone; they all just go about their business as we head to the elevator, and I push the button.

"It's kind of like they're all stuck in a mundane mediocre time loop," she comments. I nod my head but don't respond. The elevator feels stifling with her next to me. Her lips are pursed in a straight line, and I feel fucking ridiculous for wanting to make her smile, wanting to make her happy. *Could she ever truly be happy here, with me?*

The elevator dings, opening its doors, and we walk through them into the office space. Souls are working in their cubicles as Lilith looks around with interest.

"What are they working on?" she asks quietly.

"Some do the same work that they hated on earth as a punishment, others have actual jobs."

"Like..."

"Monitoring souls that have been bargained for, paperwork from sorting, reports from the pit." She nods her head, pleased with my actually answering her question. Maybe I need to be more honest with Lilith, but that involves me being vulnerable, and that sounds fucking terrible.

I don't knock, barging straight into Kirk's office. He actually has a door because he handles more delicate matters from time to time. He's been given harder tasks because he's been actively trying to be promoted to a demon for decades now.

"My lord," Kirk greets, bowing his head and glancing at Lilith. His eyes widen, and he clears his throat. My suspicions of this soul grow heavier as he glances between Lilith and me. "How may I serve you?" he asks.

"Such a gracious servant, Kirk."

I take the only available seat across his desk, leaving nowhere for Lilith to sit. She looks pissed but just stands there and watches the encounter.

"A week ago, you did the intake of all the souls. May I see it?"

"Of... Of course," he says, and I sense his fear filling up the room as he fingers through the manilla envelopes looking for last week's files. "Here you are," he says, handing them to me. If souls could sweat, I'm sure he would have some dripping down his forehead by now.

I lick my finger to turn the page and eye Lilith, who licks her lips as I glance through the paperwork. It's as I suspected; Lilith's paperwork isn't in here, even though I brought her here myself. I know I did the proper documents to make sure nothing looked suspicious. It was also a test to see if anyone was suspicious of what Lilith meant to me, and my suspicions are clearly valid as I stare at the soul before me.

"Where is Lilith's intake form?" I ask in an even tone.

"I'm not sure what you're talking about," he sputters, and I taste his lie. It's like ash on my tongue as he continues to speak. I stay sitting and don't raise my voice.

"I submitted the paperwork, where is it?"

"Sir?" he asks, trying to act like he's fumbling through the folders again.

"Has anyone come to you, Kirk? Asking about Lilith?"

Lilith's eyebrows furrow, and she looks like she wants to say something but holds back, just taking in the encounter. It's good to know that she doesn't speak everything that comes to her mind.

"My lord, I'm not sure what you're asking?"

It's then that I stand; both Kirk and Lilith track me as I slowly walk around the desk. I don't touch the soul, but I do stare at him. "Who took Lilith's paperwork?"

"I...I...I don't know."

It's not a lie; he's scared, but it's not a lie.

"Who would have had access to this?" I ask, pointing over to the filing cabinet he was leafing through earlier.

"You, high-ranking demons," he sputters.

"I see," I say with a smile on my face. "Maybe Elvor will be able to get more information from you." I clench my fist, and we watch as his soul disappears like a wisp of smoke.

When I turn on my heel and look at Lilith, her lips are parted as she looks at me and back to where the soul was standing.

"Did you kill him?" she asks.

I shake my head and adjust my suit jacket. "No, I sent him to the pit."

"Why is my paperwork so important?" she asks, her eyebrows furrowed as she holds on to her pad of paper and pen.

"Because I specifically gave it to Kirk to see who might be interested in your arrival in Hell. It appears my suspicions were correct."

She goes to ask another question, but I grab her by the arm and portal her to the fae realm before she can say anything else.

CHAPTER TEN

LILITH

I feel sick as we land on our feet. Lucifer doesn't let go of my arm, and I don't shake him off, feeling dizzy. His large palm circles the back of my neck, and I feel centered again.

"Sometimes long distances can be hard. Are you well?"

I nod my head, but he doesn't remove his hand. His skin feels ice cold against my flesh, and I nearly shiver.

"That was fucking abrupt," I scoff, and he finally removes his hand from my arm and neck. He just shrugs, making me irritated all over again. *What is it with these demons when you ask them a question?* "You would think you would want your assistant in the know so they could help you."

"You would think," he says, straightening his suit jacket. *Who gave him the right to look so damn good in a suit?* It's charcoal black and fits him perfectly. His hair didn't even move an inch from portalling here. It's embarrassing as I have to pick the jean shorts out of my ass while we walk down the path.

Whereas Hell is gloomy and gothic, the fae realm is... beautiful. The grass is the greenest I've ever seen, and the castle in front of us looks like something from a fairy tale. There are flowers trailing up the cream-colored towers, and I'm awestruck.

"You can just come here anytime you want?" I ask in disbelief.

"It's not all it seems," he retorts as we walk side by side. The gates open, and we walk through. It's then I see fae walking past us. They are all right around Elvors height. They're all slightly taller than Lucifer, and they do not look like they belong in a fairy tale.

Most are dressed in warrior regalia with blood covering their face and body. When I look to the left, I see three men hanging from what looks like a medieval gallow. Instinctively I take a step closer to Lucifer and avert my eyes from where their bodies hang. The place feels more ominous, not just because of Lucifer's words, but because of the stark contrast of how this realm looks versus the people in it.

"It's best you don't speak," Lucifer tells me as we approach the castle doors. Usually, I would retort back with something sassy, but I find his words wise, so I shut my mouth. I look up at him to see him smirking at me before the doors open, and we enter.

"Lucifer," the man on the throne says. He's a massive man with forearms the size of my thighs, and he's heavily scarred. His stance is relaxed as he sips on a stein of beer, and I watch as it drips into his ginger beard. "Who's the snack?" he asks, licking his lips and looking at me.

I instantly regret the Daisy-Duke attire that I wore to get under Lucifer's skin.

"Drugon, I'm here. What is it you want?" Lucifer demands sharply. He doesn't look at me, just faces down the fae king in front of us.

"As you know, my realm is at war." Lucifer doesn't answer, if anything, he looks bored with the conversation. "I was hoping you could spare some demon fae to come to the realm and help the cause."

Lucifer smiles. "And why would I do that?"

"My entire army will trade their souls to Hell to win this war," Drugon offers, and while Lucifer doesn't move or change his expression, I can tell he's thinking this over.

"I'll consider your offer," Lucifer says before spinning around. I stand there like an idiot for a moment before I have to nearly jog to catch up to him. Our feet hit the cobblestones, and I'm glad I at least wore comfortable shoes.

"That's it, that's the whole meeting?"

"Somethings wrong," he says softly, his brows furrowing when he looks down at me. "Fuck," he groans. He grabs my arm roughly, and I'm violently portaled again, but this time when we land I know exactly where we are.

"Why are we in Hallowsdeep?" I ask.

"Something doesn't feel right," he says again. He looks at me a little panicked as we walk down mainstreet. "Perhaps you should portal back to Hell?" he says it softly, not in his usual dickish tone.

"I can help," I reply, not knowing what exactly it is I'm to be helping him with. But in no way am I going to miss an opportunity to figure out piece by piece what's going on in this man's head.

Lucifer sighs and rubs his neck. "I'm not sure that's a good idea."

"Then I think it's probably a great idea. So what are we looking for, sir?" He stills slightly after I say 'sir', and I can't help but smirk.

So the man likes it when I call him sir, not surprising from a control freak who calls himself the 'king' of Hell.

He looks around and groans, I guess realizing that I will keep nagging the shit out of him or that he's going to have to tell me one way or another.

"A child," he says softly.

"We're here to look for a child?" I ask in confusion. "Listen man, if you're into abducting kids and bringing them to Hell this isn't going to work out. That's just wrong."

"Shut up," he growls.

"No you shut up. What kind of sick shit—"

He covers my mouth with his hand and sighs. "My child," he corrects.

My brows furrow as I take in his honest expression and look around mainstreet. "You have a kid... on Earth?"

"I... I didn't know I had one."

"So what? You came up to Earth and were a total slut and didn't know you got someone pregnant?"

"Someone fucking kill me," Lucifer mumbles under his breath. "I knew it was a possibility, but I swear I was just summoned with blood, and the only way someone could do that is if they had my blood or are of my blood."

I blink at him a few times. He looks shy and a little irritated with himself. "I mean, I guess we should start with the women you fucked while you were here." It's the first time I've seen his cheeks heat, and as cute as it is, knowing he banged half this town pisses me off.

"Okay, so maybe we're better off lining up all the children in town and seeing which ones look like you?"

"Fucking fuck," he says as he walks away from me. "Go back to Hell, Lilith. I'll handle this." He takes off in one direction, and I go the other. He storms around town like he isn't a giant lunatic. *What child would feel comfortable approaching him?* Nevertheless the opportunity to see this pan out is far too intriguing to just go back to Hell.

So, as usual, I don't listen to his instructions and start walking around town. My feelings on the matter, about him having a kid, are complicated. It's not necessarily that him having a child seems out of character, maybe I'm bothered by the idea of him being with other women. It's not like I should care that he was a complete manwhore, it's not like... *okay that train of thought got a little crazy.* I look around the town and think about where exactly a kid could accidentally summon their own father?

What would the spawn of Satan look like? As much as I'd like to say he's an evil asshole, the man is handsome. Otherworldly knee-shakingly handsome.

It's annoying and distracting.

I'm trying to find my footing in this new world and figure out how to move on, grieve over my sister and the life I had, but he makes it so damn hard. I keep wanting to annoy him and prove to him that I'm not worth the trouble. I'm not sure what he sees in me, hell knows I wish I could.

I'm so deep in my own internal thoughts that I've passed a playground and find myself by the line of trees before you enter the woods. There's a willow tree blowing in the cold air, and when I look further, I see stark black hair and hear whimpering noises. I part the willow leaves and look down to find a small child huddled under the branches, crying.

"Hey," I say softly.

Her watery gaze looks up from her knees, and she wipes her tears. "What do you want?" she snarks in an irritated tone. *Yup, this is the one.*

"Why are you hiding in here?"

"Because all of those kids are assholes," she says, and I notice a scratch on her arm.

"What happened to your arm?"

She scoffs and shakes her head. "That little turd, Clover, thought it would be funny to play Salem witch trials and said I should be the one burned at the stake. She scratched me with a stick."

"Clover sounds like a real cunt," I comment. The child's eyes glitter, and I see a small smile form across her face as she nods her head. I go over to the trunk of the tree and sit next to her. When she looks up at me, her eyes have changed to a soft yellowish color. I don't point it out, but sit exactly like she does and wrap my arms around my knees. "What were you thinking about when she hurt you?"

"How I wish I knew who my dad was so he could take me away from here."

"It's that bad?" I ask, wondering if she's being abused or if she's hurt.

She sighs and shakes her head. "I just don't fit in. The kids are mean, my mom..." she trails off, looking out at the playground.

"I've never fit in either," I say.

"Well, yeah, you're dressed like that," she says, looking at me, and I burst out laughing. The little girl follows suit, and it's nice to see a smile take over her face. "It's alright to be different, trust me." She sighs, and that's when I see Lucifer taking long strides towards the willow tree.

He parts the leaves looking at me first. "I told you to go home."

"Look," I say, pointing to the little girl. Her eyes widen when she takes in his appearance. Maybe he should have done something to not look so imposing, but Lucifer is never one to change his appearance for anyone.

In less than a few seconds, he's down on his knees in front of her, his face the most relaxed and gentle as I've ever seen it while he looks at the little girl. "Hi, I'm Luc," he says, and the little girl looks him over a few times.

"I'm Blair."

"I think we might have been looking for each other," he says. He stares at Blair for a few moments before he looks at me. I'm not sure what expression he expected to see, but honestly, this moment is so fucking cute how could I be anything but in awe.

They both stare at each other for a moment, neither of them knowing what to say when I cut in. "Blair, I think maybe you could take Luc—" I look him over and want to roll my eyes at the name he chose to give himself, "to talk to your mom."

Lucifer clears his throat. "Who—" It's my turn to put my hand on his mouth this time. What was this idiot going to do, ask her who her mother is? I glare at him but look back at Blair.

She sighs and nods her head. "Follow me," she says, standing up and walking deeper into the woods.

Lucifer and I follow behind her, giving her space.

"Were you really going to ask her who her fucking mother was?"

He grimaces and shrugs his shoulders. "I wasn't thinking. She's... she's..."

I grab his forearm and squeeze. "She's special," I tell him, and he looks down at me, smiling. It's the first time Lucifer has smiled at me in a way that's truly endearing. He isn't smiling because he knows a secret or because he's messing with me. He's smiling at me because he's happy.

"She can't know who we are." I furrow my brows and look at him as he shakes his head. "It's for her protection."

"How exactly could she summon you?" I ask as a blonde woman steps out of the forest cottage. Her nose is up in the air as she plants her hands on her hips.

He sighs as he looks at the woman in front of him. "Because she's part witch."

He walks forward as Blair's mom glares at him, then me, and then at Blair. "Stay out here while we talk," the woman spits at Blair.

The little girl rolls her eyes and stands next to me as Lucifer gives me a look that says he doesn't want to go in the cottage, but he does anyway. I try not to tell the witch she should mind who she's speaking to, but that's her own funeral. So, here I am, standing outside the cottage with a small child who happens to be the spawn of Satan.

"So you're what, his girlfriend?" Blair asks, leaning against a tree, her arms folded.

"Assistant," I reply, and she scoffs.

We hear some shouting coming from the cottage, and we both wince.

"He didn't know about me?" she asks softly, and I shake my head. Her eyebrows furrow, and her eyes turn blue. "How did you find me?"

I'm not sure how pissed Lucifer is going to be at me for doing this, but when I look down at Blair, I see so much of myself. I crouch down to get to her level, and I push every ounce of persuasion I can into my words.

"He didn't know about you, but he must have felt you calling him. You're wanted and special. Never let anyone put you down, you're meant for great things, Blair."

"I am?" she asks softly.

"Definitely."

There's some more shouting from the cottage until Lucifer storms out, no sign of Blair's mother as he calms himself and gives Blair a smile.

"Are you hungry?" he asks the little girl.

She shrugs. "Sure?"

"What's the best place you can think of, wherever you want to go."

She smiles as she thinks. "Carly's Crabs?"

"You got it," he says. "Go get cleaned up, and we'll go." She smiles and runs into the house to get changed.

"So... you're a dad."

"I guess, yeah," he says shyly, his hands in his suit jacket as he looks down at the ground. "Is that a problem for you?"

"Why would it be, I'm just your assistant."

"Right," he says, looking back at the house. "She can't remember you," he says softly.

"She doesn't even know my name," I say, trying to reason with him, and I wonder why he's being so secretive of her and me.

"It's the best for both of you. She can't know what we are or who I really am. She needs to stay with her cunt of a mother, even if I don't like it."

"Can't we bring her to Hell with us?"

He shakes his head. "She's only half demon, and I don't think it's fair to her."

I think about all the souls I've seen in Hell, and of course, there are no children. I nod my head and agree with his terms.

"Can I say goodbye?"

He nods his head and smiles as Blair comes running out of the house. "This is the best birthday ever," she says. I see a genuine smile take over Lucifer's face, and in that moment, I decide there's no way that he's the monster that I thought he was. I get down to Blair's level to speak to her again.

"So you and your dad are going to have dinner, okay?"

"You can come," Blair says, and I shake my head.

"Thanks for inviting me, but you go with your dad and have a good time."

"Okay," Blair says, looking over at Lucifer.

"Happy birthday until we can meet again," I say, holding out my hand, and she shakes it. She looks back over at Lucifer, and I watch them walk out of the woods together.

I'd never really thought of children before, and I wonder how long Lucifer has been alive, along with if this is something that he's always wanted. As I watch him laugh at his daughter's jokes, it's clear that this is a happy moment for him.

The selfish thought I have is how I wish I could be a part of this moment too, knowing damn well I have no right. I'm just his assistant.

CHAPTER ELEVEN

LUCIFER

I sit at a table in this odd seafood restaurant, staring at the child sitting across from me, who is undeniably mine. We share the same hair and eyes, and apparently, her attitude might have been inherited as well.

"Why this place?" I ask, looking at the eclectic crab shack.

"It's expensive, and I never get to come here, but it looks like you have money." I can't help but smile at her and her perceptive answer.

"How old are you?"

"I turned seven today," she says proudly, though she talks like she's much older. And with a foul mouth.

"Happy Birthday, are you having a party?"

She scoffs and shakes her head. "No, my mom told me I was lucky to be alive, and that's my gift."

My anger is on the precipice of overflowing as she talks about how Josie treats her. I remember sleeping with the witch and realizing she was powerful. She's now the high priestess of her coven, and I wonder if Josie also being magical is the reason Blair is able to be half-demon, instead of simply mortal.

Her demon nature isn't at the forefront, it's her witch side that's running the show. Her demon side is dormant, but I can feel it wanting to take over.

Everything I've ever cared about has always been taken away from me in some way or another, and as I look down at this angry little girl, I know what I have to do. And that's to protect her any way I can.

"What would you like for your birthday?" I ask, and she shrugs. Her eyes turn purple before she blinks, and they shift back to brown.

"Money is always good." I nod in agreement.

"I'm going to start a bank account for you. One that your mother can't touch. It will be your money, you understand?" She nods her head as she cracks a crab leg and eats the meat.

"So am I supposed to call you dad?" she asks.

"If you'd like."

She tilts her head and looks at me inquisitively. "You really didn't know about me?" I shake my head, and with the way she looks at me, I wonder if she has my ability to taste lies. "Okay then. I'll call you dad."

I can't hide my smile as I eat my own food. We eat somewhat quietly for a moment, sizing each other up.

"So that pretty woman, is she your girlfriend?"

"Something like that," I answer, and she nods.

"That's cool. She seems cool."

"She is."

"So what, do I get to live with you now?" she asks, and my heart sinks. As badly as I'd love to wrap her up in my arms and take her to Hell with me. Hell is no place for a child, and if I truly want to protect her, then the only people who can know about her are Lilith and myself.

"I think for now I'll just visit Hallowsdeep when I can." I watch as her face falls, and it's one of the worst things I've ever seen. As badly as I want her by my side every minute of every day, it's not safe. She's not strong enough.

But Blair just sits taller, accepting the disappointment, and nods her head. "That's fine. I get it." God, she's so young but so strong already. She shouldn't have to live like this, and I can't help but feel guilty.

"I promise to visit as much as I can."

She nods her head like she doesn't believe me. "Can you just promise me to always make my birthdays this special?"

I smile and nod. "That I can promise."

We finish dinner and head back to her mother's house. She doesn't talk much as we get to the cottage. I know what I need to do, but it doesn't make it any easier. I get down on one knee and hold out my arms. I wrap them around her, infusing her with my magic to protect her human body and mind from the demon part of her. I want her to live a full and happy life before she ever has to see where she comes from.

When she pulls away, she looks brighter; it's then I realize how much she needed me to reign her demon side in and protect her human form. This next step is going to be the hardest part. Staring into her eyes, I tell her the lie she needs to hear. "I'm your dad, and I have a very busy job. I visit as much as I can. You won't remember how we met, and you won't remember my friend. You'll just remember that I love you. Happy Birthday, Blair."

"Thanks, dad," she says.

I take her in one last time as she walks away from me, her mother glaring at her as she comes out to greet me.

"About time you decided to stop being a dead-beat," she sneers, as I look past her to confirm that Blair is in the house. I grab Josie by the throat and push her against the side of the house. Getting right into her face, I try my fucking hardest not to really kill her.

"You hit her, hurt her, or mistreat her, and I'll make sure that every moment for your eternal existence is fucking horrible." Her eyes widen as she scratches at my fist. I loosen my grip, and she glares at me.

"You don't know what it's like to parent. If you're so concerned, then take her with you."

"You don't think I wish I could. She needs to remain here until it's her time."

"So when's the next time I can expect a visit from you and your little whore?"

I snarl, gripping her throat again and hitting her hard against the house.

"You will never speak about her like that…" Another hard shove. "Again." I can see the fear in Josie's eyes when I squeeze just a little bit harder. Maybe I'd be doing the kid a favor by killing her, I could find someone better suited to raise Blair. But then I worry about what would happen if she's adopted outside of her coven. Blair needs to become the best witch she possibly can. It would make her unstoppable.

"You will raise Blair and take care of her until she's an adult. You are to train Blair to be as powerful as her potential allows. You will not tell her who I am. When I come to see her, you will not interfere. Do you understand?"

Josie nods her head, and I let her down. Her hand flies up to her throat, and I can tell she wants to hex me. Josie has her suspicions of who and what I am, but as far as she knows, I'm just a demon, and I've made it clear that I'm not one to be fucked with.

"I'm setting up a bank account in her name. If I find out you or one of your coven members have touched it, there will be hell to pay."

I walk away, my shoulders tense, and all I want to do is scream. Why did I think this was a good idea? That we could just fucking breed with humans and create demons without getting attached?

Maybe the others don't feel the same way I do because their children aren't magical. But Blair? Fuck, I can already tell her power is going to be special. She's going to be fierce and someone to reckon with. My pride for the daughter I just met is almost as overwhelming as the guilt and sadness that follows me back to Hell.

As soon as I return, I summon Toth and Milcom to my study. I've trusted both of them with multiple missions, and this one is just as important. Toth, as always, looks calm and ready, but there's something about Milcom that seems slightly off.

"I need both of you to go to Earth and see if I have any offspring that hold the demon trait."

I hand them a list, and Toth raises an eyebrow at the names on the list but doesn't say anything. "We'll split the list up and check, my lord," Toth says, making Milcom's face twitch.

"What of my work with Beelzebub, my lord?"

I arch a brow at him and let out an irritated sigh. "This is more important than monitoring the angels right now."

"Of course," he says, bowing his head as he leaves the room.

Toth stays behind and looks me over once. "Lucifer, is there something more?"

I'm overwhelmed with tonight's events and how it seems like I'll never know a moment of true peace again. Not with needing to keep the two most important people in my existence a secret.

"That is all."

"Very well," he says, spinning on his heel and leaving the office. He shuts the door, and I immediately start pouring myself a glass of alcohol.

This was not my plan when I thought about making demons on earth. I didn't plan to look at the face of a little girl with deep brown eyes and dark hair and think about how adorable she is or how I would do anything to keep her safe.

There's not much I can do to protect her except for making sure her demon side lies dormant. While there's not a lot I can do on Earth, Blair deserves a childhood. A long and happy life is far more important than having an heir or a created army.

On the other hand, I can't disband the program yet, either. Everyone will speculate, and my idiotic idea will go under fire. Maybe they would even start looking for Blair.

I've fucked up, and all I can worry about is if my mistakes and arrogance will come back to haunt the child I didn't know I had.

There's a knock at the door, and irritation fills me, thinking that Toth would like to talk some more. I roll my eyes, choosing not to answer, but the knock continues.

"What?" I growl.

"Sorry, I can come back later," her soft voice says, and I clear my throat.

"It's fine." I down the whiskey and pour another as she walks in. It's late, and she's wearing a large t-shirt, but I can't tell what's underneath. It's fucked up, but as badly as I want her here, I want her to leave as well. She saw too much. At least she didn't seem mad, but why would she? She doesn't see me the way I see her.

"How's Blair?" she asks. My eyes meet hers immediately.

"I put some protections in place."

She nods and rubs her arm. Her blonde hair is loose, falling down her back, and all I want is for her to just come sit on my lap and make everything better, but she turns. I see the outline of her panties against her shirt, and I groan.

Lilith turns back, popping out her hip and leaning against the doorframe. "If you ever want to talk about it..." She doesn't finish her offer, looking anywhere but my face.

"I'm alright."

She scoffs, shaking her head. "Are you really that unfeeling?"

I take a deep breath and look at her. "Goodnight, Lilith."

"No, not '*goodnight, Lilith*'. You have a daughter. A human daughter?" I raise an eyebrow at her, and it would usually make anyone else shut up, but she doesn't. "She just seemed sad," she says quietly.

I sigh and rub my temple. "I've had a talk with her mother, and I'll do what I can."

She looks at me as if what I'm doing isn't enough, but she nods her head anyway. "She's pretty cute," she tries again, saying it with a smile. I try to hide my smirk as I take another sip of my whiskey. "That's what I thought," she says before turning around and waving a hand. "Goodnight." She walks away, and I can't help but feel like I got played.

Lilith came in here to check on me, she didn't have to, but she did, and something about that warms my chest. As much as I might want to drink myself stupid over the guilt I feel about leaving Blair on Earth, knowing that Lilith met Blair and wasn't disgusted or angry with me is something. If anything, she seems to have a soft spot for my tenacious little spawn. I mean, how could you not?

I debate all night about what additional protections I can put in place for Blair, and if there's any way I can bring her to Hell sooner. But the idea of her not living her full life on Earth saddens me more than not having her here with me. We'll have eternity together, so for now, I'll make sure she lives. That she's happy and protected, and that she always has the best birthdays.

CHAPTER TWELVE

LILITH

*G*reat, now he's a hot dad! Is my first thought when I show up to Lucifer's office the next morning. He looks fucking good, not as sad as he looked last night. He's wearing this floor-length suit jacket with a tie that looks like it's made of leather, and his hair is pushed back. I'm not supposed to find him attractive or endearing. He's *literally* Satan. If I find him these things, what does that make me?

"Lilith," he barks, making me jump.

"Sorry, what?" He rolls his eyes at my not paying attention and sighs.

"We have to go back to the fae realm today."

"Okay," I nod and look down. I'm dressed in a floor-length, deep maroon dress with long slits up the legs. And I can't help but catch him staring at the exposed skin of my thigh as the fabric plays peek-a-boo with him. It makes my lip twitch, but I don't mention it. I sure as shit wasn't going to get caught in the fae realm looking like a pin-up for some car magazine again.

"Are you going to accept his offer?" I ask.

He smirks. "You'll just have to be patient, won't you?"

Patience is not a virtue that I have. I thought I was gaining some patience when I was going on my little murder spree, but I was wrong. I feel like there are so many secrets in Hell, and I haven't even scratched the surface. It's making me feel on edge.

He catches my forearm and portals us to the fae realm. It's the same, looking all angelic on the outside, but once you're past the gates, you can smell the violence and distraction that these people wreak.

"Remember, quiet."

I want to roll my eyes, but the truth is that this realm is scary in its own right. I'm not going to be the one to stir the pot and become a victim of whatever this place is capable of. *Now that I think of it, can I die?* This is an important question to ask, but as I watch the stony expression taking over Lucifer's face, I know now isn't the time to ask.

He doesn't knock but instead walks right into the same room as before. The giant and terrifying fae leader is sitting on his throne. Only this time, he has a small woman sitting in front of him on the floor. She looks human, pretty, but terrified. Drugon yanks slightly on a chain that's connected to a collar circling her neck and pulls her closer to him. She is basically sitting on top of his massive feet while wrapping her arms around his calves.

I wish I had my fucking dagger. I'd stab the ugly massive fae right in the heart and get her out of here. As much as I try, I can't keep my eyes off her, even as Lucifer holds a conversation with the fae king.

"Lucifer, do you accept my terms?"

"How many fae souls would I be taking to my realm?" he asks. I can see him in my peripheral vision, but my eyes still don't leave the girl. She's trying to look anywhere but directly at me. Does she think I would hurt her? I try to relax and hope that maybe some of that energy will radiate over to her.

"Easily two hundred."

"And they know of this agreement?" Lucifer asks.

"They follow under my rule; what I say goes."

"So you're bargaining with souls that aren't yours to bargain with?"

"I heard that you needed some strength in Hell, is it all gossip?" That juicy tid-bit of information has me looking away from the girl and back at Lucifer. He smirks, completely letting what the fae king says slide off his shoulders.

"Where did you hear such gossip, Drugon?" Lucifer takes a few steps closer to him. I watch as the king becomes uncomfortable, his grip around the chain loosening enough for the girl to crawl to the side of his throne.

"I can't remember the demon's name," Drugon deflects.

"That's very inconvenient."

Drugon starts to backtrack. I'm not sure if it's the calmness on Lucifer's face or just how intimidating his presence is as he continues to get closer. Drugon is bigger than Lucifer, which is saying something, but Lucifer's power makes up for any size difference they may have. It's nearly rolling off of him in waves. I can see how uncomfortable all of the fae in the room are getting.

For some reason, his power has the opposite effect on me. I find myself leaning closer to him, wanting to taste the power for myself.

"I meant no offense, Lucifer."

He smirks as the fae king says his name.

"No?" he replies. It's condescending and fucking hot, the confidence he has in this realm. "Drugon, I'm tempted to kill you and everyone in this castle right now."

"I, uh, I have a demon you can take."

"And the girl," I chime in, pointing at the girl in chains. Lucifer doesn't reprimand me, just nods his head.

"Which demon?"

Drugon holds his large fist up. "Bring him."

A blond male demon is dragged through the court and put on his knees before us. Lucifer tilts his head and looks down at the demon in recognition.

"Asmodeus."

"My lord."

"How was your stay in the fae realm?"

Asmodeus grimaces and groans. "Unpleasant."

"I find it interesting that you've had one of my demons for so long and never told me. You know, Drugon, the basis of a good friendship is honesty."

"I... I didn't think he meant much to you."

"You know what they say about assumptions," Lucifer says. He walks a little closer to Drugon, grabbing the chain from his hand and holding it out to me. I take it in my hand, and the woman looks up at me with a mixture of terror and relief. But clearly, I'm the lesser of two evils as she scurries to my side.

Lucifer grins at the king, and I barely notice the way his fingers shift into long claws. Faster than the crack of thunder, he reaches inside the king's chest and twists. A smile spreads across his face as he says, "I'm sure Elvor will be excited for the family reunion." With that, Lucifer pulls out the fae king's heart, a slash of blood spraying onto his face and all over his pristine suit.

It should be horrifying.

He just ripped out the king's heart in front of his entire village. And he smiled while he did it. I can't help but smile as I watch him drop the heart. It thuds with a squelch on the tile as he wipes his bloody hand on the clothes of the now-dead fae leader.

"Do not summon me to this shit-hole unless it's warranted. Do you understand?" Lucifer says calmly to the crowd, completely nonchalant about his act of violence. *Why is that so hot?* The fae who just watched their king die at the hands of this demon with very little effort nod their heads, and it's so quiet you could hear a pin drop.

"A little help, Barbie," Asmodeus sasses, holding out his wrists to show his shackles still tight against his skin.

I shrug. "I don't know how to take them off."

He tilts his head and assesses me. "Interesting."

"What?" I'm still holding onto the girl's chain leash, not knowing how to get her out of it, but also making sure no one takes her from me.

"Lucifer wouldn't usually bring fresh meat to something like this."

I grimace. "Gross."

"No, you know what's gross? Having to be here for a decade and not knowing why."

"Let's go," Lucifer growls. I put a hand on the girl's arm, and Lucifer takes hold of both Asmodeus and myself.

We're brought to his study, and Lucifer snaps his fingers, causing the chains holding back Asmodeus and the girl to immediately release themselves.

"Can... can I go home?" the girl questions softly.

Lucifer nods and looks over to Asmodeus. "Take her back to Earth. Then take some time off but report back in two weeks."

"Thank you, my lord," Asmodeus says, collecting the crying girl and portalling her to wherever it is she belongs.

Lucifer takes two steps towards me, backing me up against some furniture as he cranes his neck to look down at me.

"You disobeyed me," he says softly. His brown eyes are intense as he stares me down. He still has blood on his face, but somehow he still looks put together.

"I needed to get her out."

He places his hands against the wall behind me. I feel like a caged animal, and my heart beats rapidly against my chest. I'm surrounded by nothing other than him. His scent is thick, like clove and teakwood. I'm guessing he's expecting an apology, but he isn't getting one. It's not like I can think with him this close anyway.

"I would have gotten her out," he says. He doesn't touch me, and I hate myself for wishing that he would. That he would glide his massive hands down my side and show me just how strong he is. I wish that I could tangle my hands in his bloody hair and kiss him. I lick my lips with the thought, and he tracks my tongue before his gaze snaps back to my eyes.

"Do you like riling me up, Lilith?" he asks softly, almost like a taunt instead of a reprimand.

I shrug my shoulders in response. All thoughts leave my head except how close he is, how much larger he is, and how I can't stop thinking about how much I like it.

His hand is caked in blood as he touches my hair. I couldn't stop the shiver that wracks my body if I tried. "So beautiful, so defiant," he says, bringing a ribbon of hair to his nose. He inhales and lets the hair go. His fingers touch the stone of my necklace, his fingers lightly grazing my chest as he smiles at me. "We'll work on that. Goodnight, Lilith."

I don't even have a moment to question him or to reply. He's out of the room before I can even come back with a sassy retort. My breathing is heavy as I think about what just happened. My first thoughts are about how sexy he is and how he's far more complex than I ever imagined.

Then the guilt creeps in. The fact that I don't know if he was honest about Diana being an angel and how her last words to me were about me being evil and a monster.

I'm attracted to the fucking Devil, and I'm finding that perhaps it's more than just attraction. I like this job, being around him all the time. It's not just genuine curiosity either, it feels like he's the opposite side of a magnet, and no matter my resistance, he's going to pull me right back towards him every time.

I sigh, rubbing at my face and wishing for one fucking second that I could forget about the last conversation I had with Diana. If I could just speak to her one more time, we could clear the air, and then maybe I could start living this new life that I want. The life that I feel guilty for wanting.

I'm a demon, and it's about time that I start coming to terms with that.

I know that I'm here for a reason. I enjoy violence. It's not only evident in the crimes that got me sent to Hell, but watching Lucifer with his casual violence and power towards a man who deserved it, turned me on. It made me crave it for myself.

Ugh, I miss my fucking dagger. The way it made me feel powerful and warmed my hip. I miss feeling dangerous. Right now, I feel like a guilty imposter.

I still don't know if I have a gift. Really, the only demons who have been kind or embraced me in this realm are Lucifer, Kas, and Elvor. As much as I tend to linger on the past, I think I need to start working towards the future by making my place in Hell known and embracing who I can be as a demon.

As much as I want to take this step forward in this new world, I can't stop seeing Diana's horrified face every time I think about the bad deeds I can't help but seem to enjoy.

CHAPTER THIRTEEN

LILITH

This past week has been quiet, but tonight is supposed to be eventful. Asmodeus is apparently throwing a 'Welcome back to Hell' party for himself. I asked Kas if she was going, and she said she had a job to do on Earth. I could tell there was something more to her answer, and I don't care if it takes me many immortal years, I'm going to find out.

I'm in Lucifer's office, going through his schedule for the next week. The meeting with Heaven is coming up, and I've tried to be on my best behavior so that he takes me. He's been a little distant since he was all up in my personal space after killing the fae king. I'm grateful for it—I think.

"Are you going to the party tonight?" I ask, looking at him from under my lashes as he sits at his desk. He shakes his head no and swallows down another glass of whiskey. I'd say he's an alcoholic, but he doesn't seem to get drunk. Maybe it's something to do with his hands. I have other ideas about what he could do with his hands, but I shake my head, focusing back on him when he speaks.

"You're going?" he asks, arching an eyebrow, but he doesn't look up from what he's working on.

"I figured it was time to interact with more demons." He hums in acknowledgment but doesn't add any additional commentary. "Should I not go?" I ask, feeling insecure. It feels like Lucifer has sequestered me away from everyone else in his realm. I'd ask why, but I know he would either not answer or answer with some sort of riddle.

"You're free to do what you wish. Minx is here in Hell."

"Helpful," I mutter under my breath, and I watch his lip twitch. Obviously, I knew the club was in Hell, not like Asmodeous is having us all portal and party at some human establishment.

We continue working in silence, even though I still have a million questions. He still hasn't given me a straight answer for nearly any question I've asked, and the secrets between us are pissing me off. But right now is not the time to get into it. I need to be a good girl to be able to go to that meeting and find out for myself if Diana is okay. I feel like it's the only way I'll be able to move on. I need to know that she's safe and that she doesn't hate me.

Once my work is done, I glance up at him. "Is there anything else?"

He shakes his head and without speaking, leaves the room. *Such a moody bastard sometimes, I swear.*

I go back to my quarters and make myself look hot. I have demons to impress, and well, I need to establish that I'm not someone to be fucked with. I hate to admit it, but from the looks I've gotten, it's clear that most of the demons here feel some sort of way about me. They're suspicious about Lucifer's treatment of me—I guess I am too. But I need to set the record straight. I'm more than Lucifer's assistant; I can be deadly when I want to, and I won't allow the constant disrespect.

Lucifer and Kas can't be my only friends here. If I can even truly call them that. I'm in a new place, and I don't have my sister anymore to rely on when it comes to being social. It's outside of my comfort zone—making new friends, but everyone here is a demon. The expectations of my morality aren't like what they were on earth.

At least that's what I tell myself as I wiggle into the most salacious dress I've ever worn. It's deep red, so red it nearly looks black. It covers my tits, but there are strings of fabric holding it intact. My entire back is bare, and the skirt is long, but the slits are high, exposing my thighs with every movement. I choose to wear my hair down. It's long, and I swear it got softer and fuller when I became a demon. I put on some makeup to make my lashes longer, eyebrows darker, and by the time I'm done, I feel good.

More than good. If I'm being honest, I feel like myself. And as good as it feels, I'm not exactly sure what that means. *Am I fully accepting this? My life in Hell? That I'm a demon and inherently evil?*

I sigh, wanting Diana's voice out of my head for just one night. I want to be able to let her judgment go, I really do. But I don't have any closure.

My twin died right before my eyes, and the last words we said to each other are something I replay daily. Obviously, my being a demon isn't going to change, so that leaves me with only one other option; I need to change the way I feel about it. I think the only way that will happen is if I see Diana happy and she sees that I'm okay. Then the past can be in the past.

With my shoulders pushed back and my head held high I portal to the club ready to party. It's dark and gothic, just like Lucifer's home. There's red carpet throughout the space, with iron sconces on the walls and gold fixtures throughout. It's a large open space with multiple pieces of furniture for people to sit on and talk. A dance floor is in the middle of the room, but no one is currently partaking in that.

"Barbie, you made it!" Asmodeus cheers, standing next to me with a wide smile.

"I did."

He tugs me by the elbow to sit on one of the deep velvet couches. There's a clearing of a throat next to me, and Asmodeus scoffs. "Where are my manners? Judd, this is Barbie."

"Lilith," I interject, and Asmodeus waves me off.

"She's Lucifer's new asssssssistant," he says with a smirk. "Judd is Hell's local drug dealer; whatever you want, you got it."

I clear my throat and shake my head. "I'm good. Thanks."

"If you change your mind," Judd says in a bored tone with a shrug. Judd looks like he might have just gotten to Hell recently, judging by his style. It looks like he listens to Nirvana, hates everyone, and smokes weed under the bleachers. He's attractive, but he seems sad, and well, sad boys aren't my type.

Asmodeus hops up from his seat and claps his hands. "Well, friends, I need to catch up for lost time."

Judd rolls his eyes, and I blink at him. "Know of any bossy lady demons around here?" Asmodeus asks, winking at me. "Nevermind." He waves a hand at me. "I'd rather keep my dick attached to me."

"What?" I ask, but he's already walking off in the direction where a horde of women are drinking cocktails.

"Maybe Lucifer should have left him in the fae realm," Judd comments from next to me.

"Yeah, maybe."

"How long have you been here?" Judd asks.

"About a month."

Judd's eyes bulge in surprise, but his face stays pretty stoic for the most part as he takes out a small baggy from his coat pocket. Taking a small mirror out, he lines the powder into a thin line with a credit card before using a ten dollar mortal bill to snort the substance up his nose. The effects are nearly instantaneous as I watch them take over his demeanor.

He doesn't seem as laid back as before. A small smile takes over his face as his pupils dilate, and he scans the room.

"What does it feel like?" I ask him, I've never tried anything besides smoking a joint here and there. I was honestly worried about trying anything because I thought I might like it too much. I had enough problems with impulse control in my human life, I didn't need to add an addiction on top of that.

"Makes me feel excited, like I have energy. It helps with the—" he cuts himself off and shakes his head. "It just makes things more fun."

I nod my head, and I can't deny my curiosity, but right now is not the time to experiment. I need to get the lay of the land since Kas and Lucifer aren't here, and it's up to me to sink or swim.

Judd seems content to sit next to me, and I feel like a wimp using him as a sad little demon shield. But I really don't want to sit alone. He taps his foot to the soft hum of the music, and I take the time to look around the room at the mix of men and women. I can feel the danger around me, and I can't help but like it, knowing that I don't have to hide who I am, what I feel, or my impulsive choices. When I'm here around these people, I'm probably not even the worst of the worst.

"Judd?"

"Hmm?"

"Why are you a demon?"

He shrugs his shoulders. "Fuck if I know why he upgraded me, but I'm happier for it. Being a soul in Hell fucking sucks. You get to enjoy a lot more things as a demon."

I shake my head. "No, like, what did you do to get sent to Hell?" I can tell he's uncomfortable, but before he can answer, we're interrupted.

Lisa, Autumn, and Tina all stand before us. Tina looks a little lost like she doesn't realize what's going on, but she's just here for the ride. Autumn glares at me while Lisa gives me a fake smile, showing off her creepily over-whitened teeth.

"Well, look who got off her knees for five minutes to join us," Lisa says, clapping her hands together. "Looks like you found good company," she gestures over to Judd.

He doesn't even seem phased, rolling his eyes and tilting his head back, mumbling the lyrics to the song that's playing under his breath.

"Lisa, right?" I ask, and she nods her head.

"I seem to have left an impression on the little thing," Lisa scoffs, causing Autumn and Tina to both laugh at her stupid joke. "So, did Lucifer get bored yet?" she questions.

I'm not sure why it pisses me off so much. Has Lucifer had multiple demons who have served as his assistant? Am I just one of many? Or is this bitch just trying to call me a slut?

I don't let her get under my skin, giving her a snarky smile and crossing my legs. "I'm new to this whole demon thing. Is it the length of being a demon that makes you an insufferable cunt, or were you born that way?" Judd snickers next to me, covering his face with his hands while Lisa and her little posse glare at me.

"At least I earned my position. I didn't have to suck the Devil's cock to get where I am."

I smile, standing up. I'm taller than Lisa by a few inches, and I look down my nose at her. "Poor thing, it must be so fucking exhausting being so different from other girls." I lean in closer to whisper in her ear. "And you have it all wrong, sweetheart. If anyone is getting on their knees, it will be Lucifer for me." I back up, watching her horrified expression as I give her and her little girl gang a wave. "Enjoy your night," I say, spinning on my heel. Judd has a genuine smile on his face as I give him a wink and walk to the opposite side of the club.

Suddenly the necklace heats at my throat. It's so hot that it can't be ignored. "What the fuck?" I say to myself, wrapping my hands around the obsidian necklace. It immediately transports me without my consent.

It's different from portalling. The tug to the next destination feels completely different, and I feel dizzy as I land on my heels, which click against black marble floors with white and silver veins weaving through the shiny texture.

"Jesus fucking christ," I grumble, grabbing onto the closest wall for purchase.

"Didn't know it would be so taxing?" a deep voice asks in front of me. When my gaze looks up, I can hardly breathe at what's before me.

Lucifer naked in a tub. The only thing he's wearing is the same necklace as me. The tub is huge, enough to fit his large body. There are some bubbles popping on the surface, but not many.

His pecs hover above the water, and holy fuck, he looks good. There's a dark scattering of chest hair that I could spend all day staring at. That is until he clears his throat, and I have to snap my head to gaze into his dark stare.

He's smirking at me as he lies relaxed in the tub, his elbows resting on the edges like he doesn't have a single care in the world. "Eyes are up here, love," he teases, and I swallow. *I'm not going to look at Satan's dick. I'm not going to look at Satan's dick.*

I clear my throat and shake my head. "I was at a party, you know."

"I know," he says in a bored tone.

"What was so important you had to pull me away from a party to come to you when you're..." I can't complete the sentence as I use my hand to motion at his body in the tub. His beautifully bronzed, built body. It doesn't help that it smells amazing in here. I have a vision of undressing and getting into the tub next to him. As big as his body is, he would probably be able to wrap it around me like I was nothing.

I can't help myself, I look down into the clearing bubbles. Yup... his dick is huge. Like genuinely will-it-fit huge. If that's soft, I shiver, thinking about what it would look like hard. I mean, he's huge, and he's powerful, and he has a big dick. Why does the universe keep tempting me with this man? He's my boss, for one; second, he's an asshole; third, he's the fucking Devil. I should hate him. *I do hate him*. He's the manifestation of all the evil in the world... *right*?

When I glance back at his face, he's more than smirking, he's grinning at me. Proud of himself or his massive cock, I'm not sure. I mean, any man would be proud of that thing.

"The meeting with Heaven has been moved up."

"Oh?" I ask, placing my hands on my hips and willing myself to not take a deeper look at his body.

"Four days."

"Does this mean you're letting me go?"

He smiles again and licks his lips. "Yes, you can come," he confirms in a deep voice that makes me shiver, and I can't help but think he means it in more ways than one.

"Thank you," I say softly, not wanting to piss him off and have him change his mind. But more than anything, I am actually grateful. Maybe he knows I need this. I need this closure with my sister before I can really thrive here, in Hell.

"There are some rules," he says.

"Of course," I nod my head.

"The angels are to know nothing of Hell's dealings. I will handle all conversations, and you must do as I say when we get there."

"Okay." I nod my head.

"I mean it, Lilith. If I tell you to sit on your knees next to me, if I tell you to shut up, if I tell you to leave, you *will* listen."

"Yes, sir," I say softly, and watch as goosebumps cover his forearms. He shakes his head and looks back at me.

"That is all."

I bow my head and take one last greedy look at his naked body in the tub, committing it to memory before leaving his private chambers and walking back to my room. The party is completely forgotten at this point because I have a meeting and a naked, sexy forbidden man to think about.

CHAPTER FOURTEEN

LUCIFER

For the record, I know taking Lilith to this meeting with the angels is a bad fucking idea. But I also know that if I don't take her, she would never forgive me.

Something is holding her back from wanting me. I see it in her eyes when she looks at me now. Something changed the day we found Blair, and it's only gotten more apparent in the little moments when we're together. Even if most of our moments are of us bickering or trading vicious banter, there's now a flirty undertone to it. She isn't afraid of me, and she doesn't hate me.

She might not like me yet, but she's attracted to me, and that's a start. It's a start that I'm not willing to risk. It's clear she doesn't feel the same pull that I do toward her. I doubt that this will give her the closure she needs, but I'm hoping.

More than that, I'm hoping that the angels don't pull any shit while we're there. I'm in a typical black suit when Lilith comes to my office door.

"Is this okay?" she says softly. Her hair is down again, and she's wearing a more modest dress that covers her shoulders. It's tight around her chest but flares out at the waist and fans out past her knees.

"You look—" I shake my head "It's fine."

She scrubs her hands down the pleats of her skirts and nods.

"Where is the meeting?"

"Neutral ground, on Earth." She nods, seeming unsurprised. Besides her initial confusion when she came to Hell, now is the only time I've ever seen her look unsure. She's nervous as she fidgets. "You don't have to come." I wish she didn't want to. I wish I could keep her in the dark cage that is my realm. The thought of locking her away has been on my mind more than I'd like to admit. But Lilith is no caged bird; taking away her freedom would only make things worse.

"I want to," she says quickly. "I need to." I nod and hold out my arm. She loops hers around mine and grips my biceps. I try to keep my composure as I portal us to the meeting place.

We're the first ones here, of course. "Fuckers are never on time," I grumble. Lilith doesn't let go of my arm as a crack of thunder sounds in the distance, and the front door opens.

I wasn't expecting this many angels here for this meeting. And yet there are five. Ezekiel, Maddis, Rita, Jorge, and I watch as Lilith's twin steps into the room. She blinks at her sister a few times before taking her seat and looking away. As I look over at Lilith's face, one nearly identical to the angel across from us, I can see her trying to keep her composure. She's trying to push down whatever emotion she feels after seeing her twin again. She squeezes my arm before letting it go, and her arms fall to her sides.

"Lucifer," Ezekiel greets, and I nod.

"Well, let's get to it then." We all take our seats. The angels on one side of the room, and Lilith and I on the other.

Ezekiel stares at Lilith, his eyes never moving, and it makes my eyes twitch. He knows I collected her soul, but there's no way he knows anything further than that. I can't leave this room with him thinking that I have any affection towards Lilith. She, of course, doesn't notice him staring because she won't stop looking at her twin.

"Your demons are out of control, Lucifer."

I roll my eyes, crossing my arms and stretching out my legs, crossing them as well but at the ankles. "And what, pray-tell, are they doing?"

"Corrupting mortals, picking fights with collectors, just general poor manners."

"Mmm. And who is filing this complaint?"

"Heaven," Rita chimes in, glaring at me. I always hated that bitch. She's always so pinched, I would've hoped someone would have removed that stick up her arse by now. But it seems that it's still firmly in place, and she's giving no leeway. I take note of the age of the angels in this room, all are nearly ancient. I feel off-kilter and have this need to overcompensate.

I grin, flicking a piece of non-existent lint off my suit cuff. "That's interesting, is mummy back home then?" Hit them right where it hurts. She left so long ago, they've been floundering ever since, and it seems to be one of the biggest reasons they pick fights with me constantly. They so easily forget that God gave me this job for a reason; that just as much she created Heaven, she also created Hell, and someone has to fucking manage it. I would say all of this to them—but it would be all for naught. I've said it so many times, but they are too self-righteous to listen to anything but the rhetoric they have been spewing for ages.

I watch as the angels still, and my grin gets wider. It's the first time Lilith takes a break from staring at her twin to look at me. "She left, what? A millennia ago? Tired of your bullshit and what she created. Probably started all over somewhere else by now. Made new realms, ones she could be proud of."

"You shut your mouth," Rita hisses at me. Lilith's twin looks at me with pure disgust.

"What? Your little friends haven't told you that God isn't running the show?" Her eyebrows furrow as she looks at me and then at her sister. Not a surprise, I'm sure they keep new angels in line by telling them if they work hard enough, if they are devout enough, then they will get to meet God. The same one who left and is never coming back.

"That's enough, Lucifer," Ezekiel chastises.

"Always were her favorite little pet." I pick at my nails, slouching in my chair disrespectfully. This is what they expect of me. I'm the villain, so I might as well act like one. "Besides Michael, that is. *He* was her true favorite."

"Lucifer," Ezekiel growls my name.

"Don't get me wrong, brother, I know what it's like to be mummy's favorite pet. Don't forget there's a reason I got this gig in the first place." I snap my fingers, a small flame burning above my flesh. "A reason she made me so powerful," I stand to my full height, even though Ezekiel is nearly the same height as me, but he doesn't stand as he glares daggers at me. "So tell me, why exactly are you trying to pick a fight with me?"

"You've gotten out of control. Your demons are being reckless."

"Reckless would be letting them do whatever the fuck they want. Trust me, if I let them do that, *then* there would be cause for concern."

"There are other causes for concern," Rita chimes in, glaring at me and then Lilith before softly petting Diana's thigh. "Go on, darling, tell us what you know."

Lilith's twin swallows thickly, her eyes watery as she stares at her sister. "Tell us what you found in her drawer."

"It was just a knife," Diana says, and I keep my cool. I watch as a sinister grin shows up on Ezekiel's face. He was there that day, so long ago, when this punishment was placed upon me.

"And the relevance?"

"The fact that her twin says she had a knife in her drawer and I find the all mighty Lucifer taking a soul to Hell, you can't tell me it's a coincidence, *brother*," he says the word scornfully, and I realize they suspect, but don't know for sure.

"She's my latest pet. You can't deny that she's beautiful." I lean over slightly, gripping the end of Lilith's hair and wrapping it around my fist, spinning it around my closed fingers until I reach her skull. "I get so bored in Hell, sometimes it's nice to have something pretty." I glance at Ezekiel and smirk. "Not that you would know anything about that? Still practicing abstinence in Heaven?"

"This is disturbing, she's clearly—"

"Clearly fucking mine to do with as I please?" I finish for her, and I feel Lilith still underneath my hand.

Her mouth starts to open, and I shove two fingers inside of it so she can't speak. "You know how much I like the pretty ones." The angels across from me all give me disgusted glares, and Lilith looks like she wants to murder me. "The fact that she had a penchant for murder was a bonus."

"Must you put on such a heinous display?" Rita asks, looking away.

"Why do you think I brought her to this meeting? For her input?" I tug at her hair, her blue eyes meeting mine. I can feel her hatred towards me at this moment. This was supposed to help build our relationship, but it's more important to protect her. They can't know what she means to me. "I just like pretty, needy things." I lean forward and graze my teeth against her throat. "And she takes it so well."

Ezekiel clears his throat. "It must be wrong, Rita. He never treated Lily this way."

Hearing that name has an effect on both Lilith and myself. I wonder how many questions she will have once we're back in Hell. I'm sure it will be the inquisition.

"How can you let him talk to you like that?" Lilith's twin demands. My hand is still wrapped in her hair, although her attention is on her twin.

"Diana..." I tug at her hair.

"Ah, you forget yourself, pet."

"You're really gone, aren't you?" Diana asks her sister with tears welling in her eyes. Rita wraps her arm around the angel's shoulder.

"We tried to warn you, sweetheart," she consoles the angel. The hatred Lilith had directed at me is now at Rita, and she goes to open her mouth again. I lean close so only Lilith can hear my next words.

"Open your mouth again, and I'll fill it," I whisper more harshly than intended, and she firmly clamps her lips shut.

"I saw what I needed to see," Diana says, standing up and giving Lilith one last look, one filled with sadness and pity. "I hoped it wasn't true. But seeing you with him." She looks at me in disgust. "You're no longer the sister I thought I had."

She leaves the room, and I watch as all resolve and fight leaves Lilith. She opens her mouth but then shuts it right back up. I release her hair and glare at Ezekiel.

"It's clear that this meeting was just a ploy."

He looks at Lilith one more time before looking at me.

"Your demons are still causing unneeded havoc."

"Continue grating on my nerves, and I'll make sure they cause more."

"She'd be so disappointed," he says with a sigh, and a manic laugh escapes my lips.

"At the flagrant display of utilitarian dictatorship that's taken over Heaven, you're right. You fucking forget yourself, brother. She created Hell, she created me to manage it. But you, you were always built to be a foot soldier and nothing more."

His face turns red as he glares at me. I know he wants to pick a fight, and I welcome it. With how fucked up this day went, I could use a little bloodshed. With the right weapon in my hand, I could kill every single angel in this room. I would, of course, spare Lilith's twin. Ezekiel scoffs at me and instead takes the high road leaving the warehouse along with his companions. Suddenly I'm in a very stifling room with a very pissed demon.

"Take me home."

"Lilith."

Her eyes are molten with fury. "I said take me fucking home."

I grab her wrist, portalling us back into my office. Once we're free from prying eyes, she yanks her hand away as if I've burned her. I expect her to stomp her foot and go right to her room, but as always, she proves me wrong. With both hands, she shoves me in the chest.

"Why would you do that?"

"Lilith, there's so much you don't know."

She pushes again, her strength nothing compared to mine. "And whose fucking fault is that?" *Fair enough.* "The way she looked at me... this was supposed to be closure, but you made it so much worse. She doesn't just hate me, she pities and loathes me. She... she said I wasn't her sister anymore. Do you know how much of my life I spent protecting Diana? Putting what Diana needed above myself? Do you?"

I shake my head no and grab at her wrists, stopping her from trying to push me around or leave me. "They couldn't know that I care for you. Making them think you were..."

"Your personal whore," she spits, and I sigh, scrubbing at the back of my neck.

"It was to protect you."

"Well, it was for nothing because I'm nothing to you. I'll never be anything to you. I fucking hate you." The lie is small but there nonetheless. She's angry with me, but she doesn't fully hate me like she's proclaiming right now. "All I wanted was to say goodbye. To tell her I loved her, and you didn't let me say anything. You treated me like I was worthless."

"Lilith," I go to grab her wrist, but she tugs it away.

"Just shut the fuck up. You and your secrets and your precious Lily can go fuck yourself." She pushes me in the chest one more time before storming out of the office and back to her room.

I thought there was potential for things to go bad today, but this was far worse than I could've imagined. There's this nagging in my head telling me that she deserves more and that by protecting her, by withholding the truth from her, all I'm doing is hurting her further. Lily knew the truth and she still didn't care about me, even though we were fated. As much as I doubt my actions, the only way I can move forward with Lilith is if she chooses me. Nothing less than Lilith wanting me with a clear conscience is acceptable. If she doesn't want me—the thought burns in my chest—I can't and won't force her to be mine. I just need this to be her choice or I'll always wonder if what we have is genuine or fate fucking with me again.

Sleep evades me all night. I just replay the evening's events in my head. How she looked at me when I treated her like I didn't give a fuck about her. How she shouted at me and told me that she hated me. I'm not sure I can possibly fuck this up any further.

CHAPTER FIFTEEN

LILITH

I feel sick as I lie on my side and stare at the deep emerald wallpaper of my wall. The way Diana looked at me. The pity, the sadness, the hatred. I wasn't sure what to expect—but it wasn't that. I can't decide what I feel, devastated that she hates me or angry that she could treat me that way after everything I've done for her. I put Diana above myself all of the time, and she just treated me like a piece of shit. She looked disgusted at the way Lucifer spoke to me and touched me.

The way Lucifer spoke about me in front of them was clearly a show, one I'm not sure the angels bought. Lucifer isn't a man who does things without reason. But why did he have to do that? He knows how much my sister means to me, and he didn't even let me speak to her. If I'm being completely honest, I didn't mind the way he handled me, but I feel like he's lying to me, and I don't know why. He keeps trying to appease me by giving me half-truths.

He keeps saying how much I mean to him with no explanations. Half of the time his actions are tender, and there's a look of devotion in his eyes, the other half, I can't help but to feel like he knows something that I don't. None of it makes any sense.

It would have been better if I didn't go. I could just keep wondering what's going on in Diana's life, and maybe act like that last night didn't happen altogether.

It wasn't the closure I wanted, it was worse. Diana has completely disowned me; she told me I wasn't her sister anymore. I shake my head, not believing the lie. She might not like who I am, what I've become, but we will always be sisters, even if we're realms apart.

Somehow I find myself caring less about her acceptance, with the realization that I'll never get it. There's no going back to Earth, to sharing our apartment, or watching movies and staying up all night together. She'll never look at me like I'm that special person in her life. She's chosen the angels, and now I need to choose me, no matter how much it hurts. Even though all I wanted was to have hugged one last time and cleared the air, maybe I didn't deserve that closure. Everything has just gotten so much worse. Twins in opposing realms, I suppose it's something that would be written in a fucked-up tragedy.

I'm a demon. I'm everything she said I am, and I'm done fighting it. Done being sad and feeling less than because of what others think. I'm in Hell, and I'm ready to start living like it. I might not have my sister anymore, and maybe when I feel less numb, I'll grieve the loss of that relationship, but right now, all I want to do is indulge and forget.

I rip off the conservative tea dress and opt for something that shows off my back and thighs. If I'm so fucking horrible, the villain, a monster? *Then it's about time I started acting like it.*

Heavy metal blasts throughout Minx as soon as I portal here. Immediately, I grab whatever shots are on the closest tray to me and swing three back consecutively. Scanning the club, there's a new addition I notice. A throne in the front, it's gold with red velvet, and Lucifer sits on it boredly, his thumb on his temple as his elbow rests on the arm of the chair.

Lisa, Autumn, and Tina sit at the bottom of the throne like fucking carp fish begging for snacks. I'm sure they are, just begging for any little crumb Lucifer will give them, negative or positive. I roll my eyes and take another shot. Spotting Judd and Asmodeus on a deep red velvet couch, I walk over to them. I can feel Lucifer's eyes on me, but he doesn't move, not a single inch. It's like his gaze is penetrating through me.

"Hey," I say to the two demons. Asmodeus is giggling, and Judd is looking off into the distance.

"Oh hey, Barbie," Asmodeus greets.

"Judd?" He breaks away from what he was staring at to look at me. "I think I want to try," I say, trying not to ring my fingers in my dress and look like an idiot.

Judd doesn't say anything, just takes a baggy of powder and starts making lines with a card of some sort.

I clear my throat as I take the rolled-up bill. "What do I do?"

"You know, you're sweeter than you seem, Barbie. Just inhale it through your nose," Asmodeus instructs. I nod my head, leaning forward and snorting the powdery line. My nose stings and the feeling hits immediately.

It's like all my thoughts from earlier stop; it's easier to just not think and enjoy the night. Euphoria fills me, not these worries about what anyone thinks of me or questions of my morality. It's nice to just let loose. I stand there for a few minutes as my nerve endings fire off as the beat travels through me. Glancing over my shoulder, I see Lucifer sitting straighter than he was before, still watching. *Well, let's let him fucking watch, shall we?*

"Let's dance!" I shout, grabbing Asmodeus and Judd's hands and tugging them onto the dance floor.

Asmodeus laughs against my ear, dancing behind me but not touching me. "Barbie, if my soul gets fucking ripped out because of this, I'm going to be pissed."

"I'm hoping for it," Judd says, and I can hear Asmodeus laugh.

I close my eyes, just feeling the beat and moving my body accordingly. One of the demons touches my arm, and it feels nice. Nice to be touched. They should do it again.

"Do you think if I kiss her, he'll kill me?" Judd asks Asmodeus.

"Probably worse. I wouldn't risk it."

"Fuck, fine," Judd grumbles. I'm in my own world, moving my body to the rhythm, not giving a shit what the two demons near me are doing. I wonder if Lucifer would dance with me if I asked. No... no... we're mad at him.

"Ouch!" I squeal, looking down at my chest. My necklace blazes against my skin. "Motherfucker." I look over at Judd and Asmodeus. "Well, this was fun." I shrug my shoulders and grip the necklace to allow it to transport me to wherever Lucifer is. I'm not sure what I was expecting, maybe his private quarters again? Nope, we're in an empty hallway outside of the club.

I expected him to send me to my room, tell me I've been a naughty little demon, and go to bed. Nope, that's not what happens either. His hand grips my chin, and he forces my back into a wall as he tilts my head back forcibly to look at him. His eyes look darker than normal when he glares down at me.

"What the fuck was that?" he growls.

"Which part?" I ask sweetly.

His fingers dig into my jaw, and he lightly shakes my head. "Don't fuck with me, Lilith."

"Ooh, don't fuck with the big, bad Devil who talks in riddles and gets jealous when he has no right to be."

"I have every fucking right to be," he argues, and I swallow thickly.

"You're jealous?"

"Lilith," he says my name, and it's so fucking deep and gravelly. I'm not sure if it's the cocaine or this man, but I feel soaking fucking wet. The tip of his thumb drags along my bottom lip, and I shiver. *Why does he have this overwhelming effect on me?*

"I still hate you," I say back, not wanting to admit what he's doing to me.

"Lie," he says, leaning down and smelling my hair and neck. I stop breathing for a whole moment. "You know I can taste lies, little Hellfire. Yours are so fucking sweet, like sugar-coated strawberries."

I clear my throat. "I'm mad at you."

"It wasn't supposed to go like that."

"Why can't you finish a single thought? I feel like you're always keeping secrets. Like, who's Lily?"

He smiles down at me. "You are," he says, not answering the question as his hand grips my bare thigh, my slutty dress giving him easy access to my skin.

"You treated me like I was your whore."

"Don't you want to be?" he asks, his fingertips trailing up my thigh. Goosebumps cover my flesh, and he keeps moving his hand higher towards my pussy.

"No..."

He pulls back and grins. "Lie."

"No, it's not," I retort. I won't be someone's whore again, I deserve more.

He laughs and nods. "Mmm, you'd be more." His hand cradles the back of my head, his fingers lacing into my hair and pulling with just the right amount of pressure. "I'd give you everything you wanted, love."

I blink at him a few times, and I notice his eyes changing color slightly. I can't decide if it's the drugs or reality as I ask, "Are your eyes pink?"

He makes a low growling noise as his hand slides up, covering my pussy as the heel of his palm rubs against my clit. I grab his biceps as my head lightly bangs against the wall. His deft fingers slide my panties to the side as he lightly rubs two fingers against my clit.

A low whimpering noise escapes me as he grips my chin and forces me to look at him while he touches me.

"Still hate me, love?" He slides two fingers inside of me, curling them upwards. I can hear how wet I am. It's both a huge turn-on and completely betraying everything I'm saying.

"Yes," I reply, not sure if it's because I want to piss him off or because I truly do. I might not be able to sense lies like he can, but I know I'm lying to the both of us.

He grins, closing his eyes, and leans in to whisper in my ear. "You might hate me, but this wet pussy sure as fuck loves being wrapped around my fingers."

I shudder, my grip on his forearms tightening as my nails dig into his flesh. He slows his pace torturing me, bringing me so close to the peak that I desperately crave, and then taking it away.

I do my best to hold out, to not beg, and just take what he's giving me. He licks his lips, and I hate to admit how badly I want them on me. *Why isn't he kissing me?* When he leans forward again, I think that he might, but instead, he drags his teeth along my jaw and neck before going back to speak in my ear.

"You want to come, Lilith?"

My thighs shake, my need to come is more than my need to make him work for it. "Please." It's so quiet, but I know he hears it. He makes the softest moaning noise in my ear.

"I'll let you come... if you make me a promise."

"What?" I ask breathlessly. His scent consumes me, his hands feel amazing on my skin. All I want is to feel the release I know only he can give me.

"You'll never touch another demon like you did tonight," he says.

"I can do whatever I want." I can't help the defiance.

He laughs against my hair, tugging on the strands hard. "Only I can give you this, and you know it. You want to come, you want to dance. You come to me."

"But–"

"Know that if I see you with another demon, you're condemning them to death, Lilith. I don't fucking share, and you belong to me whether you want to admit it or not."

It's probably sick or fucked up, but those words are what make me come. I tremble and shake against his hold, and he doesn't relent, fucking me with his fingers and rubbing his palm against my clit.

"That's it, there's my good girl," he praises against my hair as I moan and ride out the orgasm that feels like it goes on for eternity. When I whimper that I've had enough, he pulls away, standing in front of me and looking down at me.

I open my mouth to speak, but he renders me completely speechless as he puts the two fingers that were just inside of me in his mouth and sucks them clean while holding eye contact with me the entire time. His expression is of a man who is pleased with himself.

"No more cocaine, no more touching anyone else. Do we understand?"

He finger fucked all the brain cells out of me because all I can do is nod my head in agreement. If I can follow these rules, then he'll reward me with that treatment. And that might just be worth it.

"I'll see you tomorrow morning then," he says, looking at me like he wants to say more, but he doesn't. He just adjusts my dress so that I'm covered before he portals out of the hallway.

I'm left standing here with soaking panties and wondering how the fuck that just happened. I can't help myself as a smile grows across my face, and I cover it with my hand. Maybe being on the 'bad' side of the afterlife has its perks.

CHAPTER SIXTEEN

LUCIFER

S he looked so fucking beautiful coming all over my fingers. Now that I know making her come is one way to get her to shut her mouth and listen, I plan on doing it often. I was furious when I saw her dancing with Judd and Asmodeus. They weren't even touching her, but the fact that she was so close to them pisses me off. She should only be like that with me.

I wanted to storm into the middle of the dance floor and throw her over my shoulder, but I'll never be able to do that. If this is going to work, if I'm going to make sure that she stays with me, no one can know how much she means to me.

The whiskey tastes sweeter going down my throat as I sit at my desk and reminisce. I haven't felt this light in centuries. I had to hold back when she asked me who Lily was. I could see the jealousy written on her face as much as it was on mine—It made my cock hard. I still don't understand why she denies this connection that we have, but I'm breaking her walls down slowly and piece by piece.

She might not remember her past life. But I do—I could never forget—that's why no one can know. I can give Lilith everything she wants in private. I'll treat her how she deserves within the walls of this manor, and that's going to have to be enough. While the angels finding out is the biggest threat, doesn't mean I can automatically trust every single demon.

Keeping Lilith and Blair protected is above any other duty that I have in my life. I rub my palm against my face, the scent of her cunt still lingering on my fingers. I groan, recalling the way she felt around them, so needy and wet while trying to hide from me, trying to hide how she really feels with comebacks and sass. But the way she fucking crumbled under my touch when I told her that she belonged to me, that she was mine, made this unmeasurable amount of joy bloom inside of me.

I squeeze my dick through my pants with my other hand, wishing it was her touching me, wishing that things went further and that I fucked her against the wall. Or bent her over a chair and truly showed her how much she's mine.

The memories of her whispering please and the feminine whimper that left her lips when I told her how good she was for me haunt me. I remove myself from my pants, fisting my cock, and stroking as I replay the memory over and over again.

How my thumb stroked the soft pad of her full bottom lip, the heady desire of wanting to take it between my teeth and claim her lips as mine. Her wide blue eyes as she stared up at me as my fingers fucked in and out of her tight, wet cunt.

I'm going to have to stretch her to take me. I groan, using my thumb to swipe the tip of my cock as it weeps pre-cum and use it as lube to stroke myself. I can't help but visualize the moisture of her release leaking out of her pussy; she was so fucking wet for me.

Lilith likes it rough, that's clear. But I want to give her everything, to give her vulnerabilities that I'd never even imagine gifting to another person.

Fuck. I groan as my balls begin to tighten, and I speed up my pace. The imagery of her thighs shaking around my hand and her nails leaving crescent marks in the skin of my chest as she comes is what sets me over the edge. Cum drips down my fist as I groan, jerking myself through my release.

As I look down at my mess, all I can think about is how badly I wish Lilith was here, on her knees, to clean me up.

Lilith sits at her desk across from me, and I can sense her glancing up from her work to look at me every ten minutes or so.

"Yes?" I ask with a smirk.

"You can't just finger fuck a girl in a hallway and then not say anything. It's rude."

Placing my elbows on the desk and interlacing my fingers, I prop my head on top of them. "What would you like me to say?"

"Hmm, I don't know, you were all 'you belong to me'," she says the last part in an impersonation of my voice. "'I'll fucking rip souls out that touch you', and now, you haven't said a single word," she says softly, and I realize my mistake.

"Come here." Her cheeks heat, but she stands, showing off her long dress. Her hair is in a high ponytail today, and I quite like it.

I scoot my chair back, spreading my legs wide while leaving room for her. I tap the oak of the desktop, and she props her ass on the desk. She crosses her legs, which is a shame, but with her sitting on the desk and me in my chair were nearly the same height.

"I don't mean to play games," I tell her honestly.

"So don't."

"You said you hated me, so I was giving you space." She rubs her arms, mulling that information over in her head. Her eyebrows furrow, and she sighs. It's one of the few times I see her not hiding behind a facade.

"I don't know how to feel."

I take a risk, touching her leg, and I'm pleased when she doesn't flinch away from my touch. "Why?"

She clears her throat and shakes her head. "It's mean," she says, her cheeks turning redder as she looks away.

"You can tell me."

She doesn't look at me while she says it. "If I like you, if I want to be with you..." she trails off, shaking her head. "Your reputation and what you stand for as the ruler of Hell... what does that make me if I like you?" she says it softly, and I'm not offended. The rumors, the lies that are told on Earth are disgusting. What faith and lore have turned into is merely fictitious at this point.

I abruptly stand, and she startles, looking at me. I place both of my hands on the desk, my fingers nearly touching her hips as I sigh. "I'm not good, but I wouldn't say I'm evil either. Do I do as I please and step outside of what mortals and Heaven consider morally just? Sure. Am I the ruler of Hell? Yes. But as the ruler, my job is not only to manage the dead who come here but to ensure punishment for the most evil. I don't condone certain behaviors because no one should. My soul is a deep shade of gray, and I'm okay with that."

I step back, looking at her, her blue eyes wide while taking in what I'm saying. "I'm not a person who would condemn you for how dark your soul is, Lilith. I would want you because of it. Hell, this is your chance to truly be yourself, the person you've always wanted to be. If you stopped treating it like a sentence and more like a gift, I think you'd be happy here. And perhaps even happy with me."

She rubs her neck and looks down while thinking about that. I don't make a move to touch her, no matter how badly I might want to. Her tongue sweeps out and licks her lips. "Do you have any siblings?" she asks, the question hitting me completely out of left field.

"Early on as an angel, when we were created, we called each other brother and sister. But I hold no devotion to them."

She nods in understanding. "Diana was my twin. We spent most of our time together. How everything went at the meeting the other day has me messed up. I guess I was before then too." She rubs her arm, and I have the overwhelming urge to hold her, but I don't. I give her the space she needs. "I've never cared what people thought of me." She scoffs. "That's a lie, everyone cares to some extent what people think of them. I always felt like I had a different purpose than most people, and the thoughts I sometimes had were troubling." She gives a small, stilted smile. "It felt good when I used that dagger."

The smile she gives me makes me consider giving it back to her right now. "But when Diana found out what I did, when she looked at me like I was worthless and called me a monster..." She doesn't finish her sentence but instead shakes her head and sighs.

"I'm not sure why it mattered so much to prove her wrong. After the meeting, I still don't know how I feel about it. I'm not even sure that it's sunk in that she wants nothing to do with me. That this is an entirely new life."

I nod and swallow.

"This life can be whatever you want it to be. But I can tell you that living in the past isn't going to be what makes you happy. I'd like you to consider this new life as an upgrade and include me in it."

She stares at my eyes, and I hope to shit that they aren't some crazy color right now. I'm usually pretty good at hiding my emotions, but Lilith is a different story.

Her small hands glide down the lapels of my jacket, and she sighs as she looks at me. "If I work on this." She tugs on my lapels a little harder. "Can you work on opening up and not keeping secrets all the time?" I nod, opening the top drawer and taking her dagger out, placing it on her lap. She gasps and smiles, her hand immediately palming the hilt as she looks up at me in awe. I want her looking like this all the time.

I lean in closer towards her, our lips so close that I can smell the sweet floral scent of her hair. "I'd give you everything," I tell her honestly.

Her eyes snap to mine, and I can't control it anymore. I lean forward, my lips nearly a centimeter from hers, when the door to my office slams open.

I grip the edge of my desk so hard that wood splinters underneath my palms. Lilith licks her lips as I look up to see who the fuck interrupted us.

"What?" I snarl.

"Sir, you need to come with me right now," Toth informs me. His eyes wide, looking between Lilith and me. Out of all the residents of Hell, Toth is perhaps the only one I know I can trust with this secret. I back away from Lilith, squeezing her thigh once.

"This discussion isn't over."

She nods, standing as well. Toth looks at Lilith, and his expression falls. "Lilith, you may want to stay here."

Her eyebrows furrow, and I shake my head. "It's fine, where?"

"The main hall," Toth says, looking at Lilith one more time before portalling out of the room. With my hand around her wrist, we portal there too.

The sight in front of us is a brutal one. White feathers scatter the floor, and there's some laughter and shock coming from other demons in the room.

"My lord, it's taken care of. She was attempting to get into Hell," Beelzebub laughs. His issue with the angels is getting out of hand. When I look down at the body he gestures to with a nudge of his foot, I notice that the golden spun hair matches Lilith's and is splayed on the floor with red streaks staining the blonde. The spear of Samuel protruding from her back, is one of the few ways an angel can be killed for good.

Lilith crumples to the floor in the next moment, flipping her sister's body over. Her wings lay limp as Lilith cups her face. Her twin blinks, still holding on to life as Lilith moves the bloody hair out of her face.

"Diana?" she says softly. Her twin whispers something so softly that I can't hear, only Lilith can, and we all watch as the life leaves her eyes. It's grim in more ways than I'd like to admit. Diana looks just like Lilith, it's selfish when I know that Lilith is suffering right now, but my only thoughts are of how it could've easily been Lilith, lifeless on the floor, and not her sister. I can't let that happen.

"You said any angel that attempts to come to our realm," Beelzebub says, trying to save face. He isn't wrong. But I want to rip his soul out. I look around the room, seeing that most of the demons here are smiling at the dead angel or Lilith's anguish, I'm not sure.

What I do know is Beelzebub technically was acting on my behest, and even though I know killing him would make Lilith feel better, I can't do that. If everyone in this room sees my favoritism toward her, if they know how much I care for her, she will become a bigger target. She could be the next one lying on the floor in place of her twin. I scrub my beard and put a hand on Lilith's shoulder. She shakes me off quickly as she touches her sister's face.

"Diana, who? Why, Diana!" she asks, and I can't help but wonder the same thing. Was she coming here to warn her sister about something? Why would she be so stupid?

"Sir," Beelzebub says, and I hold up a hand to silence him.

Lilith doesn't cry over her sister's body. I watch as she transforms, rage taking over every inch of her body. Her eyes grow glassy, but her jaw stays firm as she slowly stands and turns to face Beelzebub.

"You did this?" she accuses, her voice starkly calm compared to her demeanor.

"I was following orders. Any angels in Hell are to be taken care of."

Lilith moves fast, pinning Beelzebub underneath her as she whips out her dagger. She holds it under his chin, his grip firm on her forearm. It's a battle of strength as Lilith tries to slice his throat and Beelzebub attempts to protect his life.

"My lord," he begs, and I stand there trying to think, trying to protect Lilith's heart while also protecting her life.

"You nasty fucking rat, you killed her," Lilith spits into his face, her hand shaking as the dagger glints with bloodlust. "You took her. She... she's gone!" she shouts in his face. Demons are watching on with a sick fascination as they watch Lilith scream at Beelzebub while her sister bleeds out not even five feet away from her.

I take a deep breath. I can take care of Beelzebub later, but with this public display happening, I need to protect Lilith. If she kills another demon, retribution will need to be paid, and the rest of Hell won't stand for her hurting another demon over an angel's death.

"Lilith, enough," I command her. She doesn't move, the dagger still shaking wildly in her grip. "Lilith!"

"No! He needs to pay."

"Lilith," I repeat, but she shakes her head. The tears are streaming down her face now, almost as heavily as the rage that flows from her.

The blade is only a few centimeters from his neck when I make the decision. Looking to my left, I spot him, looking like he's rooting on Lilith as badly as I wish I could.

"Elvor. Take her to the pit," I say. Some demons laugh and snicker as Elvor grabs Lilith's hand, squeezing so tight that the dagger falls out of her grip. I retrieve the dagger, putting it in my suit jacket as Elvor attempts to pick up Lilith.

When he flings her over his shoulder, she points to me and glares. "I fucking hate you," she sneers.

I don't taste a lie, and I know I've ruined the best thing that could have been mine before it even really started.

CHAPTER SEVENTEEN

LILITH

"Sorry," the deep voice says from the corner. I have my arms wrapped around my legs and my face on my knees. Diana is gone... she was coming here to warn me. Her last words play on repeat, a clipped and short *'Don't trust'*. I should be thinking about those words and what they mean or whom exactly she was warning me of, but all I can think of is complete sadness taking over every molecule in my body.

I doubted her.

I doubted her love for me, what she thought of me. She lost her life coming down to protect me, and I have no clue why. I try to push down the despair, at least for now, because if I let myself fully feel the weight of what just happened, I think I may just fall apart. There's no time to fall apart right now; I need to act, I need... I don't even know what I need.

I sigh and look up at Elvor.

He's sitting casually in a chair. "It's not your fault. It's Beelzebub and Lucifer's fault."

Elvor shakes his head. "Rules."

I wave him off, not giving a shit about any rules. "I'm going to kill that rat-fucker one day," I tell Elvor, and he nods in agreement.

"I'll help," he says, and I smile.

"At least one man in this fucking hellhole gets it."

I look around the room, which is clearly a torture room in the pit, but Elvor doesn't seem to have any plans to torture me. I stand, wanting to leave this place, leave Hell. It feels like I can't fucking breathe being here. "Can I portal from here?" I ask him, and he shakes his head no. "Great."

I breathe in and out, reminding myself that I can't break here, in a fucking torture room with Elvor, but fuck if I'm not close. There are three taps on the door, and I glare at the wall, assuming it's Lucifer. One of the last people I want to see. He was in the middle of promising me the world, and then... then he abandoned me. *It feels like everyone leaves me.* I have to push down my emotions about Diana. This is not the time or the place to really let today's events sink in.

I'm sure in some small part of my brain, I know there's a reason for Lucifer doing what he did, but this is not something you do to someone you 'supposedly' care about. This isn't a way to treat someone you want to 'give the world to'.

Fortunately for me, it's not Lucifer; it's Kas standing in the doorway, and I let out a sigh of relief.

"Where have you been?" I ask her. She just sighs and rolls her eyes.

"There's been a new reason to not stick around Hell. You want to get out of here or what?" She looks over at Elvor, and he shrugs. "We're going to have to make it look convincing," she warns, and

Elvor smiles as she punches him in the gut, making his chair rock backwards. "Give me that rope, will ya?" Kas asks me. I hand it to her, and she wraps it around Elvor's body. He gives us a small smile, and she kisses the top of his head.

"You're the best, Elvor."

"He's going to be furious with you," I say to Kas, worrying about the repercussions of her actions.

"Let him. I'm honestly doing him a fucking favor before he does anything else that qualifies as being a 'complete fucking dumbass'," she says. I can tell there's a deeper story there, but I don't pry.

"Elvor, are you sure you're okay with this?" He nods and then tips his head towards the door.

"Let's get the fuck out of here," Kas says, gripping my arm and dragging me out the door before she portals us.

As soon as our feet hit the grass, the soft scent of salt and fresh air hits me. When it does, I can finally take a deep inhale and break. I fall to my knees, gripping fistfuls of dirt and grass in my hands as it all sinks in.

Diana's limp, fallen form in front of me, her chest with a deep bleeding hole, and the feathers of her wings scattered around the banquet room. The mirror image of me dead and alone on the floor.

Don't trust...

Don't trust...

Don't fucking trust who? Her last words ring in my head over and over. The two words she gave her life for, and yet they mean nothing. I needed to get out of Hell for many reasons, her last words being the biggest reason of all. *What if she was warning me not to trust Lucifer?*

I can't believe I ever doubted her at the meeting, that I took her words at face value, not thinking that maybe she was also putting on a show, just like Lucifer.

She died in my arms at the hands of a demon. One of my kind killed her while others laughed and stared at her body like it was entertainment. Not like every piece of my afterlife was coming to a complete standstill.

I want revenge to be the foremost emotion that I'm feeling, but it's not. As hard as I try to summon my hatred for Beelzebub, Lucifer, and all the people who smiled or laughed at her demise, I can't. All I feel is pure absolute anguish. My sobs wrack my body, and I feel Kas' hand on my back.

"Come on, Lilith. Let's get you inside."

I wipe my eyes with the back of my wrists and stand, wrapping my arms around myself as I follow Kas into the beach house. The home is beautiful, I'm sure, but I barely pay attention as Kas leads me down a hallway to a bedroom. It's green, just like the one in Hell. Nowhere near as lavish and nice, but it is cozy.

She pulls back the patchwork quilt, and I lie down in the bed on my side. Kas opens the window and leaves. All I'm left with is the sound of waves and my grief.

I bring the blanket all the way up to my nose while my mind just keeps picturing Diana on the floor. I'm riddled with guilt knowing that she didn't know what was coming and spent her final moments trying to warn me. She didn't deserve that. She should have happily lived her life in Heaven, not worrying about me. Yet again, I feel like I failed my sister.

It's at that moment that being immortal hits me, and I remember that I'll be spending the rest of my existence alone. Without Diana in my life, time means nothing to me. The thought of living forever without the promise of what Lucifer and I could have been or without Diana makes me feel like I'm in a void that I'll just have to figure out living in.

"Come on, bitch. You've got to get out of bed," Kas complains, and my answer is a swift shake of my head.

"No, leave me alone."

"Listen, I've got to go to Hell." She sighs and sits on my bed, picking at her nails. "Lucifer isn't dumb, he's going to know you're with me."

"Ugh, fuck him," I say, rolling on my side and dragging the blanket over my head.

"Listen, we've got to turn this sad-girl shit into something productive. Do you want to kill someone?"

"No, Kas, I don't want to kill someone. Just leave me alone."

"Well, I don't want to hear any complaining when I have all the fun stabbing some bastard."

"Okay," I groan. She just sighs, getting off the bed.

When Diana died, all I could think was about avenging her, but it seems as though I can't leave the bed. We were separated in death, but at least I knew she was living a good afterlife. But now I know she's nothing more than dust, and I'm not sure how to function. We entered and left the world together, but knowing that I still exist and she doesn't... how am I supposed to live any quality of life?

I hear the pop of Kas' portal and sit up. I've got to do something besides sit here, but I'm not sure what. Groaning, I get out of bed and get dressed in yoga pants and a t-shirt. I don't brush my hair, deciding to just put it up in a rat's nest of a bun.

I'm not sure what my intention is when I portal, but for the strangest reason, I find myself in Hallowsdeep. There's no rhyme or reason as to why I'm here. I just couldn't be in that stifling room anymore, so I walk around aimlessly. Something about the town is comforting, it's pretty fucked up, considering I died here. But I also found the dagger and found Blair here. *Maybe my subconscious knew I needed to find something again in this stupid, haunted-as-fuck town.*

When I turn the corner of the candle shop is when I hear the taunting of children.

"You're a liar, Blair. You made up having a dad. You're such a loser."

"So weird. Don't touch her, you might get cooties!"

There's a light sniffle, and I glare at the two little bitches who are teasing Blair. I didn't really care for children before I died, but as a demon, I don't really care about hitting one either. So I do the one thing that always scares children, and I act like a psychopath by leaning down and screaming bloody murder in their faces. Their eyes go wide as they turn around and run away. When I turn on my heel, Blair is smirking at me. It's annoying that she looks just like her father, but I can't hold it against her that her dad's an asshole.

"That was awesome," she gushes, squeezing her backpack straps, and I nod, fully intending to just keep walking, but she follows me. "I haven't seen you around here before." I grimace and wonder if I need to make her forget this encounter, but then I realize that since I'm not with Lucifer, I don't see how it would matter.

"No, I'm not from around here."

"That makes sense."

I arch an eyebrow, and she shrugs her shoulders. "No one cool lives here."

"You live here," I say, and she smiles.

"I'm not cool, you saw how those girls talked to me."

I turn and squat down to her height. "There's always going to be people who don't like you or will go out of their way to hurt you. Most of the time, it's because they are insecure about themselves."

"Adults just say that shit to make kids feel better."

Lucifer isn't here, and well, that means all rules are out the window. As much as I hate Lucifer right now, I still understand that Blair is worth protecting, and I will keep her a secret. But that doesn't mean that I can't help her.

I look around at the street and sigh. "Sometimes, when you're powerful, others will try to put you down, so you don't reach your full potential."

She gasps and looks at me. "But you're not—"

"No. I'm not a witch."

The shocked expression on her face is adorable as I keep walking, and again she follows. "Then what are you?"

"Not important. But what I can tell you is those kids making fun of you? They're probably scared of you."

She swallows. "I... I have accidents sometimes."

I furrow my brows and look at her. "Accidents?"

"It's like my magic can't help but to come out sometimes, and it gets me in trouble."

"Your mom doesn't help you?"

"Not really." She shrugs, tugging on her backpack straps.

"Do you have anyone?"

She shakes her head and sighs. "My cousin Stevie, but she lives a few hours away."

I hum and nod my head. "We all need allies. You've got to find someone who has your back." I sigh, thinking about how Diana and I always had each other's back. Then I feel a little melancholy when I think about Kas and how much she has taken care of me as of late.

"Will *you* have my back?"

I blink at the little girl a few times before I smile for the first time in a long time. "Yeah, I'll have your back."

"What's your name anyway?"

I'm not sure why I lie. "Lily," I tell her, and she smiles.

"So, got any ideas on how I can get back at those girls?" she asks, and when I look down at the little half-demon, half-witch, I can't help but feel like I found what I was looking for when I portaled to Hallowsdeep.

"Oh yeah, I've got ideas," I say with a smirk. I spend the rest of the day with Blair, and I hate to admit it, but it's the best I've felt in weeks.

I'm ready to portal back home, but instead, I meander down Main Street of Hallowsdeep. This town is like a beacon for the supernatural, and my gut instinct tells me that what—whom—I'm searching for will be in this town.

While Blair was a great distraction for me today, I'm still consumed by vengeance. I need someone to pay for what happened to Diana. And selfishly, what happened to me too. I want to be able to live my immortal life, but I can't do that until I feel like justice has been served for my sister.

I've thought about going back to Hell, hearing what Lucifer has to say. I know it's not as simple as him sending me away. I know he has to maintain a certain image in front of his followers. But it doesn't mean that he didn't hurt me. *Is it too much to ask to be put first?* He was just telling me how he was going to give me the world, and then the first moment he had to prove to me how much I meant to him, he failed.

It's strange how disappointing some moments in your life can feel.

I'm kicking a rock behind the post office when a voice startles me.

"Diana?"

I gasp, not having heard her name out loud from someone else's mouth in what feels like an eternity. The man is beautiful with dark hair and olive-toned skin. It's almost a familiar feeling that washes over me when he approaches me.

"Diana?" he tilts his head as he looks at me, his brows furrowing. When he's close enough, I can sense that he's an angel.

He shakes his head. "My mistake, I thought you were someone else."

"You knew my sister?" I ask.

He nods. "She hasn't returned, we've all been worried."

"Do you know why she left?"

"No, but I've been suspicious."

I step closer to him, and he's given me no indication that he knows what I am. "I... I think she was going to tell me something."

"You're Lilith?"

I can't help but smile. *Diana spoke about me in Heaven?* "I am."

"She told me she had a brave twin sister. That you had... um, ended up in a different place."

I rub my arm and nod. "Is that a problem for you?" I ask him, wondering if angels automatically hate all demons. Unfortunately, I only got a taste of the dynamic between angels and demons, not the whole picture.

"No, I just want to know what happened and why." He pauses for a moment before asking, "She's gone?" I sigh, confirming his question with a nod. He rubs his hand through his hair and sighs as well. "I can maybe poke around and see what I can find out. But no one can know."

"All I want to know is what my sister was trying to tell me."

"I'll need something in return."

"Anything."

"There's an item I've been looking for. The diadem of kinship."

I furrow my brows and shake my head. "I've never heard of it."

"That's a shame," he says.

"I'll find out, I'll do whatever it takes. I just need to know why Diana came to Hell."

He arches an eyebrow and nods. "If you help me, I'll see what I can find out. I liked Diana, it's a shame," he says.

"What's your name?" He smirks and shakes his head.

"My name is Rainn."

"How will I get in touch with you?"

He smirks and shakes his head tossing me a coin. "Keep it on you, rub it if you need me." He winks and disappears.

I'm not sure how much trust I can put into an angel, but at this moment he's the only lead I have. He could have attacked me, or much worse, but he didn't.

This day couldn't have gotten weirder. So, I portal back to the house, curl up in bed and go to sleep. Hoping that this is the thing that will help me get out of this pit of grief so I can start living.

CHAPTER EIGHTEEN

LUCIFER

"Where is she?"

It's taken every ounce of self-control to not kill Kas, or send her to the pit to be tortured.

"She's safe, as if you didn't know," Kas replies indignantly. Of course, I know, she's at a beach property that Kas owns—illegally—on Earth.

"She needs to come back to Hell!"

Kas rolls her eyes and stands up. It's the first time I've seen a look of distaste in her eyes.

"How can someone live for so long and be so fucking stupid?" My anger flairs, and in a flash, I'm on my feet towering over her as I look down at her.

"You need to watch your next words."

"You told her nothing, Lucifer. Not about the dagger or her past life, and you expect what? Complete devotion to you? Then her sister dies, her *twin* fucking sister. At the hands of Beelzebub of all fucking demons, and you don't offer her comfort or understanding. Instead, you decide to save face and send her to the fucking pit in front of everyone."

I swallow thickly and hearing it said out loud so coldly is worse than when I think about it. I had to act fast; Lilith was about to do something that couldn't be undone. "Beelzebub is taken care of."

She glares at me. "Oh, is he?"

"He's on soul collection duty."

"Oh, what a great punishment to avenge the woman you 'supposedly' love." The sarcasm is thick in her tone, and I feel like I can't win, that nothing I do in regards to Lilith is ever right. *Why can't I get anything right lately?*

"What am I supposed to do? I have to keep her safe! If the angels know about her, if demons know about her, if they see any favoritism towards her, then she could be taken away again." Even if Lilith never accepts me, the least I can do is make sure she's safe. Being tied to me shouldn't hinder her safety. I want everything for her, even if it isn't me.

Some of the anger fades from Kas as she looks at me. "Then maybe the best thing you can do is let her be on Earth for now."

"What?"

"You want her to be safe? The safest place for her is away from you as you just made very clear."

I shake my head in complete disagreement, and Kas scoffs. I both want her safe, and to be somewhere I can always keep an eye on her. I am, at my core, still extremely selfish.

"She's not okay." My heart sinks, and I deflate, sitting back down in my chair. "She needs to find herself, Lucifer. She barely got to live before she died, and she's just supposed to know how to fit into an ancient political structure? Your expectations are too high. She wasn't even out of college; she killed her last boyfriend for fuck's sake, and you want an eternity-long relationship with her?"

"She belongs here." I know I sound like a petulant child, and Kas shows her surprise with an arch of an eyebrow.

"I'm not saying she doesn't belong here. What I am saying is that everything that has happened has been out of Lilith's control. She needs time to figure out what she wants. Wouldn't you rather her want to be here willingly instead of forced?"

"I've waited so long." I pout, scrubbing my hand over my face, knowing that I sound difficult and needy. To be honest I'm not sure why I'm even arguing with Kas. As much as I hate to say it, she's right. Lilith will be safer on Earth right now, and a sick part of me wants it to be her choice to come back to Hell, to come back to *me*. Not the dagger, not the connection I feel, I want Lilith to truly and honestly want to be with me. It's why I kept the past to myself, because I want to be wanted. *Pathetic.*

I feel like a complete fool as the thoughts race through my head. Why couldn't this have all been simpler? I suppose nothing is simple when you live forever. Truly a little more time is nothing either, I can learn more patience.

"What's a few more years? She needs to figure out who she is as Lilith. She's always been a twin, and now you want her to be the consort to the king of Hell. What you're asking of her is impossible."

I rub my chin and take in the demon's words. "Will you at least update me?"

Kas rubs the back of her neck. "Will you stay away until she's ready if I update you?" I nod, knowing I can stay out of sight, but not away. But if these are the terms, then I will meet them.

"I will."

"Okay. I will keep her safe until she's ready. *If* she's ever ready." I am a patient man, but the idea of Lilith never being mine makes me sick. I nod, knowing that I hate everything about this plan, but if this is the only way for Lilith to heal, and eventually forgive me, then I'll take it. As much as I hate to admit it, being away from me is probably the safest place for Lilith right now.

I don't know what her angel sister was thinking when she came to Hell, but it had an ominous feeling to it. The only reason I would imagine her doing something suicidal like that was because she either had a death wish or there was something urgent that she needed to tell Lilith, which is equally as concerning.

"Is there anything I can do for now?"

Kas sighs and shakes her head. "No, I'll take it from here."

I sigh, pouring a glass of whiskey. She's being taken away from me again, and I wonder about the cruelty of it all. The fact that I met her in her past life just for her to be taken away from me. The creation of the dagger and having it held above my head as a constant reminder of what I lost. Then finding Lilith but her wanting nothing to do with me. It's like God is continuing to punish me every day.

Kas taps her hip once. "Any sign of Michael?"

I shake my head no, and see the anxiety flood her face. "Summon me if anything is wrong," I instruct, and she nods, portalling back home.

Tracking Lilith when I need to won't be difficult, but for now, all I want to do is sulk and think back on all my decisions. How hiding her pushed her away, how protecting her outwardly looks like I choose everyone but her. *Why would she want to be with me?* I don't deserve her, but that won't stop me from making sure that she's alright.

She might hate me, and honestly, rightfully so, but all I want to do is rewind time and make better decisions. I down my drink and pour another. Maybe if I drink enough it will make this feeling of loss go away.

A merely semi-significant amount of mortal time later...

Every single fucking day I think about dragging Lilith back down to Hell with me. Wrapping a chain around her neck and tying her to my bed. As dark as the thoughts are, I can't feed into them. Just like I can't help the fact that she doesn't want to be with me. That this pull—this fate I've been saddled with—it's one-sided, *again*. I also don't do it because she seems genuinely happy here on Earth. Seeing her happy only reaffirms my decision to let her live out her existence here in this realm. To experience more of the world and hope with every fiber of my being that she somehow chooses me. It feels like the longer we're apart, the less likely that idea becomes reality.

I can't spend much time away from Hell, but when I do, it's to see Lilith or check in on Blair.

I watch as she dances next to Kas. The club is a supernatural one, and it's not to my taste. Red beaming neon lights are what make the club luminescent. The black linoleum floor sticks to the bottoms of my shoes. This place is seedy and has none of the opulence of what I offer in Hell, but maybe that's the point. She has a glittering smile on her face, and she grabs Kas' hands as they sway to the music. It might be pathetic but I've become a bit of a stalker. I can't help myself, and it's moments like this that make me hate that Kas was right. I never saw that smile in Hell. The way that she opens up, looking so free right now, I never got that side of Lilith.

However, I'm still a possessive asshole, and my threat to her still stands. As I watch the werewolf grip her hip and dance behind her my blood heats. I have to clench my fist and dig my nails into my palm to prevent myself from going up to him right now and ripping out his heart in the middle of the dance floor. I don't miss the slight flinch Lilith makes when he touches her, but she continues smiling and dancing all the same. The dog-man scooches up closer to her, his chest pressed against her back, and Lilith pushes herself closer to Kas. I consider jumping in, but before I do, Lilith swings around. The full force of her demon strength shows as she smacks the man across his mouth, she hits him so hard that he lands on the sticky bar floor. Deep red blood pools from his mouth and stains his beard as he glares up at Lilith.

"What the fuck, bitch?"

"Don't touch me," she says to him, turning back around and dancing with Kas. I'm just itching to hurt him. For a multitude of reasons; that he touched what belongs to me, that she didn't want him to, and he called her a bitch.

Only when his large hand grips Lilith's ankle, nearly making her fall, is when Kas steps in. She stomps the skinny part of her shoe down hard on his wrist, the stiletto piercing the flesh. The werewolf howls in pain, and I can't help but smirk at the irony.

"Motherfucker! These are satin, his blood will never come out," Kas complains, shaking her head. Lilith bends down and riffles through his back pocket. The man is completely oblivious, more concerned with holding his wrist.

Lilith tosses her the man's wallet and shrugs. "That should cover it."

"Let's get out of here," Kas suggests, kicking the man one last time for good measure.

"I'm going to run to the bathroom, then we can portal home." Kas nods, and Lilith walks in the opposite direction of me to go to the bathroom. I follow her every movement, watching how tall and regal she looks in her black dress and the way it swishes with every move she makes.

"I'm guessing I can count on you to take out the trash?" Kas' voice startles me. I was too focused on staring at Lilith to even notice her approach.

"Yes," I reply, looking at the man holding his wrist and sitting down at the bar.

"This isn't healthy, you know?" she says as a pretty waitress with a tray hands her a drink. Kas gives her a lazy smile before turning back to me. "You're only torturing yourself."

"Didn't ask your opinion."

She sighs and takes a sip of her drink. "She's doing better. She's happy, she doesn't talk about her sister as much." Kas clears her throat. "If you want Beelzebub alive, however, you may want to relocate him to somewhere else."

"I don't care about him."

Kas rolls her eyes. "Do you know how much it would mean to her to hear you say that?"

"You said she's happy?" Kas nods her head. "And as far as I can tell, besides general unwanted attention, no one knows who she is. She's safer here."

"Lucifer," she sighs. "When I told you my idea, I didn't mean that you needed to stay away forever."

"I..." I shake my head as I almost forgot myself and confide in this demon. I shake my head and watch as Lilith scans the room looking for Kas. "I'll take care of the werewolf," I state flatly, walking away so Lilith doesn't spot me.

I can't believe I nearly told her the pathetic thought that's been plaguing me for too long. That I want Lilith to want me, that if she doesn't want me then what does it matter? Her safety comes before my singular want.

The werewolf is slowly healing at the bar. He doesn't heal as fast as a demon or a vampire, but it is fascinating to watch his skin slowly graft back together. *I'll quite enjoy killing him,* I decide.

I'm feeling a bit melancholy this afternoon with all that I'm depriving myself. But this—hurting this asshole—that is something I have control over. A variety of beings continue grinding on the dance floor, nearly fucking right before us as the werewolf stands. His movements are shaky as he holds his arm against his chest and leaves the club.

I follow him silently, and the sick jealousy that he got to touch Lilith is what has my feet moving. Lilith is it for me and there will never be anyone else—no one else can compete with destiny. But it appears that time is never on my side, and it won't be on this motherfucker's side either.

He startles as he attempts to put his key in the lock of his truck. "I could heal that, you know?"

"It'll heal fine," he deflects in a gruff voice.

"But wouldn't it be nice for it to be healed immediately?"

"I ain't trying to make no deal with a demon, fuck off."

"Mmm, but you had no problems putting your hands on one? No?"

"Listen, man." He spins around, looking up at me, and swallows thickly. "I think I paid enough for tonight?" he comments, holding up his arm that is still slowly oozing blood.

"Perhaps. But I'm feeling extra on edge tonight."

I don't let him respond as I extend my claws and rip into his chest, pulling out his overly large heart. It beats twice in my fist as his body transforms into a wolf one last time as he tumbles to the floor.

Like the organ has offended me, I drop it on the floor and tsk at his shifted form. He's much more likable this way, and I sigh. "I'll be seeing you shortly," I say to his corpse.

There's a pop of a portal as Ronan approaches, wearing all black. He clicks his tongue and looks down at the dead body.

"No offense, my lord, but I think you need to get more inventive with your kills."

"Why fix something when it isn't broken."

He shrugs, and I clear my throat. "Have the angels been stirring up anything lately?" I ask while grabbing my handkerchief and rubbing my bloody hand on the material.

"Ezekiel is always a fucking asshole, but nothing out of the norm."

"You'll keep me informed?"

"Always, my lord."

I give him a nod, dropping the handkerchief over the dead man's heart, and portal back to Hell only to be met by a glass of whiskey and the overwhelming desperation that follows me everywhere I go.

CHAPTER NINETEEN

LILITH

I thought I was supposed to have another meeting with Rainn today, but he bailed. He does that often. I've scoured every library possible to see what I can find out about this diadem he wants so badly, and I've found nothing. Just as he seems to have no information about Diana, or what she was trying to warn me of.

I spend half my days researching the diadem and the other half searching for Beelzebub. I'm not exactly sure how I'm going to kill him, but that's also a part of my research. The spear he threw at my sister killed her and ended her afterlife. So I've been trying to find anything I can on ancient weapons, but nothing is turning up.

My crazy thought—that turned into a crazier idea—was to visit my old pal Doug's house again. I remember all the very stealable shit he had in his home, and I'm wondering if he has anything of importance there. But I need to be smart. I need to know what I'm looking for when I break in.

So, here I sit at the seediest of seedy bars in Hallowsdeep—Eternity—hoping to gain some information. There's a very hot demon, who almost looks like a viking, and I approach him like I have nothing to lose.

"Hi," I say, waving my hand and taking the stool next to him.

"Haven't seen you here before."

"First time."

He pushes his blonde hair out of his face, and I wonder for a moment who has longer hair, him or myself. As I ponder this I can't help but sense the feeling of being watched, I look over my shoulder but no one is there. So I keep chatting up this demon, wondering if he will help.

The one thing I've learned recently is that demons are not a helpful species. It's very much every demon for themselves.

"What can I help you with, doll?"

"I'm looking for a few things."

He waggles his eyebrows, looking my body up and down.

"Not those kinds of things."

"Boo... what are you looking for then—"

"Lilith," I say my name and he smiles, not looking so downtrodden anymore.

"Elrick."

"I'm looking for something that could kill a demon."

He whistles and shoots back his whiskey. "You're going to need a can of spray paint and a rare weapon."

"I'm listening," I say and Elrik talks animatedly.

"Weapons to kill the immortal are few and far between. I know for sure there are spears laced in Lucifer's blood in Hell that can kill angels and there are daggers laced in God's blood in Heaven that can kill angels and demons. Supposedly there are a few others that have been manufactured by witches centuries ago that are powerful enough to do it too."

"Any idea where I can get my hands on a weapon like this?"

He laughs and shakes his head. "Like I said, few and far between. You're better off finding a dagger that can send demons back to Hell."

"Those are more common?"

He nods and takes a sip of his drink. "Witches have been making them for centuries, not so much anymore. It has to be a powerful witch, and the spells are complex, but they can make them."

"But then they're not dead."

He shrugs. "Probably easier to have them non-corporeal than to find a dagger that can actually kill a demon."

"Thanks for your help."

"Any hints as to what demon has you all riled up?" he asks, and I wonder why this demon was so free with his information. I watch as a bead of sweat drips down his forehead. *How peculiar...*

"Where's the fun in that?"

"Right, well, have a nice night." He swallows and sits straighter in his stool.

"Fucking weirdo," I mumble to myself as I leave the disgusting bar. Blair isn't powerful enough—yet—to do what I need. But I think I know who might be. I swallow my pride and portal in front of the cottage, knocking until Josie answers.

She looks me up and down and clicks her tongue.

"No," she says before slamming the door in my face.

This fucking bitch. I take a deep breath in, while Josie isn't immortal, witches aren't some meek supernatural species either. I'm sure she could do some serious damage.

"I'm looking for a dagger that can send a demon back to Hell," I shout through the door.

"Don't care," she yells back.

"I can pay you."

I'm not sure what spell she casts, but I'm suddenly tossed a good hundred feet from the cottage. I'm back on my feet in a moment, taking a few deep breaths before I realize I need to portal home before I lose my temper completely.

Once I'm back home, I feel exhausted. At least I learned some information, but I've hit another dead end. I'm not sure if this is even worth it. I don't feel like I'm living. I undress, and I hear the coin in my pocket pang against the floor. I sigh, taking it out and tucking it in my nightstand. I somehow feel better now that I'm in my pajamas and lying on my bed, but my mind won't shut off.

Luckily, not too long later it does, and I'm swept away into a dream.

There's a lake, one I slightly remember from Hell. Its water is inky black, and the surrounding area is covered by willows with black leaves. I sit on the grass as a large figure approaches me and sits down.

He squints at me and smirks. "Interesting."

"Well, hello to you too."

"Bad day?" Dream Lucifer asks, and I sigh.

"Why couldn't you have just been on my side? Maybe I wouldn't feel this hopeless," I admit, and he furrows his brows, shaking his head. "This is a dream, I was hoping 'dream you' would give me the answer that I wanted to hear."

"I am, and will always be, on your side. I regret how I handled that day and wish to make it up to you."

I roll my eyes and look over at him, taking in his beautiful face. *Why do I miss his face so much?* I should want to punch it in. I'm not sure why I harbor so much anger toward Lucifer, but I do. *He* didn't kill Diana, but he didn't do much to make the matter better after the fact either.

He's just as tall, put together, and stoic as I remember. Even now, looking at this dream version of Hell, I miss it. I should love being by the ocean and experiencing the four seasons, but no, I miss the gloom and otherness that is Hell. *How embarrassing.*

"I'm working on a way to kill Beelzebub."

"I figured as much."

"How do I do it?"

He clears his throat and looks up at the gray clouds. "Would you be opposed to sending him here? If he's here in Hell the options are endless."

I frown at him and shake my head. "You're just trying to keep him alive."

He sighs and shakes his head. "No, I'm thinking about true revenge."

"How do I send him to Hell?"

"You'll need a special blade, there aren't many left."

"I know this already, and I—" I almost slip up and tell him that I almost asked his baby mama to make me a dagger to kill my nemesis. Truly a low point. Man, are things getting desperate.

He waves a hand at me. "You know I could very easily drag him to Hell for you, love."

I squint and shake my head. "You didn't do it before. And, of course, you're saying everything I want to hear in a dream."

He groans and lies flat on the grass.

"You'll wrinkle your suit."

"Don't give a shite. I miss you, you know."

I sigh and lie down on the grass next to him. We don't touch, but I wish we would. "Ugh, I miss you too," I tell him honestly. If there's one place you can be a hundred percent honest, it's in your subconscious.

When I tilt my head, I see a ghost of a smile on his lips as he looks up at the clouds. I never got to see him so relaxed in Hell; he doesn't even have a suit jacket on.

"Do you know anything about the Diadem of Kinship?"

"Where the fuck did you hear about that?"

I shrug my shoulders and look at him.

"Lilith, who told you about that?" He props himself on his elbows as he looks at me.

"This is supposed to be a good dream. Where you tell me all about how much you fucked up and missed me. Not you yelling at me."

"Lilith," he says, reaching out his hand, and it's what snaps me out of my dream.

When I wake up, it's with a gasp of breath and my heart hammering in my chest. The dream was so vivid. I'm just exhausted, tired of looking for answers where none are to be found. I'm tired of Earth. It was fun at first, truly, when I was numbing the pain of Diana's death and just experimenting in the mortal realm with Kas. But now it's like sunshine and people are terrible, and Hell is where I really belong.

I stop that train of thinking before it goes any further.

I have a fucking job to do. Kill Beelzebub and find out what Diana was warning me about. Until I do that, there's no time to think about my selfish wants.

CHAPTER TWENTY

LILITH

How fast does mortal time move compared to time in Hell anyway?

"This is bullshit," I tell Kas as we sit at the cafe in Hallows-deep. "It's been how fucking long, and we haven't found him, haven't even found anyone who's seen him."

"We'll find him," Kas reassures me.

My focus on killing Beelzebub has become borderline obsessive.

Time in the mortal realm is an odd thing, I guess since I'm not battling with the idea of my morality, it seems to be moving like a blink of an eye. It's been forever since I've had any rumblings of information about Diana from Rainn, and since I haven't made any headway on the Diadem of Kinship, he seems to have lost interest. It's frustrating, but putting any faith in an angel seems pointless. Earth is beginning to feel pointless as well.

Time doesn't heal all things, but time does seem to be making things easier—even if it seems to be moving at an unrealistically fast pace.

To my core, I am an unforgiving person, but there's a piece of me that wants to forgive Lucifer... and myself. It doesn't help that my subconscious wants to forgive him too. I keep dreaming about him. Sometimes they are down and dirty. He doesn't talk much in those, and then other times, they are so sweet and domestic. I want to scream.

The idea of wanting him—that some part of me misses him—makes me feel guilty. He wasn't cruel to me, but he wasn't nice either. He gave me pretty words and an amazing orgasm—and continues to in some dreams—but besides that, he can't give me what I want. I want to be someone's everything, and I don't think Lucifer is capable of something like that. He's hardly capable of being remotely honest with me. Well, in person, anyway. Sometimes in my dreams, he's so kind and generous with information. I feel like if he was more vulnerable and honest in real life, I wouldn't feel so guilty about wanting to see him again. I hate that after all this time, my body and mind want him, it's evident in how often I dream of him. I do love my time with Kas, it's fun. She's the first person I've ever truly been myself around, and she likes me for who I am. She's just as violent as me and revels in making the most vile people pay. In many ways, Kas and I are similar. But I can tell she is growing bored. It might not be the proper term, but I think that she needs a new adventure.

I sip my coffee and glance at her. "If you wanted to take a job or something, you could, Kas. I can be left alone."

She smiles, her long black, matte nails clicking against her teacup. "I know you're more than capable," she says, making me grimace. After all this time, no other gifts have presented within me. I have the standard demon gifts of persuasion and strength, but beyond that, there's nothing extraordinary about me. "I know you can handle yourself. We'll see if any interesting jobs come up. In the meantime, collecting souls isn't so bad."

I shrug my shoulders. As much as I hate to admit it, I liked working with Lucifer more than collecting souls. Mostly because if I find out just how bad they are, I wind up killing them instead of making a deal for their soul. It's the same result, but it isn't protocol. Piles of dead bodies make suspicions grow and create more tension in the supernatural community. At least, that's the spiel I get each time I accidentally get a little too stabby on a mission.

"Does time move quickly for you on Earth?"

Kas nods and sips her coffee. "It moves quickest here, but not super fast, why?"

"Sometimes it truly feels like a blur, like I'm confused." She furrows her brows and looks at me suspiciously.

"Like how fast?"

I shrug, not knowing how to explain it. "Sometimes it feels like a month has gone by in a day."

"That's not normal." She puts her hand on my face and shakes her head. "Maybe you're missing Hell? I'm pretty sure most demons spend their first few decades in Hell before taking an outer realm assignment." I sigh, the coin burning into my thigh, but my mouth doesn't move. We can't speak about it.

"Do you miss Hell?" I ask her, and she makes a noise in the back of her throat.

"Sometimes," she says softly. "Do you?"

"Sometimes," I parrot.

"You both are so fucking stubborn," she says, shaking her head.

"Says the woman who locked her boyfriend in a different realm for a decade."

She sighs, sipping her coffee. "Lucifer and I have more in common than you can imagine."

"What does that mean?"

She gives me a soft smile and shrugs. "We have dumb as fuck ways to protect the people we care about."

"You could talk about him, you know."

"Asmodeus," she sighs. "You've met him."

"Yes, and?" I may live with Kas, and she might know all of me, but getting to the core of who she is, is a whole other story.

"It's just for the best."

"Kas," I say her name in a warning tone, but she just shakes her head.

"Let's go do something fun. I heard there's an extra handsy frat boy at the local campus. I know they're your favorite." Catching the drift that this conversation is over, I nod my head before we finish our coffee, letting the distraction of killing boys shield us from the bullshit we refuse to work through.

While killing frat boys is always a blast, it just didn't hit the spot. I lie on the couch while Kas is out doing—whatever it is that Kas does late at night. I feel like I confide in her more than she does me, but that's fine. I, at least, don't think any of her secrets involve me.

My cat hops up onto my chest, and I stroke his dark fur as his purr rumbles against my chest. "You don't keep any secrets, do you, baby?" He makes a little *meero* sound, and I scratch under his chin as he makes biscuits on my chest. There really is nothing as soothing as a cat.

I'm not tired, but somehow I find myself falling asleep and dreaming... of Lucifer... again.

"Hello, love," he says, smiling. We're at the black lake again, and I don't know why my dreams keep taking place here. Maybe because it's one of my favorite places in Hell.

"I like the dreams where you're naked better."

He smirks and shakes his head. "When are you going to realize—"

I cut him off, asking, "Realize what? That I keep dreaming of a man who probably doesn't think about me anymore?"

He shakes his head, lying down next to me and looking at the clouds. "I think of you every day. You consume me."

I groan, plopping down and looking at the clouds too. "I wish I didn't like dream you so much."

"When are you going to realize that this isn't a dream?"

"I wish it wasn't," I tell him truthfully. It's so easy to talk to him in my dreams. When he doesn't talk around what he means and when he's completely honest. I mean, it's my version of him, but still.

"It doesn't have to be, you could come back to Hell."

"But I'm not finished," I tell him.

"Avenging Diana?" When he says her name, I look over at him. His expression is soft and not at all condescending.

"She..." It's dream him. I can lay it all out there like I haven't before. "Her last words were, 'don't trust'. And I have no idea who she meant. She risked everything to tell me those two words. The least I can do is make sure she didn't die in vain."

"You think she meant me?" he asks, and I shrug.

"Maybe, I mean, she did die in your realm."

He groans and rubs his temple. "I would never hurt you, though."

"But you did."

I glare at him, and he looks back at me with a look of defeat on his face.

"I want to do better. I've made mistakes, but when you're ready, I'm ready to correct them."

I shake my head and take the coin from Rainn out of my pocket and rub it between my fingers. I'm not sure when it became a comfort item, but I carry it with me all the time like a prized possession.

"What is that?"

"A coin."

He reaches out but doesn't take the coin, almost like he can't touch it.

"Lilith, that's not—"

I'm jolted upright, a big ball of fur jumping off of me as I blink my eyes open. I'm back on the couch as Kas plops a sandwich on my chest. She squints at me and tilts her head.

"That was strange."

"What?"

She shakes her head. "It's nothing, let's eat."

I have to agree, something does feel very strange.

A blink of an immortal eye later...

My visits with Blair decreased over the years; it got easier when her cousin Stevie moved in with her. She didn't need me much anymore, and it's bittersweet. I love seeing the strong, competent witch she's grown to be.

But after the last time of persuading her that she didn't know me, it got to be too difficult. The older she's gotten, the more she looks like *him.*

Kas has been gone awhile, I'm not sure if she's on a mission for Lucifer or herself. All this time, and she still doesn't tell me shit. Time is a funny construct; when you're a mortal, it feels like you'll never get enough of it. But when you know, you're going to live forever? Some days it feels like Diana just passed yesterday, and others, it feels like a lifetime ago. I guess, in mortal terms, it would be.

I shouldn't be here, I know the risks... and yet here I am. At the bar that Blair proudly bought for herself. I've made her forget me so many times, yet, I can't stay away. If I got psychologically examined—could you imagine?—they would probably say that Blair is my tether to Lucifer, and that's why I can't let her go. But that's why

I don't go to therapy, not just because I would likely kill my therapist in a fit of rage.

Blair doesn't smile, not that I would ever expect her to, as she puts my drink on the bar top. Her cousin Stevie though, when she tells Blair something, I can't help but notice the huge smile that takes over Blair's face. I hide my own smile as I take a sip of the overly sweet cocktail she made me. The day Stevie came to live with her was the day that I knew she didn't need me anymore and that she found her person. Sometimes when I look at them, I see Diana and myself. The way Blair is protective of her or how Stevie helps Blair stay on the right path. Everyone needs that. Every woman needs a female friend who would help them bury a body. Kas is no Diana—not in a bad way—but she *is* the person I would call if I needed help. I sigh with that realization and wonder if it's fair or not.

It's then the hair rises on my neck, and I feel like I can't breathe. I don't have to see him to know that he's here. *Blair's birthday isn't for a few weeks, why is he here?* I've felt this before, his presence. Not that I've ever seen him, and maybe it's in my head, maybe it's the dreams, but there are times that I feel like Lucifer is watching me. I can't decide if I like it or not.

I stay put, drinking my cocktail like I haven't noticed his presence. No one else in the bar seems out of sorts, so I know it's just me. I don't dare look over my shoulder. *How would it feel to see him again?* I'm not sure, I've been having very vivid dreams of him lately, and it seems as though my brain has him completely memorized. It's very pathetic when I think about it. The pain still lingers from that night, just not from losing Diana. He was about to promise me everything, and he seemed genuine about it. The look on his face is ingrained in my memory, and the sting of him sending me away still lingers like no time has passed at all.

I feel like I've gotten better, that I've worked through Diana's death, but I'm still angry. I'm angry with Lucifer for not standing up for me, for not letting me get my revenge. My rage toward Beelzebub literally has no limit, but the biggest culprit of my hatred? That honor belongs to the angels.

They are the true reason why I've been back on Earth this whole time, trying to figure out their secrets. At least, that's what I tell myself. Part of me realizes that I'm a coward or making myself suffer.

Diana didn't get to live a full afterlife, why should I?

There's a ghosting of a touch on my neck, and I can't help but look over my shoulder. He's not there. I must be really losing it if, at this point I'm having phantom run-ins with Lucifer. Instead of dealing with whatever this longing is inside of my chest, I order another cocktail, knowing that in my demon form I'll need many more drinks to even feel the dull haze of a buzz.

The alcohol in Hell is so much better than this. No offense to Blair, she's doing the best she can.

To be honest, everything is better in Hell. When I first arrived, I thought I would hate it and the fact that it's always overcast in a sort of gloomy way. But I find that on Earth, I enjoy the rainy days over the sunny ones.

No place I've stayed on Earth compares to Lucifer's manor. Not to mention the overall opulence in Hell. It's like living in a different time period. Even though I was Lucifer's assistant, as far as anyone knew, I felt like royalty. *He* made me feel that way.

I swallow thickly, not liking the overwhelming intrusion that Lucifer has over me lately. Maybe I need a distraction, a new project. Maybe it's high time I started doing more when it comes to the angels.

It's about time I found one of those pigeoned-wing bitches and got some answers. As soon as that thought hits me, it's like Lucifer's presence in the bar retreats, and I can't help but feel lost without it. I shake my head. *No, I will not go back to him.* If he wanted me so bad, if he wanted my forgiveness, then he could have asked a long time ago.

I don't even give myself time to think of all of Kas' excuses for Lucifer over the years. *"He's protecting you." "He's a fucking moron, but he cares." "He had to have had a reason, Lilith."* Excuses aren't what I need. I need answers.

"Do you need another?" Blair asks me, and I shake my head.

"No thanks."

She squints and looks at me hard for a few minutes. "You look familiar, have you been here before?"

I give her a small smile and think of all the memories I have of her that she doesn't have of me. Like the time I told her to kick her prom date in the balls for getting too handsy or to set that little bitch Clover's hair on fire. Maybe I wasn't the greatest little demon on her shoulder, but we had a good time.

"No, just passing through."

She nods, but she doesn't seem convinced as she puts a hand on her hip. "Well, my name's Blair; I own the place. If anyone gives you a hard time, just come and get me." She gives the three men sitting at the bar a stern look, and I have to hide my smile at how strong she's become.

Lucifer has to be proud. I know I am.

Great, we're back on Lucifer again. I put an abundance of cash on the bartop and leave before I can get too nostalgic.

Tonight we're hatching a plan. I need Rainn to give me more information. I think about the place we met previously, and I find myself walking behind the post office. I take the coin out of my pocket and rub it. It's a fifty-fifty chance that he shows up. I fucking hate how co-dependent I've become on this coin. Especially because it's a subpar replacement for my dagger. The dagger called to me in a comforting way, like we were one. This coin, it nags on me in a festering way that I can't refuse.

I rub the back of my neck as a raindrop hit's my skin. *Odd, it wasn't supposed to rain today.*

It's as I stand outside looking at the street that I realize I don't belong here. I always thought I was meant for something other, and yet, here I am back on Earth feeling displaced. But until I have answers for Diana, I can't move on. I need to know what she was warning me about and Beelzebub's head on a spike. Nothing less will curb this hunger.

I've been a demon for long enough now, but I've never actually thought about what I want in this immortal life. It feels too overwhelming as I stand on the pavement and for some stupid reason, I think I can bargain with an angel.

There's a crack of lightning, and Rainn appears. "Lilith," he greets me, and I nod.

"I've got a lead on the Diadem."

He arches an eyebrow but seems to take the bait.

"Do tell."

"I believe it's in the Fae realm."

"And how, pray tell, did you become privy to this information?"

"That's none of your concern. But I'll need your help to get it. What do you have for trade?" I'm lying through my teeth, but I just need this to be over. Maybe if I just kill Beelzebub, I'll feel better. Sure, I'll be wondering why she came to Hell, but I can't keep living like this.

"Beelzebub's whereabouts."

My eyebrows probably skyrocket as I stare him down. "You're lying."

"I'm not, I'll bring him to you when we find the diadem."

"Tomorrow, meet me at the docks." *Shit.* I'm going to need a better plan.

He tilts his head and nods. "'Till then, Lilith."

I portal home and wonder exactly how I'm going to pull this off. Maybe I could find some sort of fake crown and give it to him. I should call Kas for backup... but for some reason, I can't speak about Rainn, no matter how much I try. It's actually quite odd; when I'm alone or with the angel, I can speak to him and remember things about him just fine, but around anyone else, it's like he doesn't exist. The coin in my dress pocket feels heavy as I lie down on the couch.

Why do I feel so strange?

I feel so stressed. Is it wrong to wish I had someone who could help me bear this weight? Suddenly my cat jumps on my chest; I smile and pet his fur as he purrs against my chest, calming my frantic thoughts that don't seem to make sense anymore.

I don't remember falling asleep, but I suddenly find myself inside of Lucifer's bedroom as he shuts a book and looks up at me. *Interesting, we're usually at the lake.*

He tilts his head to the side, complete confusion written all over his face. "Lilith?"

"Well, of course, I would have a dream about you tonight. Were you at Hex today?" I ask him. Maybe dream Lucifer will give me some answers. It's not like I'm actually going to Hell to confront him.

He blinks at me rapidly and stands. *How could I have forgotten about his daunting height?* He approaches me, his steps slow, like I'm a caged animal that might run. He looks the same as when I left him; in his fitted suit with his dark hair pushed back and his menacing brown eyes watching me as if I'm a puzzle with pieces that don't fit together.

He appraises me with his gaze, and it moves all over my body, starting at my face before dragging down my figure.

"This isn't a dream," he says, his eyes going softer than they were before.

"Sure it is. I didn't just come back to Hell on my own accord."

"You're astral projecting."

I cross my arms and look at him. "If you mean I'm projecting my irritation with you while in a dream, then yes, that's exactly what I'm doing."

"You're not dreaming. All these visits haven't been dreams," he says softly.

"Yeah, okay. Then why are you usually naked in half of my dreams," I tease, and a small smirk takes over his lips.

"Because you are mine, and if that is something that you want, it can certainly be arranged."

I hold out my hand and wave to him. "Alright, then. Take it off."

"You do realize that I'm Satan, and I don't really give a fuck if things escalate between us before you come to terms with this not being a dream. If you're willing, I'm going to do as I please."

I arch my eyebrow at him. "Well..." I wave at his body one more time. I only saw him naked in the tub that one time, but my active imagination has done wonders, filling in the missing pieces.

Especially since I can't seem to get any when I'm on Earth. I might as well take it where I can, in my dreams. All my possible sex interests either ghost me or mysteriously wind up dead.

"I won't be able to touch you," he says while he tosses his jacket onto his chair and begins unbuttoning his shirt.

"Why not?"

"Your soul is here with me, your conscious thought is here in this form, but not your physical body."

"Yeah, duh. That's what happens in fucking dreams. We've touched plenty of times before in my dreams."

"Those are your real dreams, I would definitely recall if you were asking me to undress for you, let alone fucking you. I imagine during your real dreams when you're not astral projecting, we don't speak much."

I put my hands on my hips and glare at him. "No, you don't. You're usually less chatty."

"That's because this is not a dream." *Do I even care if it's not?*

"Yes, it is. Are you going to give me the goods or what?"

He smirks and shakes his head but slowly and painfully unbuttons each button. "How has my performance been in these actual *dreams*, love?"

"Adequate." More than adequate, I usually wake up a sweaty wet mess, which doesn't happen when I have a non-spicy dream of him. Something about how we are now does seem clearer than any wet dream I've had of him before. But the needy slutty part of me doesn't care—I need this.

"Mmm, I'll have to do better than that."

"It would be appreciated." He laughs, and the smile that takes over his face is one I haven't seen before. When he looks up at me, it's like he's truly happy to see me. He never stops undressing, but he doesn't stop looking at me, either.

Once his shirt is off and I can see the full expanse of his chest, I have to bite my lip. It's not fair for this man to be this insanely hot.

"Last chance, love," he says, taking his belt out of the loops and going to unbutton his pants. "You're not dreaming. Do you want me to keep taking it off?"

I nod, and he takes it as the yes that I wish I could scream from the top of my lungs. While part of me might never forgive him for what happened that day, there's a more intrusive part of me that misses him and has been longing for him. I don't know how to explain it. It's like an itch that can never be scratched or like a fly buzzing around your ear that annoys the shit out of you and will never go away. I can't escape him, no matter how much I try. So, I should at least get a show with his infestation of my mind.

He drops his pants, and they fall to the floor; he is fully—blissfully naked. He's hard, and his cock smacks against his stomach as he pushes his pants away from himself. When he fists his length, his thumb rubs the moisture from the tip down over his shaft, and I nearly come on the spot. He doesn't say anything, just looks at me as he slowly strokes himself. It's leisurely like he wants this to last, and he's in no rush to make himself finish.

"Do you just want to watch, little Hellfire?"

I realize I'm staring at his huge dick, and when I look at his face again, he's smirking at me. *Always with that smirk.*

"You said you wouldn't touch me."

He shakes his head. "Can't, not won't," he corrects, taking a few steps closer to me. He's close enough that I can see his whole body, and it makes my heart race. "If I could touch you, love. I would be on my knees for you in a moment. I've missed you."

I swallow and look away. *When did my dream-Lucifer get so sweet?* Usually, in my dreams, we are a mix of sweat, teeth, and pants of breath. It's only in my other dreams he's this sweet. "You don't mean that."

"You just admitted to feeling my presence, how often does that happen?" He's holding his length in his hand but isn't moving as I look at his face.

I shrug, not wanting to admit just how often it feels like he's around me. Or how often I dream of him.

He clicks his tongue. "I would say you missed me too if you used your gift to come to see me. Plus, all the times you—"

I shake my head, still not believing him. If I had this so-called gift, it would have shown itself forever ago.

"Doesn't mean I'm not still mad at you."

"It seems your penchant for revenge hasn't sated over time." I shake my head and can't help but look down as he begins to stroke himself again. "Show me what I've been missing, I know you're wet."

"Am not," the lie flies out of my mouth before I can even think about it.

"Don't forget that I know when you lie, darling. Unless you would like to prove me wrong." He arches his eyebrow in challenge, and I give in. If he's not going to touch me, the least I can do is touch myself. I grab the hem of my dress and toss it over my head, throwing it on the floor.

I stand in front of him confidently and watch as his strokes become harder and faster. Fuck, it feels good to be the reason he feels that way. It might just be a dream, but in my dreams, Lucifer is obsessed with me, and he's proving it to me right now.

"On the bed, love." I blink at him, wanting to be defiant but wanting to come more. I confidently hop up onto his bed, ready for whatever he'll give me. When I look down at myself, it's like I'm glowing. *What the fuck?*

CHAPTER TWENTY-ONE

LUCIFER

Looking but not touching is the worst fate I'd been dealt in a while, but it's something. Something that I'm not willing to let slip through my fingers. She looks beautiful, but she always does. It's not like I haven't seen her; I was stalking her earlier today. Plus, the countless times she comes to see me. I thought about telling her about her gift before, but it was so easy to talk to her when she thought it was all a dream. The new information that she has sex dreams about me on top of astral projecting to see me is a bonus.

My Lilith seems conflicted. All I want to do is get on my knees and do something pathetic like beg her to come back to Hell or confess my feelings for her. The time apart has been difficult—to put it in simple terms. The only thing that's gotten me through her being on Earth is how much I check in on her. And how much she checks in on me—chooses to see me. If I didn't have these small moments with her, I wouldn't be able to function.

I know that she lives with Kas, that they are friends, and that Lilith is still as bloodthirsty as ever. I know that she's seeking revenge for her sister, and she won't feel content until she does. I even know that she's been visiting Blair. At first, I was mad at her for not listening to my orders, but when I saw them together, the way Lilith cared for my daughter when I couldn't... it meant everything to me.

I've been good, following Kas' advice so she's safe on Earth. No one has bothered her, and there haven't been any stirrings from Heaven. But I can't help how selfish I am. I need her with me, even if it is a projection and not physical. Her mind and spirit are here with me, and if that's all I get, then I'll take it.

The first time she projected to me, I thought my own subconscious brought her to me. That I yearned for her so fiercely that this vision of her was a concept my own mind made up.

Once I saw the shimmer on her skin, one that most wouldn't notice because it was barely discernible, that's when I knew she was astral projecting. The realization that she misses me as much as I miss her, even if she's not willing to admit it, means everything to me. It keeps me patient, allowing her this time to grow, learn who she is, and for her to make the choice to be with me.

I'll take her in any form she gives me, but fuck, I wish I could actually touch her right now. I've nearly forgotten how she feels under my fingertips, and I'm hungry for it.

She lies on the bed, just in her purple bra and panties. The way I want to slowly remove them with my teeth is overwhelming, but I know that I can't.

I can't help but stroke myself as I look at her body, still as beautiful as ever. Her eyes wander from where I'm touching myself to my face, and she licks her lips.

"Do you like what you do to me, Lilith?"

She nods her head and furrows her brows. "You don't usually talk this much."

"Do you want me to shut up?" I ask, and she shakes her head. "Then shall I tell you how much I've been thinking about your viciously sweet cunt?" She nods her head, and I smile. I'm so close to her, and I would give anything for it to truly be her in front of me right now. To feel the heat of her body and her skin against mine—I'm desperate for it. I'm happy she hasn't changed anything about her appearance, she's beautiful just like this.

"I think about it every day, about *you* every day," I tell her. She glides her hand over her stomach, and I don't miss the wet patch on her panties. I want to suck it in between my lips and make her come while the tight garment is still on.

"Don't lie to me in my dreams."

I shake my head. "I stroke my cock every night thinking about your pretty lips wrapped around me. Or your tight pussy stretching from my cock. It's the only way I can come... thinking of you."

She scoffs, placing her hands on the bed. "I think... maybe, I did like it when you *didn't* talk."

"If I don't talk, how can I tell you what to do?" I ask with an arch of my eyebrow. I'm so close to her, and it was already clear that she was a projection. But not being able to smell her is disturbing to me. I lean over her, my thumb grazing the head of my length, and I use the release to wet my cock.

She swallows, the column of her throat looking impossibly long, and all I can think about is leaning forward to lick and bite her tender flesh.

"What would you tell me to do?"

"Show me how you've been making yourself come."

She glances back down at where I'm touching myself, and her cheeks heat when she slides her hand down into her panties.

"Panties off." The command is clear and deep, and she surprisingly gives me no pushback as she uses her thumbs to glide the lace down her thighs.

"Such a pretty pussy," I tell her, and a small whimper escapes her plush lips.

Her hand shakes as she uses the tips of her fingers to slowly circle her clit. I keep the same pace as she does.

She moans lightly as she touches herself, but I know she's holding back. That she's not completely letting herself go. I need her to let go. It's all I ever wanted, for her to completely let go and accept this tether that ties us to one another.

"Fuck yourself with your fingers." Her eyes drift from my cock to my face before landing on the center of my chest, where the necklace dangles. I knew she wasn't wearing hers, but I never took mine off.

It's only when she sees the necklace that she does as I asked. Two of her fingers slip into her tight cunt. A keening noise escapes her lips, and her breasts rise and fall with each breath she takes, her hair spilling into a golden pool behind her.

"That's it. Are you thinking about your fingers being mine instead? How quickly you came from just my hand."

She moans and shakes her head. *Lie.* The sweet scent of strawberries and sugar still hits me. *Interesting.* I didn't know I could taste a projection's lies.

I shake my head. "It's what I think about. I think about how tight you were. How incredibly wet you were for me. How fucking sweet you tasted. How you wanted to beg for more but wouldn't."

My words send her over the edge, and as I watch her unfold before me, I can't help but speed up my pace. Lilith's eyes don't leave my body, and mine never leave hers. Both of us watch hungrily as we bring ourselves to orgasm. A mutual crescendo of release so intense and all from only watching each other.

Lilith pants, her fingers sticky with her release as she rests them on her stomach.

"I needed that," she says softly.

"So did I," I say with a smile. I would have given anything for this to be truly real, not a projection.

"You still wear it." She eyes my necklace, and I nod.

"Never stopped."

"Why?" she asks, and I glance down.

"Because *you* mean everything to me. There's more we need to talk about. The coin from the last time I saw you..." It's the first time I've had any hint that something unsavory might be happening on Earth, and I need to make sure she isn't in danger.

"What?" she asks, and I watch as her skin shimmers and flickers. When she looks down at herself, she blinks rapidly. "What the fuck?"

"Seems as though our time is up, love. Get rid of the coin, wear your necklace." She blinks again as she fades away.

All I'm left with is the memory, my cum on my fist, and the lingering feeling of disappointment.

Would she have let loose with me in any other situation? If she didn't think it was a dream, would she have opened her legs for me to show me how she makes herself cum? Doubtful.

Time, when you're immortal, is an odd thing. It moves quickly, maybe it's the revelation that time is basically irrelevant because you have an infinite resource of it. But whatever the reason, this time without her has been the slowest my long and suffering life has ever felt.

The only thing keeping me going is my realm and the possibility that one day I can provide her enough safety to have her here with me.

As I've watched her, I've realized how much she needed this time to explore on Earth. She was barely an adult when she came to me. Her experiences in life were limited, to expect her to come to a new realm and basically adapt to what I wanted her to be was unreasonable.

Lilith's safety will always be my utmost priority, but lately, I've been feeling selfish, and the only thing I care about is having her with me.

And now that I know she has some shred of feelings for me, that she *dreams* of me. I'm not sure I can just be her admirer in the shadows.

I'm not sure what I'll have to do to convince her to come back to Hell with me, but besides compromising her safety, I'd give her just about anything.

"Sir," Toth says from my library door.

"Yes?"

He plops a file down in front of me, and my brows furrow as I read over the document.

"We need to handle this," I say, looking at the amount of possessions and deaths.

"I was going to put a team together."

"Daxaddon and Asmodeus will do."

"Kas has been looking for work," he comments, and I want to roll my eyes. But perhaps making sure that Kas is preoccupied is a way to get more time with Lilith.

"Fine, but don't let them know of each other."

Toth smirks and nods his head. He doesn't leave, and I tilt my head in question.

"Something feels off about this," he says, and I look back down at the file. It is peculiar to have a demon do this many possessions instead of sticking to one vessel. *Why do they keep killing them?*

"What are you thinking?" I ask, but he shakes his head.

"I'm not sure, but it feels off."

"Set a meeting with Daxaddon and Asmodeus so they understand the importance of this mission."

"Yes, sir," he says, nodding and leaving.

I scrub my face and read over the file again. The demon doing these deeds must be unhinged or perhaps more powerful than any I've seen in the past few centuries if a human vessel can't hold them.

I place the file to the side and fill a glass of whiskey. All I can do is remember last night. the way she looked at me and spoke to me, the way she has doubts about how I feel about her.

I plan on making sure she knows just how much I care for her.

Exactly how do I plan on doing that? I have no fucking clue. But perhaps I need to upgrade from stalking from the shadows to stalking right in front of her face.

A sudden burn hits the center of my chest.

"Fucking hell."

When I grab the chain around my neck that rests under my clothes, the crystal burns against my fingers. She's wearing the necklace and is summoning me to her. I smile to myself, gripping the crystal and portalling directly to her.

I land with a smile on my face, but when my eyes connect with Lilith's and those who surround her, all I'm filled with is a devastating amount of rage.

CHAPTER TWENTY-TWO

LILITH

When I'm back in my body, I realize that Lucifer was telling me the truth about astral projecting. To give him the credit he did give me multiple warnings letting me know that I wasn't dreaming. Not that I regret it, but I feel confused. The way he looked at me and spoke to me, it was reverent and of someone who truly missed a lover.

It wasn't the way I thought he would look at me. Like the demon he threw aside to protect Beelzebub.

It was unexpected and hotter than any dream I've had of him. Even though we didn't physically touch, knowing that I have that power over him, that I made him come from just watching me, made me feel powerful and desired beyond anything I've ever felt. No other sex dream had ever felt that intense, I know he was telling me the truth. I have to take a moment and decipher which moments were truly dreams and which ones were me astral projecting. It doesn't take long to sort out my consciousness, and I sigh, touching my rapidly beating heart.

The realization that all of these times I thought we were having conversations in my dreams were truly me seeking him out and projecting to him. The Lucifer I wished I could be with was real. I sigh heavily trying to gather all of my emotions about the man I thought discarded me. He's actually been here all along, giving me space while also being there for me.

I knew before I left Hell that there was a cosmic connection between Lucifer and me, but after this time, when I thought we were growing apart—we were actually getting closer. Maybe I *can* trust him. The idea that he was the person Diana was warning me about has rung less and less true the more I've had time to think about it.

But the more and more I think about it, I know one thing. I want to be with Lucifer, and I think it's about time I accept that reality. He's not the man I originally thought he was. Sure, he's complicated, stoic, and a routine pain in my ass... but this longing for him? Those conversations I've had in my dreams, they've kept me sane while I've been parted from Hell.

I'm not sure if I'm ready to go to Hell and have this discussion with him. I still have work to do. I need to find out what Diana was coming to Hell to tell me and who is responsible for her death—besides Beelzebub. Lucifer said he would help me with that slime-ball, and I believe him, but we need to find him first.

One of the things that shocked me the most was that he still wears the necklace. That little connection we have together, he carries it with him everywhere he goes.

Call me a sentimental sap, but somehow that meant more to me than him saying he misses me. He all but said he's been stalking me, and I wonder if all this talk of protection Kas has been giving me is valid.

I scrub my face in the sink and open the drawer. The jewelry box is a symbol of me taking a step forward. My life has been stagnant on Earth, it hasn't felt meaningful without Diana or as effortless as my short time in Hell felt.

I open the black box and grab the necklace, looping it around my neck. A sense of belonging fills me as the cool crystal lands between my breasts. Lucifer's warning about the coin rings in my mind, so I put the coin Rainn gave me into the box. I don't feel comfortable doing it like I'm misbehaving or something, and as I walk away from the drawer, the tug of the coin feels less heady, especially as I toy with the crystal on my neck.

While I might be projecting back into Lucifer's private quarters tonight, I have a promise to fill. I need to avenge Diana; it feels like until I do that, I can't move forward. I feel selfish for how desperately I want to move on and live life for myself. While I know my life will be extraordinarily long, I can't continue to have this weighing on me.

I put on a pair of jeans and a t-shirt, groaning at the firm material of the jeans and wishing I was wearing one of the luxurious dresses I had in Hell. I'm not sure when I became a whore for luxury, but damn, do I miss the effortless elegance in Hell.

Stop it.

We're not thinking about Hell, Lucifer, or the way he came looking at me.

I'm going to kill Beelzebub today, and after that, maybe I'll astral project into Lucifer's bedroom and watch him masturbate. I have holy water, a charmed noose, and a standard dagger in my purse. Not enough to kill Beelzebub, but likely enough to push him off-kilter and portal him to Hell. I'll take him to Hell, and Lucifer will help me. I smile at the thought.

It's a cooler evening, especially by the docks as I walk around. It's eerily quiet, making me worry that Rainn's playing me and I'll be on wild goose chase for the rest of my life. Seeking vengeance for someone who's no longer here and will never return. The idea of needing closure is what fuels me. It's the only thing that will allow me to move on.

There's a bang against one of the shipping containers, and I walk over. The containers are stacked in rows of ten wide and four high. The noise comes from the far left, and I open the door with ease. The creak of the metal is the only sound I hear. The inside of the container is dark and damp as I walk in.

The door slowly shuts to partially open, but the dreary daylight from outside doesn't help me see anything in the metal box. There doesn't seem to be any cargo, and once I go to turn around, I find that I physically cannot move. It's like an invisible wall is set between me and the exit of this container.

"Rainn?"

"She's all yours," I hear Rainn say, his voice floating around me. I watch as two forms exchange what looks like to be a glittering diadem. Well, it looks like it is real, and it's clear I was playing him. *Fuck me.*

"Heard you've been looking for me," the deep voice rumbles, shaking the container walls. I look at the floor, vaguely seeing the outline of a Devil's trap. *Motherfucker.*

Kas told me to be careful, to always pay attention when I was walking into a building or room. The first time I try to do something without her, and this is what my dumbass does.

Suddenly the container illuminates from what looks like white Christmas lights hung around the edges. When I spin around, I find none other than Ezekiel sitting on the chair in front of me. His white wings spread, and the smug look on his face makes me want to slap it off of him.

I decide to play it cool, letting my temper flare or my true intentions come to light is not the way to play this.

"Where's Rainn?" I ask softly and in the nicest tone I can possibly conjure.

He scoffs and shakes his head. "Sorry, dear girl, it seems *Rainn,*" he pauses, accentuating the name dramatically before continuing, "Wasn't getting what he needed out of you. He loves a good trade, and I had what he needed. So why would he be willing to barter with you?"

"You were at that meeting, did you send Diana to Hell?" I ask, his face making me angry, and right now, he should feel really lucky that this sneaky little trap is holding me back from breaking his nose.

"I couldn't tell you why she attempted to go to Hell. She was told not to. It's clear that blind action is a hereditary trait in your family,"

I breathe in and out deeply. *I will not snap, not when we don't have the upper hand.*

"I find it interesting that you're here, Lilith," he says my name like it's a nasty swear word.

"Where? In a stinky shipping container?"

"No, on Earth. I thought that Lucifer would hold his mate a little closer."

I blink at him, confused. "What?"

"That explains it. I thought he was putting on a show during that meeting. It's clear he hasn't told you anything. It was so evident who you were to the angels. Lucifer doesn't deserve happiness with the hatred he spills every day on Earth. Not just among the humans but toward the angels. You know, he was my favorite brother until he started to change. He thought he was better than all of us. It's why God sent him away, she had enough of his posturing and sent him away."

I tilt my head and take a good, long look at the angel in front of me. I might not have the ability to taste lies like Lucifer, but everything he's saying feels like a lie to some extent.

"Well, I'm not with Lucifer, never was."

"Ah, but he would care if something happened to you."

"No, he wouldn't," I reply quickly.

He clicks his tongue. "Don't worry, we will make it quick."

Three more angels walk into the container, skirting around the outline of the white Devil's trap I'm standing in. I recognize the woman—Rita.

She was rude, but comforted Diana during the meeting. She has a look on her face like she's smelled something foul; she's pinched in every way. I don't recognize the other two angels, but the look on their faces are ones of clear malice.

"What's your goal here? To piss Lucifer off? Because I gotta tell you, it's really not that hard."

"Oh, I don't want to just piss him off. I want to hurt him so deeply that his only recourse is war."

"Shouldn't angels want world peace and all that shit?"

Rita scoffs and shakes her head. "The only way to get some semblance of peace is to overthrow Lucifer. It's time someone else takes over the throne of Hell, someone that Heaven can work with."

I turn my head to look at her.

"And who's going to do that? Not one of you, I assume."

"Of course not, we don't want to live in that dreadful realm. But things are coming together now, and it's time to hit him where it hurts."

I blink a few times, trying to understand what they're saying. *They have someone powerful enough to take Lucifer's place? And I'm a pawn in this scheme to what? Cause an uprising in Hell when Lucifer freaks out over my death.*

I now know that the man cares about me, more than I ever realized. I think back to what Ezekiel said, and I wonder if I am his... What did he call it, his mate? Like his soulmate?

"Well, this plan sounds wonderful and all, but where do I start when it comes to all the flaws?"

Ezekiel stands, and the chair drags against the floor until it's in the Devil's trap.

"Sit," he commands.

"Mmm... I'd rather not."

"Sit!" His voice rumbles and shakes the containers. He tilts his head at the angel to the left of me. He's able to walk in the Devil's trap with no issue and grabs my arm.

I don't even think before I act, grabbing the knife from the cuff of my jeans and slicing off his ear completely. The cartilage falling to the floor has him hissing in pain. I know he'll heal quickly, but he really is hamming up the pain as he cries like a little bitch.

The other angel grips my arms. And unfortunately, the neanderthal is twice my size, meaning he's way stronger than me, and easily ties me to the chair. He's rough, and the ropes are tight, but not in a fun way.

"Are you done?" Rita asks in a condescending tone.

I just stare at them and blink, keeping my mouth shut, and running through all my options. *I can't portal in this fucking trap. I haven't talked to Kas in a few weeks; plus, she has no idea where I am. Lucifer...* the necklace. I need to get my hand around it and call his name.

Fuck.

Why didn't I do that as soon as I was thrown into the trap? Probably because I haven't worn it in such a long time. I forgot what it could do, how much protection it could offer me. I need to get my hand free.

"We need some specifics about Lucifer's Manor."

"Mmm... it's big."

"I told you this was pointless, you should just kill her. *He* gave us enough information." My head tilts at the mention of a he.

A traitor? I can't help the first name I think of—Beelzebub. I'm so going to kill that rat-bastard.

"He hasn't been in Lucifer's private quarters. We don't know what we're getting into."

"Yeah, you wouldn't want to run into the hellhounds," I lie. I haven't seen any true creatures in Hell, but they don't know that.

Rita blinks a few times and tilts her head. "The hellhounds?"

"Seriously, your little rat didn't tell you about them? Perhaps he's not as good of an informant as you thought. I'm sure he didn't tell you about the warded rivers either." *Just keep coming up with dumb things for them to worry about.* If I can keep them talking just a bit longer, maybe I can rid myself of my bindings and call in some reinforcements.

"She's lying," Ezekiel accuses. I can read the frustration on his face as he steps up to me and smacks me across the face. The smack is so audible in the confined shipping container, it makes my ears ring, and I taste the tang of metallic blood in my mouth.

When I straighten my face, some of my hair falling loosely around my face. I'm sure I look insane as I give Ezekiel a bloody smile, and spit some of my blood onto his cheek. He wipes off my tainted blood from his face and smacks me again. The chair nearly falls over when he hits me, and I know I need to push every button I can.

"Let us end this, brother," Rita pleads. Her tone is bored and bitchy, but I see the rage and anger written on Ezekiel's face. He still has a few specks of blood on his chin, and it makes me smile. I need to make him as angry as possible. Best case scenario is him knocking this chair over. I *need* to get to the necklace.

"Knife," Ezekiel demands, holding out his hand to one of his minions. They hand him my blade, and I grin at him again. *At least my blade won't kill me.*

"Oooh, fun. Do you like knives as much as I do? I didn't think a top angel would love violence so much. What does your God think about that?" I taunt him, not showing any fear.

"Shut up!"

He slices across my arm, making the bindings loosen just the tiniest bit. I'm hoping, with my strength, I might be able to break the binds. The slice fucking burns, and I watch as my skin starts to slowly knit itself together. It's taking longer than usual, and I start to worry about how much time I have.

"Is it frustrating being so self-righteous? Tell me, does mommy let you out of your cage often?"

That infuriates him, and he starts hitting me so hard that I nearly black out. I don't give in but stay awake as his fists hit different parts of my body. A ridiculously hard hit to the chest has me falling, and the chair breaks in the process as I land hard on my side.

I laugh maniacally as Ezekiel pants, my blood decorating his fists. My body aches in a way I've never felt before, but as I watch his eyes widen, I can't help but laugh even harder.

"Oh, you're going to pay," I warn him, and he scoffs. Rita doesn't look shocked at the beating I just received from an angel, but she does look irritated that this is taking so long.

"Can we please wrap this up?"

"Leave if you're so impatient." She rolls her eyes and presses her hip against the metal wall.

I'm weakened with my body trying to heal multiple injuries at once. I'm bleeding in multiple places, but I do my best to shimmy.

"Give me the Hell blade," he requests, and Rita finally smiles. I'm using all my strength but I have no idea what the fuck these binds are made of. I'm worried about the capabilities of the blade he's switching to and if this could be the end. The end before I ever truly let myself live. My mortal existence and my afterlife have been dedicated to Diana. Out of fear and vengeance, I've forgotten to live, and I might truly pay the ultimate price.

When the blade hits my side and knicks the rope, I have a moment of relief. That's until he removes the blade from my side. It's not healing. My blood flows rapidly out of the wound, and all I want to do is apply pressure to the injury.

Ezekiel smiles down at me, he holds the knife like a prized possession as he stabs me again. It hurts so bad that I can't help the horrific scream that escapes my throat. It goes completely through me, through my front and out my back. It hits my wrist, freeing my left hand. I can barely breathe. I'm bleeding so fast and not healing.

"Stop toying with her, strike her in the heart," Rita commands, her eyes filled with violence and hate.

"Shut up Rita, I'm having a little fun."

Ezekiel looks like he's about to stab me again, but I quickly grab the crystal necklace around my bloody fist.

"Lucifer," I say his name so quietly I wonder if it'll even work.

"What was that, demon?" Ezekiel taunts. My face is pressed to the floor, and I feel like I just might pass out right about now.

But I don't.

The loud crack of his immediate portal has me blinking slowly as I watch Lucifer take in the room. He acts immediately. With a stroke of his hand, it's like a shiny glimmer that covers the container.

It's actually really pretty, I think in my haze.

It's only then that I realize he's made their ability to portal out of the container impossible.

His eyes take in my broken body before he swivels towards Ezekiel. The way Lucifer grabs the wings on his back, ripping them off, shouldn't be so attractive, but it is. I watch the blood drip from his back and splatter over Lucifer's perfect face. The contrast between his proper suit and the blood on his face is the most attractive thing I've ever seen.

Ezekiel attempts to stab Lucifer with the same knife he used on me, but Lucifer is faster, grabbing it and shoving it through Ezekiel's neck. The squelch of his blood dripping down his chest from his throat is satisfying.

The sound is pleasing, but not as gratifying as the gurgling in his throat and watching his blood leak from his lips. Lucifer kicks him in the chest, sending him to the floor before he moves on to the other angels. He avoids the Devil's trap but moves with such elegance and finesse that I'm in awe. If I wasn't bleeding out and near losing consciousness or possibly my life, I would probably be clapping and cheering him on.

He works quickly, ripping Rita's heart from her chest and stabbing the heart with the knife from earlier. I can barely see by the time he gets to the two other angels, but he's quick. I hear thuds, blood dripping, and screams. I'm pretty sure he stabs them all with that feisty little dagger that has me spilling my guts everywhere right now.

I'm glad he was able to get his revenge quickly. That's important. That's nice for him.

There's a loud thud, and I realize the ground is shaking, the lines of the Devil's trap crack, no longer forming a perfect circle.

Large arms wrap me up, and I'm placed against the warmest and largest chest imaginable.

"You better fucking hold on. You *will not* fucking die."

"That's nice," I reply.

"You better hold on. I will kill every demon you care about if you don't live."

"That's not nice," I counter, shutting my eyes and leaning against his chest. I feel dizzy as we move. *Why is he walking like that?* Mmm... but he must be walking fast because soon my back is placed on the softest and coziest material I've ever felt.

"Get me her knife," he says.

It's the last thing I hear before everything goes dark.

CHAPTER TWENTY-THREE

LUCIFER

When I first felt my necklace heat, I assumed that Lilith missed me because of what transpired the other night. I didn't expect to find her beaten and bleeding at the hands of angels. She's been so safe on Earth for years, why did they attack her now? She's barely lucid as I lay her on the couch in my library.

It's reminiscent of when I brought her soul here, the day she was reborn as a demon. The bleeding won't stop, and as I look at the dagger the angels used, I know exactly what I must do. My blood is the only thing that can heal a demon in this condition, just as God's is the only one who can heal an angel. Luckily for me, none of those angels I left in that shipping container will be able to seek help. Not just because of the wounds I inflicted but because of the fact that God has been gone for years.

Lilith moans and clutches her side where she was stabbed.

"It's alright, I'm going to fix it."

"Hurts," she moans as she tries to curl into herself, but the pain is too much.

Toth comes back to me with the dagger, the one that connects us; one with magic just as powerful as the weapon used to inflict her wounds.

I cut a path down the length of my forearm. The deep red of my blood flows freely as I place it over her wounds with the intention of healing her. She gasps but is no longer moving her body like she's in unbearable pain.

"That's good, just a little more."

"Fuck," she hisses as I spread my blood on all her different wounds. Toth stands by in the corner, his eyes wide in wonder. I've never cared enough to save another demon's life, let alone like this. If they were dumb enough to get themselves killed, I was under the opinion that they deserved it. But with Lilith, the only person to blame is myself.

I shouldn't have let her go in the first place. I should have been more forthright. Even if I kept her a prisoner here, at least she would have been safe and not in this condition. It's like I've willed history to repeat itself. While the angels held the dagger, I created the opportunity to make this happen.

In my own efforts to shield her, and anyone else from the truth, I've isolated her. All the years I could have had her to myself are gone because I was afraid.

As I watch her wounds heal and the blood dry on her perfect skin, the only thought I have is how I'm not going to be afraid anymore.

I'll chain Lilith to my bed if I have to. She's not leaving Hell; she's not leaving me ever again.

Her skin is fully grafted together, and the color of her skin looks healthy again, but her eyes are still closed.

"Lilith?"

"Mmm?"

"How do you feel?"

"Tired."

"I'll take you to bed." She makes a noise of understanding as I take her in my arms. Toth looks on, at her in my arms longingly, but I can tell he's not lusting for Lilith. Perhaps Toth has been longing for a companion after all of these years. I've never seen him with other demons, he keeps to himself.

I don't concern myself with Toth's feelings for long because when Lilith's face presses against my chest, all I can concern myself with is her presence.

I run the scenarios in my head. *How do I get her to stay? Is this close call enough for her to want to be here?* Deep down, I know that if I force her to stay here, she will resent me. Truthfully if it came down to it, I would do it. But in reality, I would rather her care for me than hate me. But I will do whatever I have to in order to keep her safe.

"Let's get you cleaned up."

"Okay," she softly agrees.

When I'm in my bathroom, I place her carefully in the tub before extending a claw to cut her clothes off from her collarbone to her waist.

"I like those," she mumbles, staring down at my hand.

"You would."

She blinks at me, her hair and face, tacky with blood. "This is real, right?"

"Yes, you're really here."

"And you're really looking at my tits right now?"

"I've seen them before."

She moves her hands to cover her chest; clearly, the healing is working quickly now that my blood is fully in her system.

"Would you rather clean yourself? Or are you going to be a good girl and let me clean you up?"

I watch as she shifts at the words good girl and suppress a smirk. She drops her hands from her chest and helps me remove the t-shirt. I don't get the pleasure of ripping her jeans in two as she unbuttons them and rolls them down her legs.

It takes every ounce of me to not react to her body, even in this state. I clear my throat and turn on the faucet. The warm water fills the bath quickly, and I shiver when Lilith moans as the warmth laps at her beautiful flesh.

Lucky fucking water.

"What about the bubbles?" she asks.

"Bubbles?"

"When you summoned me here that one time, there were bubbles."

While the idea of adding an obstacle to seeing her like this makes me want to scream, I hesitantly grab the bag and toss it into the tub. Flower petals float to the top as the aroma of lavender and rosemary fills the room.

"That's nice." She hums, resting her head on the lip of the tub. I don't ask, just take the loofah and begin cleaning her body. She doesn't object, but I feel her body tense as I touch her.

"Are you okay?" I ask her, and she opens her eyes to look at me.

"You killed them all?"

I nod, and she closes her eyes again, relaxing in the tub. "Then, yes, I'm okay. They weren't going to help me anyway."

I already know what she was looking for, but I mention it anyway. "You wanted to know why your sister came to Hell?"

She nods, not opening her eyes, and I realize what I must do to keep her here. But I'm not sure how to approach the conversation. I very slowly continue cleaning her body. If she notices how long I'm taking to finish, she doesn't say anything. We sit here in silence, no doubt each of us lost in our own train of thought.

When I've finished her body, I lightly trace my finger along her jawline. Her lips part, and the little gasp that escapes her makes me shiver.

She blinks at me, and I hold a piece of hair between my two fingers. "Your face and hair are next." She nods, sinking under the water and holding her breath for an extremely long time. When she breaks the surface and takes a deep breath, I sigh in relief. She scrubs her face before I drain the water. She groans, so I refill the tub with fresh water and throw another bath bag in there.

Spoiled. It's my first thought, and I smirk to myself. All I want to do is spoil her... if she'll let me.

"Will you stay in Hell?" I ask, no longer able to hold the question back.

She blinks at me. "I'm not sure I want to," she states, and I can taste the lie, but I don't call her out on it.

"What can I do to convince you to stay?"

She tilts her head, her hair soaking wet and dripping off the side of the tub.

"I'd want my old job back."

"Done."

"My old room too."

I think about how badly I want her in my room, but down the hall will suffice.

"Fine."

"I want my cat from Earth," she demands with an arch of her eyebrow.

"Okay," I agree, wondering how I can make this cat immortal.

"And no more secrets. If I come back to Hell and stay here, you need to be honest with me. I think you owe me that."

I swallow thickly and nod. "I can do that."

"Also, I want to use this tub whenever I want."

My head bobs, and she smirks.

"There's one more thing."

"Anything."

"I want Beelzebub." I search her face but eventually give her a single nod.

"Okay," I sigh.

Her mouth parts, and she looks at me in shock. "Seriously, just... okay?"

"I've told you already that I would help you. I just couldn't do it in front of everyone in Hell. Technically, he didn't break any rules. But since he's left Hell, I worry what he's been up to. If you want him, he's yours, love."

Her cheeks heat as she tilts her head, accepting my honesty. "Could have saved me a few stab wounds and shaved some years off my Earth Rumspringa with that information." I ignore her jab and glare at her.

"How are your wounds?" I ask her, and she shrugs her shoulders.

"I feel completely fine. Can your blood heal anything?"

"Different ancient weapons do different things. The dagger they used can be a weapon against angels and demons. It can inflict life-threatening injuries that can only be healed by God or myself. There are other daggers that can send demons back to Hell. Or your dagger can kill by just penetrating flesh. Your dagger would not kill an angel or a demon, though."

"They have to be living," she interjects, and I confirm with a nod of my head. "I tried to stab the vampire that killed Diana, and it didn't work," she tells me, and I nod.

I stand up, taking one last glance at her naked form before putting a towel on the counter for her. "Take your time."

"How long do you think it will take you to meet my demands?" she smiles, and I can tell she's enjoying toying with me.

"Not long. Your cat, where is it, and what's its name?"

The grin that takes over her face is feral as she says, "At mine and Kas' place. I'm assuming you know where that is." I don't answer, because yes, I do know where she lives. "And his name is Lucipurr."

My eyebrows furrow, and my mouth slightly parts as I'm stunned into silence. Lilith's laugh echoes through the bathroom, and I can't help the happiness that overshadows my irritation. I've missed her laugh, her playfulness. I've even missed her misbehaving and pushing my buttons.

It seems I have quite the to-do list, and I don't plan on giving her any time to change her mind.

"I'll be back shortly."

Her laughing fit doesn't stop as I portal to her seaside home.

I have to forcibly knock down the front door of their home. Kas is not here, as I suspected. I have her on a mission right now, which I'm trying not to regret. Perhaps if I didn't send her to handle this rogue demon, then maybe Lilith wouldn't have gotten hurt. But if she didn't get hurt, would she have ever come back to me?

Her lie about not wanting to be back in Hell was evident. But Lilith is stubborn, and she probably would have resisted me for as long as possible. I might have let her as well, telling myself that as long as she was safe, then that's all that mattered.

It's not all that matters.

What is an eternal life worth if I'm not able to spend it with the person who makes me feel alive? I've been floating through this existence, managing Hell and doing the duty that I was assigned. But she's come back to me, and I'm very much trying to *not* fuck it up.

Something feels off at her home, almost like I can't remember why I'm here or what I'm looking for. I shake off the feeling and refocus on the fact that I have somehow become so whipped that I'm here to fetch a cat. The term pussy-whipped takes on a whole new meaning.

I make an embarrassing pst-pst noise to try and find the creature. I swear, if she actually named it Lucipurr, I may have to renegotiate our terms because there's no fucking way I'm calling a cat that. I don't even like animals, and this little prick with my namesake will be roaming the manor halls, throwing up on the carpet and scratching curtains.

When I turn the corner in the living room, I see a small black blob. It blinks its green eyes, and I have hope that it's a semi-docile creature. Then its mouth opens, exposing his fangs as he lets out a sharp hiss.

"Let's go."

As I reach out a hand to pick it up, but it bats away my fingers, it's claws scratching my skin.

"You'll fit right in, you little bastard." I grab the cat by the scruff and tuck him under my arm, portalling back to Lilith's bedroom. He's just a cat for now, I can't do anything to him until he passes. As far as I know, all pets go to Heaven and all that bullshit. But surely, I'll figure it out.

She's wrapped in a robe, and her beaming smile when she sees the little twat under my arm makes it worth it. She holds out her arms, and I pass her the cat. The little shit purrs immediately and rubs its head against her chest, clearly marking his territory.

"He's difficult," I say to her, and she kisses the top of his head.

"I like difficult."

"His name—" I start, gesturing to the cat, but her laugh, along with the shake of her head, cuts me off.

"Oh, you don't like Lucipurr?" she teases, tilting her head and holding back another laugh. I give her a look that clearly demonstrates that I, in fact, do not appreciate the flattery of this copycat. She laughs again, petting the small black cat. "Don't worry, his name is actually Doom."

"How fitting," I comment, glaring at the cat who gets to rub up against Lilith's tits.

Am I really at the point that I'm feeling jealous of a cat?

"So, job, room, cat. What do you want to tackle next?" she asks, arching a brow, as if I was bluffing about the whole ordeal.

I smirk at her as I walk backwards out the door. "I suppose we'll start with no more secrets." I have the door half closed before I give her one last glance. "Tomorrow."

She blinks at me as I shut the door, leaving her with her cat and her thoughts. I'm sure she still has a lot to work through. She seems to be handling the event with the angels well. I'm not too surprised. Lilith isn't afraid of violence, and clearly, she didn't want to die, or else she wouldn't have summoned me.

Now, all I have to figure out is how to tell Lilith the whole truth while making sure I keep her safe. I lie awake all night wondering if it's possible to have everything I've ever wanted. My mind also runs every possible scenario as to how it could get fucked up.

CHAPTER TWENTY-FOUR

LILITH

Doom sleeps curled up on my legs, and I can't help but smile. Seems the move from Earth to Hell wasn't too much for her. I make a note to ask Lucifer if he'll still have a cat's lifespan or if it will be longer in this realm. Maybe I should be a little more shaken up after what happened with the angels, but I'm no stranger to violence. Plus, they're all dead. Not to say that more angels might not come after me, but I feel safer in Hell—safer with him.

It was inevitable that, at some point, my quest for answers would come and bite me in the ass. And after the day's events, I have no doubt in my mind Diana was coming to Hell to warn me of the angels and their intent. Then what did I do? I trusted a stupid angel with a stupid fucking name to help me. I was so blinded by revenge that I desperately turned to him. It's clear I should have turned to Lucifer first, but it's all behind me now, I've grown in a lot of ways while I was away and living in the mortal world.

My life on Earth has been subpar, and I can't help but feel like I belong in Hell. Is it because I feel more secure around Lucifer? Or maybe it's the gothic ambiance of the manor or just the people here in general.

Sure, I'm judged in Hell. I definitely haven't missed Lisa and her merry gang of skanks, but I'm not judged for being a bad person; they simply just don't like me. Which is fine, I don't like those bitches either.

I will miss Kas, but I imagine that she would come visit me. At least, I hope so.

The feeling of my heart being tugged on has stopped now that I'm here. Now that Lucifer has touched me, saved me, and bathed me.

I shiver when I think about his gentle touches, so contradictory to the hard man that he is. He's reverent with me. The only other time I've ever seen him gentle is with Blair. Clearly, in a different way, but something about being a soft spot for the Devil does something to me. Before I left, he promised me the world. I'm still unsure of his intentions, and I wonder how much is going to come to light now that all of our secrets are coming to an end.

Nervousness is probably the main feeling when it comes to knowing all of Lucifer's secrets. But to be honest, I'm excited more than anything. What prevented me from giving in before everything happened was not only my internal struggle with my morality but his inability to be forthcoming.

Could this really be the fresh start I was looking for?

Living my life in Hell the way I see fit? Falling for the man no other would even consider because of his reputation? I can't help but think about the overwhelming possibility, especially when Doom purrs. Lucifer—Satan—Ruler of the Underworld brought me my fucking cat to make me happy.

I pull up my shirt and look at the spot where my wound no longer exists. He saved me, he wants me, and most of all, he will do anything to protect me.

Doom rubs his forehead against mine, waking me up. I stretch, and I can't help but run my hands along the expensive bedspread.

I missed these sheets.

After I shower and enter my closet, I smile, looking upon my old friends. All my luxurious clothes which Lucifer picked out for me—at least, that's what I'm assuming.

I chose a black silk dress that shows just the right amount of cleavage while the entire back is made of hanging black gems and crystals. It's heavy, but it will be worth it.

As soon as I open the door, I find Lucifer standing in the hallway. He's wearing a black suit as usual, his hair slightly loose and not pushed back. I can't help when my mind wanders to what he was wearing when he saved me, how he was splattered in our enemies' blood. He sullied his expensive outfit to avenge me—who said romance is not dead?

Is there anything that's more of a turn-on than being violently avenged by an attractive man?

I blink... nope, we can't go there. We still have no secrets and Beelzebub to cross off our list before we give in. *I can't give in, no matter how good he looks.*

"Sleep well?" I nod my head, and he smirks. "Was my performance adequate?"

My mouth gapes as I glare at him. "You can not use what I said when I thought I was in a dream against me."

"Did you really think you were dreaming, darling?"

"Yes, now what are we doing today?" I ask, trying to change the subject. Sadly, I didn't have any fun dreams last night.

"A date."

"A date?" He nods and holds out his hand. I slip mine against his. My longer dark nails contrast against his skin, and I can't help but to toy with a silver ring on his finger. This feels nice, comfortable, in a way that I thought would have faded after time and distance apart.

"Where does the Devil take one on a date?" I ask, knowing he hates the term *Devil*, but I enjoy getting under his skin. *Is there any stronger form of foreplay than being a brat?*

"I suppose he would want to take his date somewhere she had never been before. But I'm not sure if he should reward a smart mouth."

I tug on his hand, catching his smirk. "Oh, you like it. Let's go."

He pulls me closer, our hands still locked, and his other hand wraps around my shoulder blades. It's disorienting at first; it always is when someone else brings you along, but when I blink, taking in the world before me, I'm in awe.

"It's the realm of the fated," he informs softly.

"What does that even mean?"

He clicks his tongue and sighs. "Let me show you."

It's like we're in a futuristic tropical paradise. All the colors of the trees, water, and ground are far brighter than anything I've seen on Earth. The trees' leaves are so brightly green that one melts into the next. The sky is cloudless and the brightest shade of blue I've ever seen. Two stark suns sit in the sky, and it almost feels like sensory overload. It smells like honeysuckle, and there's a low lulling of birds chattering in the distance. We're walking down a carved-out path, and my focus is on the view surrounding us, but it's impossible not to feel Lucifer's presence.

It's only when we reach the end of the path that I see what a futuristic planet this is. I'm still not sure about the difference between a realm and a planet, but I fear it's too late to ask at this point.

It's a metropolis of people wearing simple a-line outfits in bold colors like magenta and periwinkle. The men all have gray trousers and similar-colored tops. The people look human, but not quite. They are taller, their eyes and ears larger. It's like they took humanity and made everything better here.

One thing I notice immediately is how everyone is walking in a couple, different gender pairings, but everyone is with someone.

"Everyone has a fated mate here?" I ask, and Lucifer nods his head.

He continues to hold my hand as we make our way to a futuristic pod-looking vehicle. The door automatically shuts behind us once we take our seats. It's just large enough for two people to sit comfortably. The back is white, and the entire front is glass, so you can see where you're going. I take in everything around me, from the tiny differences between this species and humans to how beautiful everything on this planet is. Everything is just close enough to being like Earth that it's not too jarring, but everything is more colorful and less tainted than Earth is. The inhabitants of this planet clearly value it, at home all of these trees would have been taken down, but yet here, they thrive. Lucifer watches me as I take in the world around us, and I let him. The silence should be stifling, but it's comfortable.

I should wonder why he brought me here, I'm guessing the scenery has to be the reason. I'm definitely not complaining about the location for a first date.

The pod lands by a lake that is nearly crystal clear. There's just a light tint of aquamarine to the water, but you can see the rocks, crystals, and fish clearly from where we stand.

Lucifer unfolds a blanket placing it on the white sand next to the water. I take that as my cue to sit next to him.

"It's beautiful here."

"It is."

"Why are we here?"

"You said no more secrets?" I nod, and he clears his throat. "This is where I first met you."

I furrow my brows as I look him over, knowing damn well I've never been here before. "What?"

"Well, a version of you." He glances over at me before looking back at the water. I can't help but feel that we're both overdressed for this little lakeside adventure. "I was already this," he says, waving to himself. "But I came here to see the realm. Not many of the creatures here end up in Hell, it's very rare. So I wanted to understand why. That's when I met you."

"What are you saying?"

"That you're my reincarnated fated mate."

I blink at him and let go of his hand, feeling like he's full of shit. I've seen that Heaven and Hell exist. I've seen a myriad of supernatural creatures. But reincarnation?

I take a breath and nod. "Go on."

"Everyone on this planet is destined to be with someone. You usually find them early on in life, it's uncommon to not find your mate. Back then, your name was Lily." I blink at him, thinking about my code name with Blair, and when I asked him who Lily was, he said that it was me. "You never found your mate, not that you were old, but when I came here to visit, it was clear that we were destined for each other."

I wave my hand, urging him to go on, not sure what else to say.

"Most people here didn't understand and didn't approve. Most of all, *you* didn't approve. You were innocent and sweet, being caught up in my darkness was a challenge for you."

"Maybe let's stick to Lily and not me. I don't have any memories of what you're saying. So I don't think it's fair to call me Lily."

He sighs. "I suppose you're right. You two aren't similar." I swallow thickly, thinking about how much he must like this other version of who I was better. Even if I don't completely understand it. His thumb tilts my chin as he looks at me, his dark eyes soft and his face relaxed. "I like you just the way you are. I wouldn't change anything."

I sigh, but I nod and let him continue.

"I visited often. I cared deeply for Lily, but she had a decision to make; to live her life here or to come with me to Hell to be a demon."

"What did she choose?"

"She chose to stay here until it was her true time to come to Hell. Unfortunately, she never got the chance. She never chose me, and I don't quite blame her." It's at that moment, Lucifer's stoic facade falls, he's never been chosen by someone. Fate has always decided for him, and all he wants is for someone to care for him for who he is. I swallow thickly as I stare at him.

His eyes look out at the lake, and I wonder how I truly compare to Lily, if we're the same to him or different. I don't think I like being compared to someone, even if we are the same but in different lifetimes. I can't help but to feel that I'm giving him something Lily never could have—genuine affection. The thought makes me shiver as Lucifer continues.

"God was mad at me, perhaps jealous. I'm not sure."

"She killed her?"

"She did. Not only did she kill her, she taunted me with the chance of getting her back."

"The dagger?" I ask.

"It's what she killed Lily with, said that if the dagger was ever awakened again that it would be her gift to me. A stronger version of Lily, a version that could handle my darkness and represent her forgiveness for what I had become."

"How long ago was this?"

"A few thousand years. There were a few centuries where I was a little out of control with power and bloodlust. I needed to be reeled in, but I still don't think the means were just."

"I forget how old you are," I say without thinking, and he scoffs.

"So that is why I have been the way that I am with you. I've seen a version of you taken away from me, and I can't let it happen again. I can't lose you again." He says it softly and in a tone so genuine that I can't help but stare at him. He looks right back at me, his expression is one of a man who has gone through torture, who has been alone for so long, and I'm that last speck of hope.

"So I'm your fated mate?" I groan as I admit what I've always held back. "I've felt it," I admit to him, and he smirks. "It's like a tug against my heart pulling me towards you. I thought maybe I was just pathetically missing you, but it's something more."

"It's much more. It's everything."

"Then why did you let me leave?" I ask one of the biggest questions I've always had. *Why did he not take my side when Diana was murdered? Why did he send me away with Elvor?*

"Partly because I thought you were safer on Earth and that you needed time to learn who you are, I also wanted to give you a choice. But mostly because I can't risk anyone knowing."

"Know what?"

"About us. I can't have people knowing that we're together. That you're my fated mate. The risk is too high. It puts your life in danger, just as you saw yesterday." I swallow thickly. I can't deny that I very nearly lost my life to the angels the other day. But the thought of being his secret... I'm not sure I can handle that either. "I want to give you everything, Lilith. All that I ask is you let me protect you, and the only way I can do that is by not making this known."

"But Kas and Toth know," I say. I know I sound petulant. I promised myself a long time ago that I wouldn't be someone's secret.

"They're extremely loyal and trusted friends. In the manor, we can be everything we want to be. We can travel to places where we can be affectionate openly with each other, as long as it's safe."

"But in court, in front of other demons?"

"You'll need to be my assistant."

"What if they just think I'm your plaything?"

"Look how that turned out with the angels," he says plainly, and I sigh. I don't like it at all, and I'm sure that he can read it on my face. "I can't lose you, Lilith. Please."

I'm sure the word please is so rarely used by Lucifer that it was nearly painful for him to say. The larger than life man in front of me has so many facets and insecurities, just as I do. He's lost someone before, just like I have, so I can understand his protectiveness. I sigh and nod my head. "I still get to hurt Beelzebub."

He smirks and nods. "For all of eternity, once he's found, of course."

He pushes my hair off my shoulder and looks at me like I'm the most beautiful thing he's ever seen. "You won't compare me to Lily?" I ask.

He smiles and shakes his head. "There's no comparison, love. My darkness calls to yours."

CHAPTER TWENTY-FIVE

LUCIFER

The first thing I wanted to do when we portalled back to Hell is take Lilith to my bed and finally lose myself inside of her. Finally, show her that I'm truly hers. She still has this dreamy look on her face as we walk through the halls, heading toward my quarters.

"Sir," Toth interrupts, and I hold back a groan. "Asmodeus and Dax are here."

"Can't it wait?"

Toth shakes his head, he looks between Lilith and me. I sigh dramatically but trust that Toth wouldn't waste my time.

Lilith looks to me for guidance, and I gesture with my head for her to follow. We all enter the meeting room, and the tension is thick. Daxaddon and Asmodeus look as though they might shit themselves. Lilith, Toth, and Milcom stand in the corner as I try to tamper my mood.

"Update?" I bark, wondering why the fuck they've interrupted my evening.

"We found one of the possessed. It's clear that when they're possessing, the mortal is present throughout. The mortal woman said she witnessed evil deeds while she was possessed, said the demon's name is Mara."

I flinch at the name and glance over at Milcom. Beelzebub and Milcom reported that I had no other children, gifted or otherwise, that were currently alive. I tap my chin, wondering how I will make him suffer. The decision to hand over Beelzebub to Lilith has just gotten easier.

I have another daughter, and she's been living on Earth—suffering. There's a pain in my chest, and I rub the spot as I look back at Asmodeus and Daxaddon's confused faces.

"When you find Mara, you are to capture her and bring her to Hell. Her soul is not to be destroyed. She is to be brought to me intact. Do you understand?"

"Yes, Lord," they say in unison.

"Milcom, a word?" I tip my head, dismissing the two demons in the room, assuming they will portal out of the meeting room. Milcom, Toth, and Lilith follow me out of the room, and I do my best not to fully snap.

As soon as we're in the hallway, I grab Milcom by the throat, pinning him to the wall. Toth and Lilith watch with wide eyes but don't intervene.

"You said she didn't make it to childhood."

"It was Beelzebub, sir. We split up duties so we could get to Hell quicker." I taste the lie as he speaks, but don't call him out on it. Milcom has been around a long time, he knows a great deal of the inner workings of Hell. I trusted him, and this is how he repays me?

"If I find you are lying, you will suffer. Do you understand?" Milcom nods his head, a bead of sweat rolling down his temple. His face is red from the grip of my hand. "Bring me Beelzebub."

I toss him down like the disregarded piece of shit that he is and storm off to my room. I hear the clicking of Lilith's heels behind me but don't slow my pace. The noise that escapes me is horrific and nearly animalistic as I swing my door open, tossing my jacket along with my cufflinks to the floor. I can't breathe.

The collar to my shirt feels so fucking suffocating that I aggressively rip it to mid-waist. I sit on the edge of the bed, my elbows on my thighs and my fingers tugging on the strands of my hair.

I nearly forgot Lilith was here until she's kneeling in front of me, her small hands on my thighs as she looks at me with compassion and adoration that I don't fucking deserve.

"Who is Mara?" she asks softly. I rub my eyes roughly with the palms of my hands.

"My daughter."

She stills for a moment until she rubs my thighs again. "We'll get her back," she insists, and it makes me look at her in a new light. She should be telling me what a fuck up I am. How I can't take care of anyone who is truly important to me. I don't deserve Lilith or my daughters. But to my core, I'm a selfish bastard, and I plan on somehow making this right with all of them.

"I... I didn't know."

She nods her head and takes her heels off, but she never stops touching me. "Do you trust them to bring her back safely?"

"I'm not sure."

"Do you want me to go?"

I shake my head, not able to conceptualize the thought of her leaving too. "No. If this is too much…"

She squeezes my thighs. "It's not. I love Blair, and I'm sure I'll love Mara too."

That makes me smile, and I shake my head. "You know I was aware that you were seeing her?"

She shrugs her shoulders in a way that tells me she didn't care how I felt about her checking in on Blair all these years. "Besides just caring for her as a person, I think she was the thing that kept me close to you while we were apart."

My fingertips push her hair back and trail down her face, tilting her chin up to me. "I don't deserve you, Hellfire."

"I know." She smirks. "But I'm here anyway."

"Kas," I say, and her eyebrows furrow. "Kas is on the case as well."

Lilith smiles fondly at the name of her friend. Who I semi-hate solely for the fact she is part of the reason Lilith and I were separated for so long. I know it's mostly my fault, but it's easier to blame others.

"I can speak to her," she says, and I shake my head.

"No, I'll contact her."

She tilts her head but nods. All the delicious thoughts I had earlier are gone. All I want to do is flagellate myself for my failures. *How could I be so careless? Am I still being careless now?*

Blair seems happy, and that's because I protect her from afar. Honestly, I wonder sometimes if she would be happier if she just never knew about me. Maybe it's best for Mara if I just help her with becoming a full demon and then leave her alone. Why does it feel like everything I touch fractures?

"Come on," Lilith encourages, tugging me onto the bed. She lies next to me, placing her head and palm on my chest. Her scent and presence center me a little bit, although I can't help but feel lost.

Am I truly destined and undeserving of love? Is that why these things keep happening?

I've contemplated numerous times on if I should go to Earth and fetch Mara myself. But each time I consider that idea, I can't help the nagging amount of guilt and self-loathing that follows me. It's evident everyone around me is aware of my mood.

Toth keeps his distance while Milcom has been hiding in the pits, in fear of my wrath, I'm sure.

The only person who doesn't hide from me is Lilith. She's not aggressively in my face, but she keeps her place at my side, doing her job as my assistant and my partner. I guess we didn't put a particular label on it, but she's mine even though I don't deserve her.

My first meeting of the day is with Ponds, and all I want to do is kill the little narc as he sits across the table from Lilith and myself.

"My lord, Elvor's behavior is only getting worse."

Lilith scoffs next to me. "How does somebody torture someone wrong?"

"You wouldn't understand. You've been a demon for what, two minutes."

Lilith rolls her eyes and smirks at Ponds. "Haven't you heard the phrase 'no one likes a snitch'?"

Ponds looks over at me, only to notice that he's clearly getting no help from me. I'm honestly quite tired of his complaints over how the pit is being handled. Having Lilith take care of it is much better.

"I'm just trying to make sure things run smoothly," he tries again, sitting up a little straighter.

"Mmm, to me, it sounds like you want Elvor in trouble. Why is that, Ponds?" She says his name in a droning voice, and I look at the ceiling, taking a deep breath.

"I... I'm not sure what you mean."

"Did you know Elvor is my friend?"

"I..."

"Did you know Elvor told me you have a crush on him, and he wasn't interested? So now you do everything in your power to take him down a peg."

"That's not true."

"Elvor is a man of few words, none of them have ever been lies," I comment, backing my partner up, and Lilith looks at me with pink cheeks. I stand, adjusting my jacket, placing my hand on the back of Lilith's chair. "I assume you have this covered, darling?"

"I do," Lilith confirms, nodding.

"Good girl," I say, leaning forward and kissing the top of her head. Her cheeks are flaming red, and when I look over at Ponds, his mouth is gaping wide open. "Fuck," I groan.

I snap my fingers, ripping Pond's soul from his corporeal body. The shadowy dark soul whines as his body crumples to the floor. I open my palm, the soul reluctantly wisping into my hand before I place it in my mouth and swallow it whole.

Lilith blinks at me as his soul sinks to my stomach.

"Did... did you just consume his soul."

"I did. Disgusting little soul."

"You killed him because he saw us together?" I nod and sigh, bending so my face is in front of hers.

"Ponds couldn't be trusted."

She nods, and I can't tell if she's disgruntled or turned on.

"Well, at least he won't bother Elvor anymore." I roll my eyes at the affection my mate has towards the fae demon.

I smile at her regardless, and I lean forward, my lips nearly a breath away from hers, when Toth storms in. It's unlike him to not knock.

"We need to go to the pit, now," he says. No formal greeting, no asking, just telling me.

"Stay here. I'll be right back." Lilith frowns at me and crosses her arms. But Toth and I portal together to the pit. When I see who the poor soul is on the floor, I can't help the feral smile that takes over my face.

He whimpers in a corner, no longer fully whole.

"Beelzebub, don't worry, lad. I'll make you whole again," I coax in a soft tone. The soul unfolds, and I hold back my true intentions. Having consumed Ponds not that long ago, it's easy to just use a drip of my own blood to give him his body back. Since Beelzebub is such a simple-looking demon, with shit for brains, it doesn't take much to make him corporeal.

"My lord," he croaks.

"What happened?"

"Kasdeya and Daxaddon, my lord. They are out of control."

"Hmm, unacceptable. Toth, why don't you fetch the demon a chair and a nice glass of water."

Toth smirks, grabbing the chair next to him, and Beelzebub sits. Toth hands him the water.

I conjure my shadows, locking him to the chair before I'm in his face.

"You've betrayed me, Beelzebub. Now... I can make your suffering endless and painful, or I can rid you of pain and suffering if you tell me the truth."

He sputters, a tear trailing down his face.

"I didn't want to, my lord. I didn't want to."

I grip his throat to the point that his face turns red and swollen. "Didn't want to do *what*?"

I have to release him for a moment so he can speak. "The angels, they want a new ruler of Hell. They thought she could do it."

"Whom?" I already know, but I need him to tell me everything. I know he was lying about not wanting to betray me, but his confession about the angels rings true.

"Mara, she's bloodthirsty and powerful, made from your blood. We thought she could take over."

"You planned to usurp me with my daughter, who you previously told me was dead? How long have you been working against me?"

I hold out my hand, and Toth puts a dagger in my palm without me verbally needing to ask for it. As I hold the blade, ready to stab him in the side, he breaks.

"Wait, wait. I'll tell you everything."

"Go on."

"The angel. It... it was a diversion." I nudge his skin with the tip of the blade. "The day that angel fell. That was the start of it."

I tilt my head at him. Lies. He was in on it before then.

"Where is Mara?"

"I don't know, but they can't be far from her. She... she knows about you." That is the truth, and my heart sinks.

"I'm assuming you told her this?"

"And..." He swallows, shaking his head.

"And what? You fucking useless cunt!"

"She wants to take over Hell."

"I'm sure your meddling treachery had nothing to do with this?"

"My lord–"

I smack him across the face and stand tall, turning to Toth.

"Toth, make sure he stays put. I'll be back momentarily."

I compose myself to the best of my ability. If I let my feelings get the best of me, I will kill him too soon. And I have a promise to fulfill.

CHAPTER TWENTY-SIX

LILITH

O f course he just popped away for an emergency without bringing me—figures. I lie on my bed, petting Doom. He seems to really like it in Hell, and I don't blame him, I like it here too. Even more so since the air has been cleared between Lucifer and myself. I can't deny that I'm disappointed that more hasn't happened than a few soft touches and some obvious flirting.

But since he learned that he has another daughter, things have been hard. Is it wrong to say that it's one of his traits I find the most endearing? He can be a real asshole, don't get me wrong, but to know that there is a soft side of him reserved for his daughters—and for me.

I'm hoping that everything gets resolved soon, not just so that Lucifer has some peace of mind but so that this can really start to move forward.

Where is the leader of Hell who pushed me against the wall and fingered me so hard I saw stars? This time I wouldn't be resistant, not even in the least. I've seen what Lucifer is working with, and I want it. I want all of him, and it's hard to admit to myself when I still feel like a failure. I feel like I let Diana down. But I'm not an idiot. What the angels attempted the other day, that has to be why Diana came down here. To warn me that they would attempt to use me against Lucifer, maybe she even had the knowledge that I was his fated mate.

If only.

If only Beelzebub didn't kill her. If she got that message to me, all of these years wouldn't have been wasted, and she would still be here.

I roll over onto my side, scratching Doom's chin as his purrs rumble over my fingertips.

"At least you love me, Doom," I tell him, and he rubs his face against my hand. There's a knock at my door, and before I can even say anything, Lucifer swings the door open. He looks... excited?

"I've got a present for you," he announces with a smirk on his face. He looks down at Doom, who hisses and jumps off the bed, going over to his black cat tower to hide.

I smile at him. "Is that so? What is it?"

"Wouldn't you rather be surprised?"

"Is it another dress? I wouldn't turn down another dress."

"Good to know, but no. It's far better."

Please tell me it's something sexual. Maybe my present is copious amounts of orgasms and him bringing me so close to the edge that I break, begging for him. He stills next to me, pushing my hair off my shoulder so that it spills down my back.

Lucifer's touch is like nothing I've ever experienced. It's all-consuming as he looks down at me and smiles.

"Maybe some of that later, but this present can't wait."

I blink up at him a few times, my mouth falls open before quickly closing again. "How?"

"How could I not know when my soulmate wants me? Now, come on." He lets out a small laugh at the end, and I swear I nearly expire on the spot.

All thoughts of arousal fade to the background as he portals us to the pit. I'm facing a wall where Toth is standing with his arms crossed.

"That will be all, Toth," Lucifer says to him with a nod. His right-hand nods back, giving me a half smile and walking out the door. When Lucifer grabs my shoulders and spins me around, I swear my heart stops beating.

Beelzebub sits before me, his lip bleeding, and he's tied to a chair. His eyes are wide as he looks at me and then to Lucifer.

His touch is gentle on my shoulders and the curve of my neck. It's a unique feeling having a man fulfill all the promises he made to me. This was the final one. The thing I needed for closure.

Not that a piece of Diana won't live with me forever. But to make sense of her death and to get revenge against the people who harmed her will make that piece hurt less. Lucifer already killed the angels who tainted her mind, and now I get to hurt the man who took away her afterlife.

"Are you pleased?" Lucifer asks against my ear, and I nod my head, just staring at this gift before me.

"How is he here?"

I can feel his lips near the shell of my ear. "Your friend Kas may have something to do with it."

I smile, and Beelzebub winces. "I didn't know she was your sister," he whines, and I shake my head.

Lucifer's hand glides down my arm, and I miss the feeling of his flesh on mine until he hands me my dagger. I don't have to look down to know it's mine. Its weight and the feel of the handle are ingrained in me at this point.

His palm is wrapped around mine until he lets go. "Give 'em hell, love." He steps away, and I turn to watch him. He casually props his large frame against the wall, just watching me.

It hits me then that I've found someone who truly accepts me and that nothing I can do will scare him. I can be authentically me, and Lucifer won't think I'm a monster or a bad person. If anything, he embraces this side of me that I've always hid away from. I bite my lip, and he nods at me, giving me his blessing.

Encouraging my darkness.

I smile at Lucifer before pushing my shoulders back and looking down at Beelzebub. He's such an unfortunate demon. His hair is thin and balding, his eyes are beady and filled with deceit. But right now, I watch as his whole body tenses, and I truly can't wait to make him suffer.

Looking down at the dagger, I remember what Lucifer said about magical weapons and how each possesses different abilities.

"It won't kill him?" I ask, not looking at Lucifer.

"Just for the evening. Then he will reanimate tomorrow."

"Hear that, rat? It's going to be a long eternity for you and me."

"My lord, I didn't mean it. Please forgive me. I made a mistake. I'll do whatever you wish."

I take two steps forward, my heels clicking loudly against the cement floor as I stand before the demon who took my sister's life.

"He's not the one you should be begging," I tell him, and his gaze travels from my face to Lucifer's in the corner.

"My lord?"

"You heard her," he replies, and I have to shake off just how attractive that was to me. I look back to the demon in question, and his terror is palpable. I feed off his fear, it excites me. He should fear me. There's no holding back, this isn't just my violent heart seeking a sacrifice. This is years of pent-up and unsatisfied retribution, years lost to grief and guilt. Beelzebub feels like the symbol of everything that has been hurting me these past years.

"Where should we start?"

"Please, I'm sorry. I was just doing my job."

"My friend Elvor likes to start with fingers, maybe we should start there." I hear a snicker from behind me, and I smile as I catch Beelzebub off guard. I'm so quick he doesn't even see my blade coming down on his tied hands, severing off his middle finger. Beelzebub wails in pain as he looks at his bleeding finger. Symbolic, should have gone for his ring finger, that would be full circle.

"I don't deserve this."

"No, you're right, you don't." I watch him sigh, and panic begins to leave his features. "You deserve so much worse."

Needing to make this last, I'm efficient with my slice along his throat. Deep enough to bleed but not deep enough to kill him. He chokes as blood stains his shirt, and I'm sure there are some flecks on my own skin. But I don't stop there, I continue slicing his flesh, cuts that alone are not deep enough to kill but together will cause him unbearable and lasting pain.

"You know, I've thought about how I would kill you all these years," I tell him, still holding onto my dagger while speaking with my hands. "But you know the beauty of it?" He looks up at me, looking like an absolute bloody mess. It's beautiful.

He gurgles now that he's lost his ability to speak, and I take that as his acknowledgment to continue. "You won't actually die." I laugh and plunge the dagger into his lung. He wheezes and cries as I smile at his ugly face grimacing in pain. "I'll get to live out every single way I've thought of killing you, and the days I'm busy? I'll send someone else to do it. The rest of your existence is going to be painful and brutal, and you have no one else but yourself to blame. Until next time."

I turn the knife, likely nicking his heart, and I watch the life leave his eyes. It's single-handedly the most satisfying kill I've ever had, and the adrenaline coursing through my body is unreal as I watch him slump in the chair.

It's like a weight has been lifted off my chest, the revenge I've been seeking for so long has been fulfilled, and I can do this whenever I need. I drag the bloody blade along Beelzebub's shirt and turn around.

Before I can even search for him, his hands are on my face, his thumb stroking my cheekbone as I look up at his face.

"Magnificent," he says before his lips are on mine.

I can't be certain if it's the excitement of what I just did or having Lucifer kiss me for the first time, but it feels revolutionary. Like no other kiss between two people has ever compared. Lucifer's lips on mine are all-consuming. His lips are softer than I imagined, but he isn't gentle, not that I would ever expect him to be. His kiss is aggressive and demanding as he parts my lips and explores me with his tongue. I can't help the moan that escapes me, and he hungrily devours.

His large hands are firm, one cradling the back of my skull and tangling with my hair as the other tilts my jaw to him. He has to bend down significantly to kiss me, and I hear him groan. I sigh as his hands leave my face, but I find quick relief as he grabs me by my hips and uses one hand to swipe off everything on top of a nearby table. The clanging of weapons and tools is jarring as they hit the floor but is easily forgotten as his hands are back on my face.

I never want to be without his touch ever again, I decide. When his skin is against mine, I feel whole.

"This needs to go," he says, his finger trailing along the scalloped sleeve of my dress. I feel devoid of words as I swallow and nod my head. He smirks, and I watch his finger morph into a claw.

I inhale as I feel the pointed edge glide down my chest as he cuts the dress clean off of me.

"I like those."

"I know," he replies, leaning forward and sucking on my lace-clad breasts. I moan and push my chest against his mouth. His hand is back to normal, one gripping my hip and the other fisting my hair.

He sucks on my nipple hard, the line between pleasure and pain fully met, and I can't hold back a whimper that morphs into a moan.

I fist his hair in return, holding him to my chest, and he makes such a masculine sound of approval I nearly come on the spot. His hair is soft beneath my fingers, and I greedily direct his face to my other breast.

"Wouldn't want her to feel left out," he jokes, following my direction and giving my other nipple the same treatment.

His hand leaves my hair and travels down my body, leaving goosebumps in its wake. *How can someone's touch be so significant?* It's like my skin is on fire, and the only thing that can put it out is the same person causing the sensation.

Lucifer easily moves my body towards the end of the table, his hand shifting down my stomach, and the back of his fingers graze along the lace covering my cunt.

"Tell me, love, what has you wetter? Was it ending his life with your knife?" He kisses my chest and looks at me. "Was it my claw devesting you with the removal of your pretty dress?" Another kiss lands on my shoulder as his dark eyes meet mine. "Or was it simply my touch?"

"Everything," I say in a breathy tone.

His fingers still run up and down the lace of my panties, and all I want him to do is slide them to the side and have his way with me.

"Please."

He arches his eyebrow. That smirk that I've grown to be devastated by takes over his face as he looks down at how embarrassingly wet I am for him.

"What do you want, love?"

"Anything, everything, just touch me."

"Am I not touching you right now?" he taunts, making me want to both smack him and fuck him at the same time.

"I need more than that."

"You want to come, Hellfire?" I nod. He stops touching me, and I nearly want to cry. That's the opposite of what I want. He leans forward, his arms wrapping around my back. He takes my bra off gingerly, the polar opposite of how he took off my dress, and licks his lips as he takes in my exposed breasts. Lucifer's deft fingers push back all my blonde hair behind my shoulders, leaning in so that his lips are touching the shell of my ear. "Where do I start? Should I slide my fingers inside of you and feel your wetness drip down my hand? Or should I have your cunt gushing on my tongue? Or perhaps I should just sink my cock deep inside of you like I've wanted to from the moment we met."

I'm panting, his words ringing in my ears. "All of it," I say, gripping his hair and forcing him to look at me. "I want everything you'll give me."

He smiles, and my heart melts. I know this smile is reserved for only me, and I can't help but smile back. He tugs my hair, and his lips finding the column of my throat, kissing, biting, and licking. I feel like I'm being toyed with in the most delicious but frustrating way. His lips are warm on my skin, and he takes his time. Nibbling my flesh and then kissing away the pain. I want his lips everywhere, against mine, on my neck, my chest, my pussy. I want to get on my knees and beg him to just never stop touching me. "Please, sir,"

I feel his body quake between my legs as his teeth drag up my throat. I make a noise of protest, and his teeth tug lightly on my ear lobe. "Not here."

We both look over at Beelzebub's crumpled body. I legitimately forgot his corpse was here as soon as he touched me.

"Your room or mine?" he says.

I push his hair back and know immediately where I want him to take me. "Yours." He nods, and I'm shocked by the cool greeting of his claw as he slices off my panties, leaving me completely bare in front of him, even though he's still wearing his suit.

He licks his lips, grabbing me by the ass and making me wrap my legs around him, my arms looping around his broad shoulders as he portals us to his bedroom.

My back meets his luxurious sheets as he eyes my body hungrily.

"Fucking beautiful."

My body is on fire being under this powerful man's gaze, and all the things he's been saying has my ego growing five times its normal size—which is saying something.

He grips the back of my thighs once more and pushes them to my chest. I nearly squeak from the sudden movement, but that's short-lived as I feel his warm tongue lick me from my entrance to my clit. I swear he growls, and his grip on my thighs feels near bruising. I welcome the feeling with open arms.

CHAPTER TWENTY-SEVEN

LUCIFER

My dick strains against my trousers as I finally taste her—my soulmate—my complete other half. Sure, I tasted her on my fingers all those years ago. But this—tasting her warm and wanting cunt while she whimpers under my touch—is exquisite.

I explore what she likes, swiping my tongue along her clit and fucking her tight and slick pussy as she moans, making her back arch off the bed.

Her hand wraps around mine on her thigh, and I decide I like that—a lot. I want Lilith's hands on me every moment I possibly can. Too much has separated us, too many frivolous and ridiculous things have kept me away from her—from this.

I swipe my nose against her clit, and she moans. I quickly roll my tongue against the bud before wrapping my lips around the small bundle and sucking. I don't let up, switching from sucking and licking the spot that's making her shake.

Needing to feel her clench around me, I free one of her thighs, and it falls on my shoulder as I push two of my fingers inside of her wet, needy cunt. She's so tight as I curl my long fingers inside of her, hitting that fleshy patch that has her legs shaking. I pick up the pace, sucking her clit and fingering her pussy.

"Lucifer. So good." I shiver when my name falls from her lips in a moan of ecstasy. Her hand presses against the back of my head, holding me against her pussy, and I smile as I lap at her center. I need Lilith to want me, beg me, be rough with me. I need everything she's willing to give. I know now what true desperation is as Lilith comes on my tongue, her one thigh shaking against my face and her cunt milking my fingers. Her moans are feminine and soft as she says my name while she comes.

I will never tire of the sound, and I make it my mission to hear it as many times a day as hellishly possible. I don't stop licking her and fucking her with my fingers. She nearly screams, trying to push my head away, but I'm stronger, and frankly, I need her to come again because I don't know how long I'll last once I'm inside of her.

She writhes under my touch. "It's too much, I can't. I can't!"

My mouth is too preoccupied with her perfect pussy to tell her she can take as much as I give her. She pants, saying my name over and over as I suck her sensitive clit.

"Oh... Oh... Yes... Lucifer." The last time she says my name, it comes out on a sigh of contentment, and I lose all control, curling my fingers inside of her as I watch her break, giving her another orgasm. She cries out, her back fully off the bed like I've possessed her.

She's panting, a sheen of sweat coating her chest as I climb up her body. Her eyes are hooded and soft as she looks up at me. Her thumb trails along my chin, collecting her wetness before she pushes it between my lips, and I taste her release on the pad of her thumb. She smiles widely at me as I look down at her. I quite like that, no drop of her should be wasted.

"You're still dressed," she comments.

"Undress me, then." She tugs me down by grabbing the lapels of my jacket and kissing me so fiercely that I don't think about anything else. My guilt, my fears, they're all gone; the only thing I can think about is this perfect creature is unequivocally mine. Her blue eyes are like pools of the clearest water as she licks her lips. I can't help the self-satisfaction of her tasting herself and enjoying it.

Her touch is gentle as she unbuttons my dress shirt. I like watching her throat bob as she swallows while she takes in my exposed chest. I help her by shrugging off the jacket and shirt. Her small hands explore my chest, and I hold back a shiver. Until her nails drag down, leaving pink trails behind them.

"Cheeky little demon. Are you going to be my good girl, or are you going to be my little brat tonight?"

"I'm always a good girl," she counters in mock shock.

"Then take out my cock for me."

She swallows and nods, unlatching my belt, leaving it in the belt loops as she unbuttons and unzips my trousers. I have to get off the bed to remove them, leaving us both completely naked together, and this time we can touch.

"What now, love?"

She licks her lips and looks down at my weeping cock that is ever so eager to finally sink into our mate.

"I... I want to taste you."

"Oh, you certainly are being a good girl." I smirk at her, and she surprises me by dragging her naked form over the bed, her back pressed against the soft cushion. Her flushed skin and blonde hair contrasting perfectly against the black sheets. She tilts her head over the end of the mattress, and I can't help but touch myself as I watch her. This beautiful creature is ready to please *me*.

"Please," she begs once her face is fully upside down and she's ready for me, her soft plush lips parted.

"Fucking Hell."

I stand by the bed, the height perfect for her to take my length. Her one hand is wrapped around the back of my thigh as the other grips my ass cheek. She licks the tip and wets my cock with her saliva before opening her mouth fully for me to slide down her throat. In this position, she can relax her throat completely, and I watch with complete rapture as I watch my cock slide down her throat.

"Pinch me if it's too much, love," I tell her, and she hums her agreement around my cock, making me groan. Her hair tickles my thighs and shin, and her grip on my ass and thigh is rough. This woman was fucking made for me.

"You're doing so well, darling. Look at you swallowing my cock."

Her grip tightens, and my hand drags down her chest, my thumbs circling her taut nipples. The suction of her lips wrapped around my length has me moving my hips, and she takes each thrust eagerly. My hand glides down her soft skin, wrapping gently around her throat. My thumb is right at the center, and I can feel her taking my cock.

The sounds she's making while sucking me are obscene, and as I visually see her throat taking me, I don't think I can take it anymore. I need to be inside of her.

"Fuck, love. You're so fucking good, but if I don't fuck you right now, I might die."

I push off of her, and she pants for air, taking deep breaths in and out as I help her sit up. My thumbs brush the underside of her eyes, removing her smudged makeup, and I pick up the corner of the sheet to wipe her mouth. I lean forward, kissing her forehead and face. Pulling back, I notice her eyes are glassy, and her chest is still rising and falling at an increased pace.

"So fucking beautiful. My perfect," I pause, kissing the side of her head. "Violent," Another pause and another kiss, this one to the underside of her jaw. "Magnificent, little demon," I finish.

She doesn't shrivel at the word demon, all I can see is pride written on her face while she basks in my praise. Her fingers wrap around my neck, the tips of her fingers toying with my hair as we shift on the bed. She falls back onto the mattress, taking me with her.

I don't waste any time as I fist myself and rub the head of my length along her wet and ready entrance. Her hips thrust up to mine, begging to be stretched. It's like our bodies are already so intuned with one another's needs as I slowly push inside of her. Her cunt grips me tight as I push into her inch by inch.

Her beautiful blonde hair is everywhere on the bed, and I can't help but fist it while cradling her head as I get down on my elbows.

She stares at me, her supple lips parted as she exhales wispy breaths. I move slowly in and out of her, letting her adjust to my size. It's unlike anything I've experienced; nothing has ever felt this significant with another individual. Her hand comes up, stroking my jaw, and I kiss the inside of her palm. Her cunt clenches at the small affection, and when I meet her eyes, all I want to do is spew out all of my feelings. I hold them back as she moans when I hit the right spot.

Words seem unnecessary as we stare into each other's eyes, watching how much the other is enjoying this moment—how much we enjoy each other.

"I... I..." she can't get out her sentence as I continue fucking her leisurely like I never want it to end.

"What do you need, love?"

She blinks her watery eyes as she shakes her head. "Just this," she answers. I nearly spill into her at that moment, but instead, I place more of my weight on top of her. Our chests rub together, and I feel the wetness and friction of her cunt against my pelvis. She moans against my ear, and I can't help but feel like it isn't close enough.

No matter how much skin we have touching, I simply will never be as close to Lilith as every fiber of my being requires. But this is as close as it physically gets. Her cunt clenching around me, her breasts rubbing against my chest, the scent of her hair going straight to my brain, and her lips nearly touching my ear.

My hand cradles her head as my pace quickens, and her sharp nails dig into my back, urging me to fuck her faster.

"Are you going to come for me one more time?" Her pants hit my ear, but she doesn't answer. "Give me one more, Lilith. I need to feel that sweet cunt of yours gushing around my cock."

It's then, when her nails cut the skin of my shoulder blades, and her heels push against my ass hard enough to bruise that I feel her clenching around me. Her moans are loud against my ear as she holds me tight, and I fuck her through her orgasm, chasing after my own.

The scent of her hair assaults my nose, and with her soft smaller body beneath mine, I trail kisses up the side of her throat up to her ear. The noise I make as I finish is feral. There's no other thought in my mind except how lucky I am at this moment. My soulmate is in my arms, her satisfied pants echoing in my ear, and the masculine satisfaction of knowing I made her come three times tonight settles into my bones.

I pull back, but she doesn't let me, holding tight against my shoulders. I don't resist, not wanting to pull out of her, not wanting this moment to end.

Mortals spend all of their short, miserable lives searching for what they think Heaven will bring them. But I know if they got to experience even a fraction of what I just had, they would know utopia isn't in the clouds but inside of a beautiful woman who means more than any world ever created.

I try pulling back again to look at her, and she smiles at me. I love when she smiles. I've never felt more like a pathetic sap in my life than I do at this moment, but I couldn't care less.

"Bath?" I ask, and she nods her head. I'm up on my knees, pulling out of her when she winces. She goes to put her legs down, but I hold them up and watch in awe as my cum drips out of her beautiful cunt, pooling against the stark black sheets.

"Seriously?" she asks, rolling her eyes, but a playful smile is still on her face.

"Seriously. Have you seen how perfect you are when my cum is dripping out of you?"

She blushes, shaking her head. I let her put her legs down, and I enjoy watching her walk to the bathroom with a mix of me and her running down her thighs. I turn on the faucet and throw in one of the bags she likes. The water fills quickly, and the scent of lavender wafts around the small bathroom.

"I didn't think the Devil would be a bath bomb type of guy."

"It's not a bath bomb." I roll my eyes hating and loving when she calls me the Devil. Especially after what just happened between us. It's not a word she uses in contempt anymore. She knows who I am and accepts it, my darkness and all.

"It sure seems bath-bombish."

"Just get your ass in," I retort. Standing in the tub and holding out my hand. She accepts it and steps in, moaning as her skin hits the warm water.

I sit first, my long limbs taking up most of the tub as she sits in front of me, her back pressed against my chest.

"This is much better than the last time I was in your tub," she says, and I have to conceal my anger. Their deaths were far too humane. I wish I could have drawn it out, made them suffer, but we were under a time crunch.

"I like you here," I say instead of talking about the way I could have desecrated her attacker's bodies.

"I like being here too."

"I know."

"You knew I was lying about what I needed to stay in Hell, so why didn't you say anything?"

"And deny you the things you want?" I question, wrapping an arm around her waist and placing the back of my head against the tub.

"I'm gonna warn you now, you can't just stop spoiling me now that we've fucked."

I laugh and shake my head, squeezing her side and making her jump slightly in the tub. "You don't have to worry about that."

"So what now?"

"I'm hoping you'd like to stay in my room with me," I say. Maybe I come across as needy, but I don't really give a fuck. It's been too long since I haven't been denied this, and I don't really care to waste any more time apart.

"Only if my cat can come too."

I take a deep inhale. "Fine, but not on the bed."

"Uh-huh," she says, shaking her head and leaning closer to my chest.

We stay like that for a while, just letting the warm water soothe our muscles until I scrub off a fleck of blood that was in her hair.

"Do you feel satisfied?"

She laughs. "Yes, after three orgasms, I feel satisfied."

I shake my head and sigh. "No, with Beelzebub."

She sinks a little more into the water, gliding against my half-mast cock. "I'm not sure I'll truly ever feel vindicated when it comes to Diana. But knowing that he's going to suffer for a long time and that you took care of those angels does make me feel better. Like I can move on." She turns, her legs bracketing my waist as she cups my face. "I think I'm ready for forever now, I'm ready to be me."

I smile, grabbing her face and kissing her. I don't think this all-consuming feeling is going to go away anytime soon.

CHAPTER TWENTY-EIGHT

LILITH

I blink a few times and bring the soft fabric to my face. Lucifer's sheets must be made from angel wings or unicorn hair, I don't think there's a softer sheet in all of the universes. When I look up, Lucifer is by the fire, his legs spread out while he pets Doom, who is sitting on the table, soaking up the warmth of the fire.

"I knew you liked the cat."

His hand is off the cat, like his fur burned him, and he takes a sip of his whiskey before shaking his head. "I don't like the cat."

"Mmmhmm," I say, getting out of bed. Wearing nothing except one of Lucifer's shirts, I stand between his legs. His hands immediately wrap around the backs of my thighs, stroking the skin lovingly. "So am I just going to want to fuck you all the time now?"

He smirks and nods. "I hope so."

"What has you up so late? We just went to bed."

"Something doesn't feel right," he admits, and I stroke his face, his stubble rough against my hands. I can't help but love the just rolled-out-of-bed look he has, even if he did put a dress shirt and trousers on just to sit by the fire.

"Can I make it feel right?"

He nods and slides me onto his lap. The kisses he trails down my throat are tender and slow. Lucifer is not one to rush himself when it comes to sex, or so I've learned. I thought maybe we would have had a quickie last night after our bath, but that turned into him making me come four more times before sinking into me again.

I'm spoiled, and I adore it.

I tangle my fingers in his hair, and he tugs the shirt off my torso, exposing my skin before kissing and nipping at my shoulder. I'm fully grinding on him at this point as a cracking noise jolts us both, and I look up to see Dax portal into Lucifer's room with a bleeding Blair in his arms. We're both on our feet in an instant.

"What is this?" Lucifer demands in a panic, walking over to where Blair is crumpled on the floor in Dax's arms. "Why have you brought my daughter to Hell, Daxaddon?"

Dax's brows are furrowed as he looks at Lucifer, then down at Blair. "Mara is your daughter?"

Lucifer strokes Blair's hair affectionately and sighs. "They both are," he says. "Lilith, love. Fetch Milcom for me." I take a deep breath, wondering just how in the fuck one of Lucifer's daughters possessed the other one. Lucifer is keeping calm, but it's clear he's nervous. He's been worried about Mara, and having her finally in Hell under these circumstances is not ideal. I look down at Blair's face, schooling the worry that I feel in my gut. Lucifer knows what he's doing, he'll make sure she's okay.

"Yes, sir," I say immediately, grabbing some pants and portalling to Lust, the place I know that scum bag is likely hanging out at this time of night.

I'm proven right when I find him balls-deep in some demon I don't recognize.

"Milcom, Lucifer needs to see you immediately."

"Yeah, and he sent his little bitch to come collect me?"

I bite my tongue, because I already know Milcom likely won't be alive by the end of the night. He thrusts one more time into his companion and shudders before zipping up his pants. I grab hold of his forearm, because there's no way I'm touching his hand, and portal us away.

We land back in Lucifer's room, and I take note of how both Dax and Lucifer are looking at Blair. I have a feeling Lucifer isn't going to come around easily to his daughter dating one of his trusted demons, but out of all the demons Blair could have picked, Dax was a great choice. Now that I see them together, I honestly couldn't have picked a better match.

"Milcom, my lord," I announce, and Lucifer nods his head.

"You've asked for me, my lord," Milcom says, and he audibly swallows. He should be nervous. My man is totally about to kill him; it's going to be awesome, and I can't wait to watch.

"Yes, well. Once my daughters wake up, we can discuss. Lilith, love. Will you get me some smelling salts?" Lucifer asks. I smile and nod.

"Yes, sir," I reply, and I see his lips twitch. *Oh yes, he enjoys all his titles.* Sir is just one I can say in public. Maybe he needs a cute pet name for when we're in private.

"Thank you, love. You are dismissed." I can't help but pout. *What the fuck?* I don't get to watch the Milcom murder, help Blair, or be here when he meets his other daughter. He's all 'we're soulmates and shit', but now that it's a family matter, I'm kicked out? "Now darling, what have I said about pouting? I'll see you momentarily."

"Yes, sir," I say with so much sass, no longer making the word hot. He's going to pay for this later.

I can't help but mumble to myself as I go and wait in my own room. "Fucking asshole. Here let me wow you with my big dick and stabbing this demon you hate. But wait? Actual family drama happens, and you're *just* my assistant again. Fucking secret bullshit."

I groan as my back hits my bed, these sheets suck ass compared to the ones on his bed—our bed? I know where Lucifer is coming from when he says he doesn't want everyone to know about me. I witnessed it when that gang of pigeon-winged fuckers tried to murder me. *So why does it still hurt? Why do I still feel like a dirty secret?*

Suddenly my necklace heats, and I stick up a middle finger I know Lucifer can't see.

I portal right to him, back to his room, where I see Dax, Blair, and another woman who looks a lot like Lucifer—Mara, I assume. I give her a soft smile even though she looks slightly confused. There's no Milcom in sight, and Blair looks completely healed, though Dax hovers over her in an extremely protective way.

I missed all the fun stuff. I glare at Lucifer as he speaks to me.

"Love, can you show the girls their rooms?"

"Now that I'm allowed to be a part of the conversation, I would love to. Please follow me." I glare at Lucifer before I turn my back to him and walk out with Dax, Blair, and Mara following me.

When we come up to the first room on the left, I speak to Mara. She is beautiful, but clearly, not all there when I speak to her.

"Mara, this is your room. If you need anything, please just let me know."

"You're really pretty and nice. Are you my... um... stepmother?" Mara is in her early twenties, but I suspect her maturity might be stilted due to her losing her mind and possessing people for so long. Time will only tell.

"Heavens no, but we can talk more later," I offer, holding back a gag at the term stepmother. I mean, Lucifer has called me his love, his soulmate, but he hasn't given me an actual title. That title surely isn't going to be stepmother.

I guide Blair and Dax to their suite, and I know it's petty and unreasonable, but there's a part of me that wishes she remembered me. Even if I am the one who took her memories every time we saw each other. I wonder if there's a way to reinstate them or if it would do more harm than good. We can always start over; Blair and I have always been similar. At the very least, now I don't have to lie to her all the time.

"Thank you," Blair says, and I touch her arm, giving her a light squeeze when I see the pain in her eyes. I feel it too, sometimes. For her, she wants to understand why Lucifer didn't give her more, and sometimes, I wonder the same thing. He cares deeply, but his protectiveness always outweighs his heart.

"Give him time. If anyone can confirm he cares, it's me," I say, giving Blair a small smile before turning on my heel and leaving the room.

I march down the hall back to Lucifer's room. He's on the edge of his bed, his elbows on his knees as his palms rub his eye sockets.

"And what in the fuck was that?"

"What?"

"*You're dismissed*?" I say, imitating his voice, and he shakes his head.

"Lilith," he groans.

"No, don't you 'Lilith me'. You're all *stay in Hell, love, my darkness calls to yours, you're so important to me.* But the minute the shit hits the fan, you send me away?"

"I'm sorry," he says, and I have to blink a few times.

"What?"

"You're right. I'm sorry."

I put my hands on my hips. I was ready for a fight, for him to tell me that he's the king of Hell and he can do whatever the fuck he wants.

"So next time?"

"Next time, you're involved. You're part of this family."

"Like your girlfriend?" He scoffs, shaking his head.

"Come here." I step in between his legs, and he holds me by my hips. "No words suffice for what you are to me, Lilith, but I'm far too fucking old to be someone's boyfriend."

I cup his jaw and pinch his cheek. "You're right. You are old. How will you ever keep up with your much younger lover?" I tease.

He smacks my ass and grips the flesh roughly. "I don't think stamina is a problem."

"I don't think so."

He kisses the side of my face and sighs.

"So... your daughters... they're both in Hell."

He groans, letting go of me and flopping down onto the bed. I easily crawl onto the bed and straddle him.

"I'm not sure who I need to apologize to first."

"Just give them time. Let them know you care and be honest with them."

"That's all I need to do?"

"It's a start." He groans again, and I lay on top of his large body, liking his warmth and size. "And be nice to Dax."

He puffs out an irritated sound while rolling his eyes. "Fine."

I sit up and look down at him. "I'm going to get a few things done. We can all have breakfast in the morning."

He nods, and I lean down to kiss him before leaving the room.

Satan himself just apologized to me. I feel a whirlwind of emotions, but gratification is the highest on the list.

CHAPTER TWENTY-NINE

LUCIFER

It's been an absolute cluster fuck these last few days. I had to threaten some witches to get Blair's magic back, come to terms with the fact that she's with Daxaddon, and accept that she doesn't want to live in Hell full-time. Not that she's explicitly said so, but it's clear. It's disheartening, but I always wanted her to live fully, and I completely understand that it's hard to live that way in Hell.

Mara, on the other hand, is a completely different story. She seems to like it here; more than like it here, she loves it here.

Lilith is sleeping next to me, the cat curled above her head, and I pet the little fucker, making him purr lightly.

"Knew you liked the cat," she taunts sleepily, and my hand immediately flies off the fur.

"I don't like the cat."

"I can taste your lies, and they're so sweet," she replies, imitating me, and I can't help but tickle her side. She jolts up, trying to escape, but it's no use as I pull her onto my lap. Her hair is an absolute mess, but she looks perfect like this. She looks truly happy, and the realization that I'm part of that happiness means everything to me.

"What are you doing today?" she asks.

"You're my assistant, you tell me."

"Your daddy-daughter date with Mara."

I roll my eyes and nod. "I'm not sure what my read on her is. Blair is simpler, she forgives me, but she's still bitter."

"The women in your life are very petty. Maybe you should reflect on why that is."

"Mmm," I hum while kissing her exposed shoulder.

"I don't think Mara is that complicated," she says, shrugging her shoulders. "I think she's been lost for a long time and finally feels like she's somewhere she belongs."

"I failed her."

Lilith pushes my shoulder. "You're so annoying sometimes, you know. Mara doesn't want your guilt or your self-loathing. She wants a Dad, she wants to be loved, and she wants to live. Can you imagine what it was like to live from possession to possession for all those years? You finally gave her a body, and from the way she's constantly checking herself out in the mirror, it's clear she likes it. Sure, tell her you're sorry, but don't dwell on it. She's more eager for the future you'll share together."

"When did you become so wise?"

"While I haven't had all eternity," she says, jabbing my chest. "I think I know a little bit about Hell being the place where I fit in the most. I think Mara feels the same. Just tell her how much you care, that's all she wants to hear."

She pushes my loose hair behind my ear and kisses my cheek. "You better go get ready."

"I have ten more minutes."

She laughs as I flip her on her back and pepper kisses along her face and neck. I realize that at this moment, I've never truly felt happiness. And while my heart is fuller than it's ever been, my peace of mind is forever shattered because of the precious people I now need to protect with every ounce of magic I have in me.

I sit at the black lake with Mara, not sure why I picked this place on the manor grounds. Perhaps it's because it's where I was most vulnerable with Lilith when she would astral project to me.

"How are you feeling with your new body?"

She turns to me and smiles. "It's amazing, thank you."

"I can't apologize enough for everything that's happened, Mara. I didn't know, if I had known about you, I would have taken care of you."

She nods and swallows. "Beelzebub told me a lot of things about you that I now know are lies. I don't know Blair yet, but I'm hoping she forgives me for the whole possession thing and joking about sleeping with her boyfriend." I grimace, and Mara shrugs her shoulders. "But it's clear she thinks you're a good Dad, even if you lied."

"I've gotten caught up in a few lies over time. Ones that I regret deeply, I want to be better."

"That's all I can ask for. Honestly, this is the first time I've been able to think clearly in years."

I try to swallow down my guilt like Lilith told me to. Mara doesn't care about that, she wants the future. "You like it here?" I ask her.

"Oh yes, it's very cozy and creepy, but in an expensive way."

I laugh and shake my head. Taking a sip out of the thermos that Lilith packed each of us. "I think you should start training then."

"Training?"

"Learning all the facets of your power, what you're capable of, and how to handle your corporeal body."

"I handled myself perfectly fine on Earth."

"I don't doubt that," I tell her. "But I would feel better if you were properly trained in defending yourself and learned more about the history and inner workings of Hell."

"Like a protege?"

"Exactly like that."

She sits up straighter, looking at me. "You're not fucking with me, are you, Satan?"

I raise my hands up in mock surrender. "Definitely not fucking with you."

"But you don't even know me."

"I want to," I respond genuinely, which makes her smile back at me.

"You're definitely not what I imagined."

"Oh?"

"I thought you were going to be this big hulking asshole who eats souls, rips people's hearts out with your bare hands, and crushes people's hopes and dreams."

I clear my throat. "I may do some of those things, but not for the people I care about."

She smirks, and it's like looking in a reflection. "And how long is that list?"

"A list of three," I tell her, and she nods.

"I can definitely live with that. And actually, I think ripping people's hearts out is pretty cool."

"Maybe I can show you sometime?" That's clearly an appropriate daddy-daughter bonding activity, right?

"I'd love to! I also want to explore Hell more, get a feel for the place."

"I'd like to wait until you're more settled and have more time training with Toth, if you don't mind."

She looks at me the same way Blair does when she's irritated but suddenly perks up. "Toth will be the one training me?"

"Yes. He and Lilith are the only people I'd trust with something so important."

"I'm sure I could learn something from both of them. I want to live in my own body with a sound mind and never let someone take advantage of me ever again."

Anger fills me when I think about everything Beelzebub possibly told her about me, about Hell, but I tamper it down. "No one will ever second guess the princess of Hell ever again."

She grins at the title and takes a bite of her sandwich. Today went far better than I could have imagined. Mara doesn't look at me like she hates me, she looks eager to learn and get to know me. It's far more than I deserve, but I'll take it.

CHAPTER THIRTY

LILITH

The next few days at the manor have been magical and odd at the same time. With both of Lucifer's daughters fully in his life now, there are definitely some growing pains. Mostly adjusting to sharing the manor and Mara learning how to be a normal, functioning demon.

"When do I get to torture people?" she asks as she lowers her teacup to the table.

"What?"

"I thought that was the whole point of being a demon, torturing people," Mara says matter-of-factly.

"I'm sure if you want to work in the pit, your father will arrange it."

"So you and my daddio, huh?" she questions, changing the topic suddenly.

"Yes," I reply, and she takes a sip of her drink.

"You two don't leave the manor much. I guess it's difficult when you're banging like feral animals." I gape at the pretty demon.

"Um, right. We just leave from time to time."

"Interesting. My father said Beelzebub's soul was destroyed."

I swallow at the lie and wonder why he didn't tell her that he's basically the human-like punching bag that I visit every night. *Perhaps he doesn't want him tainting her mind further?*

"Right."

"Shame, really. I would have enjoyed torturing him."

I go to answer her when Toth enters the room. As soon as he does, a huge grin spreads over Mara's face.

"Mara, it's time for your lesson," he informs her, and she nods.

She leans over so only I can hear. "Are all the male demons this fucking hot?"

I clear my throat and look over to Toth. "No, not all of them."

"I can't wait to get out of this mansion and see what else is out there."

"Your father said not yet," Toth replies, and Mara rolls her eyes.

"I know, warrior-demon-daddy, you want to keep me all to yourself, but I'm not a one demon kind of a girl. You'll have to learn to share."

"We're just training," he says, looking frustrated.

"You keep telling yourself that," she replies, shaking her head.

The circus leaves the dining room, and I close my eyes while sipping my tea. Mara isn't wrong, I do feel like it's been a long time since we've left the manor.

Lucifer comes into the room, kissing the top of my head before sitting next to me. "What's going on?"

"I think I'd like to go out tonight."

He sighs and scrubs his face. "The club?" he guesses.

I nod, and he grabs a pastry from the table. "Fine, but you know there will need to be rules, right?"

"I know, no one can know about us outside of the manor."

He nods, and I push down my disappointment. Maybe it's my ego or my pride, but when Lucifer said there wasn't a word fitting enough to describe what I am to him—the word queen seemed pretty fitting to me. But we're new, it's all still so exciting, and maybe he'll come around and realize that I'm not leaving Hell, and the longer I stay here, the stronger I feel. I can protect myself from threats, and if I can't, he will.

"I think Mara wants to explore Hell as well."

Lucifer winces. "I don't think she's ready for public consumption just yet." I hold back my laughter and nod my head.

"Wear the black off-the-shoulder dress with the cape tonight," he says, and my body heats. I nod at his orders, but I know damn well that is not going to be the dress I wear tonight. He kisses my head before portalling to Hell-only-knows where.

I did *not* do as told and wore the blood-red satin gown that shows far too much chest and leg instead. It clings to the upper half of my body like a second skin, and the bottom flows down to the ground.

I have to be careful that the midsection doesn't slip, or everyone at the club will get a show.

Perhaps I want them too. Maybe I'm being indignant, but all I want to do is make Lucifer confess in front of everyone that I'm his.

Safety concerns be damned.

Lucifer shows so much passion and care towards me in private, is it that wrong to want that in front of others as well?

He told me to meet him there, that coming together would be too suspicious. I rolled my eyes, and he clicked his tongue, so I already know I'm on thin ice. Pushing him is becoming my favorite pastime. I'm just not sure where the edge of his patience is.

I portal to the club and notice that nothing has changed in all of these years, not the furniture or the people. My heels click along the dark marble until I see Judd.

He gives me a small smile.

"Hey, Judd."

"Hey Barbie, it's been a while."

I shrug, and we both look at the center stage, where Lucifer sits on his throne. His glare towards Judd is intense, and I can't help but enjoy it.

"Still have a death wish, Judd?" I ask, looking back at him and ignoring Lucifer's stare.

"I don't think I do," he says, lining some coke on the table in front of him. "You want a bump?"

I shake my head. I might want to push Lucifer, but not that far. "No thanks. Where's Asmo?"

Judd laughs and shakes his head. "I don't think I've ever met a more pussy-whipped demon in my life." I furrow my brows, and he tilts his head. "Not BFFs with Kas anymore?"

"I just haven't seen her in a while."

"Seems like a common theme lately," Judd says.

"You seem different," I comment, looking him over, and he shrugs. "Is Elvor coming tonight?"

Judd shakes his head, leaning forward and taking a deep inhale of the white powder before sitting up. "No, he's been working overtime since Ponds suddenly went missing."

"Hmm, shame."

Judd laughs, and when I look over my shoulder, I can see how rigid Lucifer is as he watches us. I wish I could enjoy the moment of his jealousy, but it's short-lived when Lisa and her two flunkies approach his throne. I can't hear what they're saying, but Lucifer looks bored.

I don't like them around him at all. I look back to Judd.

"Do you want to dance, Judd?"

He shakes his head, laughing. "Sorry, Barbie. I no longer have a death wish, remember."

"Boo." I look around the room; a lot of familiar faces, but no one I truly know. I would kill someone to have Kas here with me right now. I mean, I would kill someone for a lot less, but I miss my friend.

I make my way closer to where Lucifer sits so I can hear what Lisa is saying. I'm not shocked to hear her flirting with Lucifer. She's as shameless as she is plain.

"My lord, if there is anything we can offer you to relieve your stress, we'd be more than happy too."

"That is unnecessary," Lucifer rejects her offer in an uninterested tone.

"Everyone needs some stress relief from time to time."

I can't help it. "Are your ears working, Lisa?" I draw out her name, and she turns, scoffing when she sees it's me.

"I don't see how this is any of your concern. Maybe you should go back to wherever it was that you fucked off to."

"But then how would I put you in your place?"

She scoffs again, the violent urge to stick my heel through her eye socket crosses my mind, and I'm taking off my shoe before I even realize it. Lucifer is standing with a grip on my arm in the next second.

"Lilith." His voice is commanding.

"What?"

"This behavior is uncouth."

"Yeah, well, so is Lisa's face."

Lisa crosses her arms, looking at me like I'm being scolded and she won. That is until Lucifer speaks again. "It doesn't matter how unattractive she is."

Her face falls, and it takes everything in me to not stick my tongue at her like a child would.

"Fine. I won't gouge her eye out with the heel of my shoe," I concede.

"That's progress." Lucifer looks back at Lisa and her friends. "You're dismissed." Lucifer's hand hasn't left my arm, and when he looks back at me, he sighs. "Lilith."

I tug my arm out of his grip. "I can't do this." I know I'm acting like a brat, and usually, I'm okay with that. I'm more than happy to push Lucifer's buttons, but right now, it feels like I'm pushing my own. Being a secret... I'm not sure it's something I can live with. All I wanted to do was wrap my hands around his neck, climb his body like a tree, and kiss his face.

But no, in public I'm just Lucifer's assistant.

I fucking hate this.

I'm feeling murderous, and my heels click against the tile of the club floor before portalling to the mansion. I debate on which room to go to, but I go to Lucifer's, even though I'm pissed. I'm feeling insecure, and I can't deny that I don't want to be around him.

I'm barely in his room when his arms wrap around my waist.

"What was that about, love?" he asks softly.

"Nothing."

"Didn't feel like nothing."

"I don't like her speaking to you like you're just down to fuck whatever demon bats their eyes at you."

"You know you have nothing to worry about when it comes to my fidelity. It's only you that I want."

I sigh, leaning the back of my head against his chest. "I know."

"Do you need a reminder of my devotion, little Hellfire?"

SARAH BLUE

"Maybe," I sigh, even if I'm feeling conflicted, I know having his hands on me will make everything feel better. The fact that he left the club to chase after me already has me feeling a lot better.

His fingers trail down my throat to my collarbone, and I feel the tip of his finger tug at the dress strap.

"This isn't the dress I requested."

"No, it's not."

"Does defying me make you wet, darling?" I swallow but don't move or respond. "I think you need to see what it's like to be my bad girl tonight."

"I can be good."

"Mmm, we shall see. Remove your dress."

He usually undresses me, but I push back my irritation as I remove the red satin, and it pools onto the floor. I wore nothing underneath, so I know he's looking at my bare ass as I turn around to face him.

"Perhaps you need a lesson in clearing your mind."

I swallow. "What?"

He snaps his fingers, and when I turn to the left, there is an X-shaped device in the corner. Lucifer's hand glides down my back before gently cupping my ass. "Back against the wood," he instructs, and I look at him, blinking a few times. "Now," he says in a tone that warrants submission.

The cross is padded in fine leather and is cool against my skin as I stand naked against it. He's still fully dressed in his all-black suit, looking absolutely delicious.

"What is this?" I ask, worried that he will be irritated with my speaking.

"A St. Andrews Cross," he answers with a smirk. My mouth parts, and he laughs. "The irony is not lost on me."

"What are you going to do?"

"Help you to stop thinking so much," he says, taking my wrist and locking it above my head before doing the same with the other.

"I don't think too much," I retort, and he arches an eyebrow at me. He leans forward, but doesn't touch me as his elbow presses against the wood behind me as he looks down at me.

"I'm going to take away most of your senses. You need to just let yourself feel and not overthink it."

He places a ping-pong sized ball in my hand. "If at any time you want to stop, just drop the ball, love."

"Wait." He stops what he's doing immediately and looks at me. "You'll stop right away if I drop the ball? If I don't like anything?"

"Yes, but be sure you want me to stop."

"You won't hurt me?"

He shakes his head, kissing up my throat and nipping at my jaw. "Only in the ways you'll enjoy."

I sigh, goosebumps covering my skin as I nod. "Okay."

Suddenly smoke clouds my vision, and I let out a soft gasp. "My shadows will ensure you can't see anything. I think I'll let you keep your hearing for now."

"Okay."

His thumb trails along my lips before I feel soft material slide between my lips, hitting my tongue before wrapping around the back of my head. "As much as I love this smart mouth, I think I'd like to hear your noises of pleasure while you gagged." His tie is tight between my parted lips, but not painfully so. My mouth already waters, wetting the fabric, and as humiliating as it should feel, all I feel is turned on.

I'm tied up, blind, and can't speak. I've handed over the complete power of my safety and pleasure to Lucifer, and the thing is, I know he will provide.

"Where should we start, love?" I feel his fingers wrap around my ankle, and I gasp, though it's muffled with his tie between my lips. "Silly me, I forgot about these ankles." I swear he kisses my instep as he locks my ankles into place. The only movements I can make are to lift my back and bottom off the back of the cross. But I'm so overwhelmed by the new sensations I don't move at all.

"I think we should start with your punishment for wearing the wrong dress."

I make a noise against the tie, which was supposed to be a retort about choosing whatever the fuck I want to wear. I hear his laugh, and I know he isn't laughing at me but enjoying my being submissive to him.

"Let's start with delayed gratification."

I swallow the spit pooling in my mouth as I breathe out of my nose. There's a buzzing noise, and when something touches my clit, I jump slightly from the sensation. This isn't a build-up of sensation, it's a full-blown assault on my clit. My toes curl as the device circles my sensitive bundle of nerves, and I just know I'm about to come embarrassingly fast.

Lucifer holds it there until I'm on the cusp of coming before moving it off my clit. I feel the buzzing against my nipples, the wetness from my pussy covering my left nipple. I suck in a sharp breath as it's taken away, and Lucifer's lips replace it, sucking and licking my essence from my chest.

"You look stunning wrapped up in my leather and shadows, Lilith." He does the same motion with my other nipple, putting the toy against it, and getting my nipple hard and wet before sucking on it.

He's still playing with my nipple when he drags the toy back on my clit. This time on a lower setting. It's too low, just enough to entice but not enough to make me come. When I groan against my gag, he lightly nips against my breast, making my back straighten.

"That's no way to ask to come, love."

He inserts two fingers inside of me while still using the toy on my clit. This... This could definitely work.

"You're so fucking wet, nearly dripping down your thighs." I can picture what he's saying, I even feel the sheen of my wetness against the inner part of my thigh. His fingers are curling slowly inside my pussy, and I feel so close I want to scream. The vibrator is hitting my clit at the right angle, and I pant, knowing my release is going to come. But then he pulls his fingers and toy away from me at the same moment. My head falls forward, and I can barely hear the whimpering noises I'm making around his tie.

"My poor, sweet, little demon. Making a mess of yourself and not being able to come," he taunts, and all it does is make me wetter.

My skin feels like it's on fire, and I wait for moments that span far too long, just waiting for him to touch me again, though he doesn't.

I'm trying so hard to be patient and not whimper pathetically against the gag.

When his tongue trails from the side of my knee to the outer lips of my pussy I nearly cry out. I can only imagine how beautiful and powerful he looks on his knees for me, cleaning up the mess of me he's made while he continues to deny me my release.

I'm so close to dropping the ball and begging him to fuck me, to do anything to me. I can't take it anymore, but I know if I drop this ball, then the game is over. The small sphere feels like it weighs a million pounds in the palm of my hand.

He bites the inside of my thigh, and it's like all my nerves have been rewired. I moan and thrust my hips involuntarily at him. I can't imagine what a simpering mess I must look like for him right now.

"So fucking beautiful," he says. His hands land on my hips as he climbs up my body, leaving a trail of wet kisses up my thighs, stomach, and chest. I nearly feel like crying as he kisses up my throat and behind my ear.

I want to beg him to please give me some relief. When it feels like I leave my body.

Lucifer laughs, and somehow I see him... and myself.

"Oh, love... you cheeky little cheater."

I blink at him and look down at my body... well, sort of. Lucifer looks at me in disbelief and arches his eyebrow. "Can you still feel?" he asks, and I watch him as he fingers my pussy. I groan and shake my head.

I realize that in my distress, I must have astral projected, and I can see everything in this form. I see what I look like in his eyes and at his mercy. I look like I'm going to gush on his fingers, but at the same time, I can't feel it. I let out a sigh. "How do I get back in my body?"

He smirks and shakes his head.

"Better figure it out soon because I think I just may let you come."

I don't know if it's the promise of relief or how turned on I am watching him toy with my body, but I close my eyes and think really hard, willing myself back into my body.

When I open my eyes, I see nothing, and I sigh with relief. Every sensation feels ten times better; the smoke blinding my vision, my saliva pooling in my mouth, but most specifically, Lucifer's fingers fucking me so hard while hitting the right spot. I don't think I've ever felt this good.

"That's my good girl. Are you going to make a mess on me, love?" He kisses my throat before pulling back, no doubt watching how his fingers fuck me. The imagery is enough to send me over the edge. A gush hits my thighs as my legs quake and my brain goes hazy. My orgasm is so strong enough that I feel like I might pass out. He doesn't stop either, pushing me to the edge until I'm a shivering, over-sensitive mess.

"So perfect," he says, gliding his fingers out of me. His wet fingers touch my cheek as he removes my gag, and the smoke clears from my vision. I blink open my eyes and breathe loudly now that my mouth isn't full. Lucifer quickly removes all of my bindings and scoops me into his arms.

My hands fly up to cup his face, pulling his lips against mine, and he groans. He still has all his clothes on. "More," I beg, and he bites my lip before placing me on his chair next to the fire. I've never seen him undress as quickly as he does now. His clothes are flung around the room as if he was a tornado. He turns me so my knees are on the chair, and my hands grip the back. He wastes no time, kissing the back of my neck and filling me with his cock.

"You were magnificent. Such a good girl. Do you want more?"

"Please," I beg, and the stretch of him entering me has me moaning.

"You want me to fill you up with my cum? Remind you that you're the only one I have eyes for. Is that what you need, Lilith?"

I nod my head, and he bites the back of my shoulder lightly.

"How could I ever want anything else when I have you and this perfect needy pussy."

I don't think I've ever come so fast from just penetration. I don't know if it's from his words or the delayed gratification from earlier, but I welcome it completely.

Lucifer moans at my back, his hand spreading my ass as he spits, and I feel the wetness gather. His thumb rubs against the tight hole, and he slowly pushes into me, his thrusts in sync with his thumb. I can barely hold myself up against the chair as he fucks me.

"So fucking tight. So good, aren't you, love?" I nod my head frantically, and his thrusts are so hard the chair squeaks as it slides against the floor. It doesn't deter him as he breathes against my neck, moaning when he fills me. His grip tightens around my hips as his orgasm hits him completely. It was fast and dirty, and I can't help but love that I'm the one who makes him feel this way.

We stay like that for a moment, both of us just breathing heavily. A sticky sheen of sweat on both of us as he pulls out. I already know what to expect when he spreads my cheeks, and I feel the sensation of his release dripping into the fabric of the chair. He groans before scooping me back up in his arms.

I feel so relaxed that I can't even remember what happened at the club, just that I feel safe in his arms and the assurance that Lucifer will always give me what I need.

CHAPTER THIRTY-ONE

LILITH

I t's a gloomy day in Hell, as it is most days. I love it, but today feels different. When I'm alone and in my bubble with Lucifer, everything feels fine. But when the day comes, I can't help but feel defeated.

We're at breakfast, and it's an exciting one since Blair and Dax decided to join us. They sit next to each other. Lucifer is at the head of the table with me on the opposite side, while Mara and Toth sit next to each other.

"Blair and Dax, you are doing well with your assignments?"

Blair smiles and nods. "I'm really enjoying it."

"Good. Mara, how is your training with Toth going?"

"Oh, it's revolutionary." She sucks on her spoon before putting it back in the teacup and putting her hand behind Toth's chair.

Toth lightly chokes on his breakfast and shakes his head.

"Toth said you are doing well. Since you have decided to stay in Hell, the choice is yours; you can live your life as a demon, and no one has to know your connection, or if you would like, I will name you my heir apparent."

Heir apparent rings in my head like a fucking alarm.

He would announce her to the world? But keep me hidden.

"I think I'd like to learn the ropes, so I could help you out around here," Mara says.

"Blair, it is up to you how you would like to live, as a demon or to be known as my daughter. There are costs with being directly associated with me. You both need to know this before making your choice."

"I think I'd like to remain unknown for now," Blair says, and Lucifer nods his head.

"And me?" I ask, not even caring that I'm interrupting.

"We've discussed this," is his response, and I want to scream. I push my chair back, and it audibly screeches against the expensive floor. *I hope it scuffs it permanently.* "Where are you going?" Lucifer asks, getting out of his chair and following me down the hall.

"You're giving them a choice to come out as your family but not me? How do you think that would make me feel? Can I not handle it? Am I not strong enough? Or are you just not wanting the world to know that I'm who you're with."

"Lilith."

"No. I need some time to think. Go spend the day with your daughters. I'm sure they miss you."

He sighs, rubbing the back of his neck. "I can't lose you."

"And what? You can lose your daughters?"

"They can't die."

I blink at him rapidly. "What?"

"Mara accidentally stabbed herself with a few of the daggers, seeing what they could do."

I blink, but it tracks; Mara would think it would be a great idea to test out what weapons could hurt her.

"And?"

"Just like me, they do nothing. It seems my curse has passed to my daughters."

"Your curse?"

"Of living forever. Never dying."

"But I can die," I say it plainly; I've been close to dying already, we know that certain weapons definitely work.

"With the proper weapon, yes."

"I... I still need a moment." A moment to breathe, to gather my thoughts. *Why do I feel so hopelessly insecure about this?*

He groans and steps into my space, grabbing my cheeks. "Promise me you won't leave Hell."

"I promise." He kisses the top of my head, his hands trailing down my hair before I look at the ground and walk away. I'm not running from him or this. I just need to collect my thoughts. There's no better place for such thinking than the black lake, but it's far enough from the manor that I need to portal.

The clouds overhead are dark and ominous as I sit on the grass and look at the inky water of the lake. I'd considered putting a toe in there once but thought better of it. Maybe Mara will get curious enough to test it out and report back.

There's a crack of a portal, and I turn around to see Kas. I can't stop the huge smile that takes over my face when I see her. She walks over to me and sits down, even though she glares at the grass before doing so.

"Where have you been, bitch?" I ask her, and she pushes her shoulder against mine before resting her head on my shoulder.

"I've got to go away for a bit."

"Why?"

"Family drama."

"That doesn't answer where you've been."

She sighs and sits up. "I reconnected with Asmo and met the sweetest little witch." My eyebrows furrow, and it's the first time I've ever seen Kas close to crying. "I should have known better. That it was too good to last. I never should have let myself fall to begin with."

"Kas, what are you talking about?"

"I told Lucifer to give you space in the beginning, Lilith. I thought I was protecting you like I'm protecting them."

I look over at her. I'm not mad, we needed that time apart for me to realize what I wanted. "I'm not mad at you."

"I know, I just needed you to know. I need you to understand why *I'm* leaving."

"Kas, you're not telling me anything."

She pushes up her knees, she's still dressed impeccably as she wraps her arms around her legs and rests her head on her knees. "Remember when I said having an angel sibling wasn't all it was cracked up to be?"

I nod my head, and she sighs, opening her mouth to continue. But suddenly, a few raindrops hit my face. I look up at the sky and wince. It's usually gloomy in Hell, and it rains every three days on the dot.

Today is not one of those days. There's a crack of thunder, and when I look to my left, I see the angel Rainn standing there.

Kas is immediately on her feet, and I follow suit as we stare at the angel before us. When I glance back at Kas, I realize now why Rainn looked so familiar to me. My mouth parts as Kas takes a defensive stance.

"Coming to Hell is really bold, Michael."

"You forget, I was trapped here for a few decades. A shame Beelzebub met his demise, or so I'm told. He was a very helpful little rat when he needed to be."

"You're Kas' brother?" I say, but Rainn—Michael—whatever his name is doesn't say anything; he just continues glaring at Kas.

"She's not my partner, you can let her go."

"But you love her, you care for her. Do you remember my promise, sister?"

"I'm sick of this game, Michael. It's been centuries. Why can't you let this go?"

He laughs cruelly and shakes his head. "Let it go? One doesn't simply forgive. There's a reason why you were sent to Hell, Kasdeya. So what do you choose? I can let blondie walk away, but that means your little witch is in for a special treat."

"Kas, go. I can handle myself."

She shakes her head. "He's an archangel. His power has only grown. Can you summon Lucifer?"

"Oh yes, let's add another sibling I loathe into the mix."

"Kas, go. I can handle this," I tell her, but she shakes her head. "Go warn Asmo and your witch. I can handle this," I say again because I can see the fear that Michael has instilled in her.

"Don't be fucking stupid. Do you have a weapon?"

Yeah, my dagger... *which is basically useless to Michael. I need something that can take down a fucking archangel.*

"My dagger, what do you have?"

"Something stronger," she says. We stay close, keeping our distance from Michael the best that we can. It's all coming together now, why Kas is always running, and why she thought I should stay away from Lucifer all this time. She cares about protecting the ones she loves, and apparently, she is protecting them from her psychopathic archangel brother.

"I suggest you leave. Lucifer should be here any moment."

"How unprogressive of you. Do you need a man to save you? I guess it's unsurprising, you did fall for all my tricks. How pathetic." He tosses the coin on the ground, and as soon as it's near me, I feel confused, and that's when time picks up. "You really thought an angel would be on your side? That I gave a single fuck about what happened to your twin?"

"Why did you toy with me for so long?" I ask, and he laughs.

"I suppose I'm a bit of a sadist. I never truly knew how much Kasdeya cared for you. But when the angels were talking about Lucifer's mate and disrupting the hierarchy of Hell, I decided you were of no use. Clearly, my siblings in Heaven were unsuccessful. How predictably boring."

He steps closer to me. I know that I can grab my necklace and call for Lucifer, but there's a part of me that needs to prove myself. Kas is right next to me, her mouth in a hard line, trying to figure out our next move.

We can do this. I can do this.

I'm powerful, and Kas is strong.

I'm a fucking demon, and it's about time this angel learns a god-damn lesson. It's difficult, but the toe of my shoe is just able to touch the coin, and I kick it as hard as I can, but it's not far enough. Fortunately, Kas takes the next step and kicks it into the black lake, the black sludge sucking it deep into its depths. As soon as it's away from me, I feel instantly better.

"What the fuck was that thing?" I ask Kas.

"One of Michael's favorite tricks, it makes you forget certain things and is used as a tracker."

"Kas, I had that at the house," she looks irritated but not concerned. I'm guessing she hadn't brought Asmo or her witch to the house.

"I don't need magical assistance, do I, Kasdeya? How many loved ones have I taken from you now?"

"Michael, this has to stop."

"Like how you stopped?" he yells at her.

"It's been centuries, Michael."

"Not long enough for me to forget or to collect."

"Just take me instead," Kas says, pleading with her insane brother. His focus is completely on her as I step more off to the side, creating a trap where he's between both of us.

"And miss out on all of your beautiful suffering? I think not."

It's then that he lunges for Kas. As they fight it out, it's clear his aim is to hurt and not kill. Both of them have so much anger towards each other as they fight, and both have a blade in their hand. Neither of them have been cut yet, but there have been some heavy punches in the mix. Kas' nose is bleeding, and Michael has a black eye. They are both healing at an extreme pace, just to get hurt all over again.

With Michael distracted, I jump on his back and stab him in the shoulder. His elbow hits me so hard in the nose that I'm thrown back at least ten feet. My nose is bleeding, and I wipe it off with my forearm.

His rage is surprisingly focused all on Kas. "You made me like this!" he screams as his wings flair out while he's on top of her, strangling her. "I didn't want this. *You* did this." He screams and cries in her face. He's so completely unhinged and singularly focused that he doesn't expect me. I know my blade won't do much, so I pick somewhere it will really hurt.

I slash against his Achilles tendon as hard as I can. He howls, and his grip loosens just enough for Kas to stab him in the shoulder.

His tendons are an absolute mess from where I cut him. Blood gushes everywhere as he falls to the ground. "Fucking bitches," he hisses.

Kas is just about to stab him when Michael gives her a bloody smile. "This isn't over, my dear sister." He grabs at a necklace that is similar to my own and whispers under his breath. Just as Kas is lowering the blade to end his life, he disappears, and all the blade hits is a dead patch of grass.

Kas pants and it's the first time I see her break. She doesn't cry, but something akin to it. "He's never going to stop."

"So then stop him," I say to her in a fierce tone.

"You saw him, he's strong."

"Kas, we just left him bloody and portalling back to wherever he came from. He might be strong, but he can be wounded; he can be killed."

She wraps her arms around her knees and rests her head on her legs. "I don't want to kill him," she says so softly, like it's a secret she's never wanted to say out loud.

"Then we'll come up with something. Go back to Asmo and your witch; the best way to protect them is to be with them."

"Is that what you're doing?" she asks.

"Planning on it," I tell her. If I'm telling Kas to face her fears and not run or hide, I should be able to tell Lucifer, right? "You should probably head out."

She wipes a bit of blood off the corner of her mouth. "When the fuck did you get so smart, huh?"

I lean against her, bumping our shoulders together. "I learned from the best."

"Oh, fuck off, Lilith," she says jokingly, bumping back into me. "So, you and the big man are happy?"

"We will be," I promise her.

"That's good. If I need your help in taking Michael down again?"

"You don't even have to ask," I say, tapping her knee. "Now, don't be a stranger and go get your lovers back."

"Ew, don't say lovers."

"Grow up," I reply, rolling my eyes.

"I guess if you have, I should too."

"Especially because you're dealing with two. I can't imagine."

"Oh, I certainly have my hands full." She dusts herself off as she winks at me. "Give 'em hell."

Oh, I plan too. Today was the last thing I needed to solidify the fact that I need to talk about how I'm feeling with Lucifer. About how I can't just be somebody's secret, that for this to work, we need to be true partners. While I'll never delude myself into thinking I'm anywhere near as physically powerful or as gifted as Lucifer, I know now that I can handle myself. I also know that I have friends and people who love me, who have my back unconditionally. If it's enough for me, it should surely be enough for him.

I sigh as I wrap my hand around the necklace and call his name. The fury written on his face when he lands right in front of me is palpable.

He rubs some blood off of my face and frowns at me. "What happened?"

"Kas and I got into it with Michael."

He gapes at me, his grip on my face tightening. "You fucking took on an archangel?"

"Yes, I did. And no, he's not dead, but he isn't doing so hot either."

"Why didn't you call me sooner?" Lucifer demands angrily as I walk back to the manor. His first response isn't I'm proud of you or asking the finer details of the fight; it is how I should have called him first, how I need him to protect me. I'm so frustrated I want to scream.

"Lilith," he says my name harshly, coming to stand in front of me quicker than a flash. "Why didn't you call for me?"

"Because I'm not helpless. Because I'm not some damsel in distress for you to lock away in a tower." I don't know why tears fall from my eyes as I shout at him. "I'm strong, I can take care of myself."

"I know you're strong and brave, it's what I love about you."

We hadn't said it yet, sure he calls me love all the time, but he's never outright told me that he loves me.

"You love me?" I reiterate, and he nods his head. "Then why can't you love me the way I need to be loved? I can't be your secret, stealing affections in the manor or only in front of your trusted friends. I want to be with someone who is proud to be with me. I want to be loved openly and honestly."

His head is downcast as his eyes look up at me. "I can't lose you, Lilith."

"If you keep using my safety as a reason to hide me, you will." I don't mean to be harsh, and I don't want this to feel like an ultimatum, but I guess it is. I can't live the rest of my life feeling insecure and like another person feels ashamed to be with me. I've spent too much of my life dealing with that.

"You've seen before, angels aren't afraid to come after you."

"Yeah, and you saw how I handled myself. Can you trust me and trust yourself to protect me? I'm willing to compromise, but being your dirty, little secret isn't part of the deal."

"You're not my dirty, little secret."

"Aren't I? I want to be able to kiss you in front of a room full of demons. I want them to know how proud I am of you and to be yours. Can you say the same?" He opens his mouth, and I put a hand on his chest. "Don't answer; just think about what I've said, and once you know what you can handle, come find me."

"Lilith," he sighs my name, but I shake my head.

"Just think about it." I wrap my arms around his waist, and his hand comes up to cup the back of my head as he portals us back to the mansion, me going back to my room and Lucifer going to wherever he needs to go to think.

CHAPTER THIRTY-TWO

LUCIFER

*S*he feels like a dirty secret.

That she needs our love to be public in order for this to work. If I were a mortal, I would think I was having a heart attack the way my chest aches. I suppose she has some points. If Michael knew of her as well as the other angels, she's truly not a secret. I, of course, worry about my own demons. But as she pointed out, I can protect her, and she can take care of herself.

I suppose my trauma of losing her before—not truly her—losing Lily has jaded me. The feelings and connection I had with Lily are nothing like I have with Lilith. Lilith pushes me, she's strong, funny, and beautiful. I groan as I walk into the training area. Mara has Toth pinned beneath her and is pointing a dagger to his chin. As soon as he sees me, he clears his throat and tosses Mara off of him.

"My lord," he greets.

"Sorry to interrupt."

"Oh, I was just kicking your second-hand's ass, it's fine," Mara teases and Toth rolls his eyes. "Is something wrong?"

"Lilith," I say as I sit on one of the training benches.

"Obviously," Mara says, picking up a dagger and tossing it at the wall. It lands in the wood with an audible thud and a splintering of the wall.

"Obviously?" I ask.

"Yeah, no girl wants to be someone's secret," she is speaking to me but glances at Toth.

"She's not a secret."

"Oh, do you take her on dates? Does she have a title? Can she tell whoever she wants about you two?"

"I need to protect her." Mara rolls her eyes.

"Listen, Pops, I know you've been alive for like a really long time, but us lady folk can take care of ourselves. Honestly, I'm surprised she hasn't stabbed you in your sleep for insinuating she can't protect herself."

"I know she's strong."

Mara throws another dagger, and it lands in the same spot as the previous one, clanking against the embedded knife, making the hole gapping at this point.

"So then why are you treating her like she's made of glass? Also, from what I hear, there are some real bitches in Hell. Of course, she wants to openly claim you as hers."

My brows furrow because Mara hasn't left the manor. I've made it clear that she shouldn't until we figure out what she wants to do. I worry about the death toll when we let her loose. It's why I haven't told her about Beelzebub being kept in the pits. I plan on telling her, but only when I'm sure she's here to stay and that demon hasn't tainted her mind.

"Where have you heard this?"

She tosses a dagger in the air and catches it by the handle, pointing the end at Toth, who looks shocked by her pointing the finger—or dagger, in this case—at him.

"I see."

"My lord—" Toth starts, and I wave a hand at him.

"It's important for Mara to know the social aspects of Hell. It's fine, Toth."

Mara throws another dagger, landing in the same spot alongside the other knives, and it's a relief to know how well she's doing with her training, how powerful she is. I find myself not worrying about her allegiance, she genuinely seems to want a relationship with me and to learn everything there is to learn about Hell.

"So what do I do now?"

Mara rolls her eyes. "A grand gesture, duh."

"A grand gesture?"

"Yeah, you need to let her know that you're all in."

"All in." It still creates a pit in my stomach, and I realize that I'll never have peace of mind as long as Lilith is mine. The least I can do is provide her the title and love she deserves.

"And soon, girls don't like to wait." I smile at my daughter and nod.

"Your coronation is tomorrow, but it suddenly seems like we need to push it back."

Mara smiles and nods. "That's the spirit."

The 'coronation' is set up in the banquet hall of the mansion. It's separate from my personal quarters, and no one can explore elsewhere unless invited. Lilith slept in her room last night, and the worst part was she didn't take her cat with her. The little fucker slept nestled between my legs. *I didn't enjoy it—not for a moment.*

Mara told me I needed a grand gesture, and I couldn't think of one better than this. I asked Toth to stay here with Mara, and I didn't invite Blair or Dax. There are some things your children don't need to see.

We've been careless around the mansion, but that's about to change.

I'm still not sure how to battle the emotions of everyone knowing about Lilith. I liked her being mine and safe, but she's been attacked twice, so how safe has she truly been? While immortality may seem long, I've spent too much time preoccupied with duty and possession than actually living. I'm ready to finally start my life with my soulmate by my side and watching my daughters live their long and happy lives.

I arrive in the banquet hall first, the room going quiet as I enter. There must be three hundred demons in attendance this evening, but there's only one I truly care about.

Considering the fact that I've killed two of my inner circle lately and asked Toth to stay back with Mara, the only person standing next to my throne is Lilith, and Elvor stands tall next to her.

She doesn't look at me right away, but she looks stunning. She always does. She's wearing the black dress that I asked her to wear a few days ago, and I wonder if this is her peace offering or if she will accept mine.

I wore my crown tonight, something I hardly ever do, though it is made of the finest metals from multiple realms. I don't need the symbol of my powers, just my presence is usually enough, but for this moment, it's needed.

"Citizens of Hell," I say, standing in front of the throne. "I know you're curious as to why I've gathered you here, and for a coronation, no less. Lately, my status has been challenged, and I hope you have taken note of what happens when someone disrespects me. I would suggest you ask Beelzebub or Milcom, but seeing as they are dead, that would be impossible." There is a light chatter in the room filled with gasps and mumblings.

"I want to make myself crystal clear; if you in any way threaten me or my family, there will be no second chances. You will find yourself in the pit for all of eternity, or your soul will simply be destroyed." I pick at my nails, looking around the room. "Elvor has been feeling very restless lately," I say, nodding to the fae. He grunts and nods his head in acknowledgment. "So let's just say that my preference is eternal torture and not mercy, especially when it comes to those I deem important."

I glare at the crowd that is now bowing on their knees, letting a moment of silence linger throughout the hall. "There has been some commotion with the angels recently, and I want to assure you that it is being dealt with. I expect complete transparency in this realm. If there is even a whisper of coercion with the angels, know that you alone have sealed your fate."

The room is silent, and I look over at Lilith, who has her head down; her blonde hair is wavy, falling over one shoulder and down to her waist.

"Now that I feel you have been properly warned and made aware of my expectations, it's time for the celebration." I pause for dramatic effect, and my eyes never leave Lilith as I say my next words.

"I would like to announce the new Queen of Hell—prosecutor of crimes against women—Lilith." She looks up with her brows furrowed as her mouth gapes open. Then she looks at me with wide eyes before looking around the room.

"You've got to be kidding me," I hear a demon say. When I look down into the crowd, I realize it's Autumn. When I make eye contact with her, she starts shivering. Her two friends take two steps away from the idiot.

I snap my fingers, her soul ripping from her body and traveling right into my mouth. I don't savor her soul at all as I consume her. The tension in the room rises, and everyone looks at Autumn's crumpled body.

"Take that as a warning to never disrespect your Queen."

I hold out my hand, and Lilith takes it, a look of complete disbelief written on her face as she blinks at me.

Elvor hands me her crown; it's black and dainty, with obsidian crystals hanging in an intricate pattern. "Take your throne, love."

She still doesn't seem to gather everything that is happening, but I walk her to the throne where she sits, crossing her legs and exposing nearly the whole length of her leg. I compose myself as I place the crown on her head.

"Magnificent," I tell her as she sits tall on the throne she deserves. I don't know what I was thinking by keeping her to myself. She was meant to be my equal, to entice fear in others. I told her that my darkness calls to her, and as I see the power she exudes, I know that we were truly fated to be together.

When I get down on one knee in front of her, I hear the gasps around the room, but nowhere as loud as Lilith's.

"You know when I said I didn't want to be a secret, I meant like take me out on a date or dance with me at the club."

"But as I said, you deserve *everything*," I remind her, and she smiles.

I grab her ankle and kiss the inside before kissing up her leg. I can feel the shock and intrigue throughout the room. Lucifer, the Devil, Satan himself, is on his knees for another demon. But she isn't just any demon. She's my soulmate, my true counterpart, and she should be treated as such.

"Lucifer, what are you doing?"

"Worshiping you."

"In front of everyone?"

"They need to understand that I bow to you, and they should too," I explain, kissing up her leg. I watch as her flesh pebbles under my lips, and she looks out towards the crowd, no doubt every set of eyes watching us with unblinking interest.

Her hand covers mine on her thigh, squeezing gently.

"Shall I show them how I get to worship you, love? A way no other being can?"

She looks out to the crowd again. I'm not sure what she's searching for, but as soon as she sees it, she smirks and looks down at me. Spreading her legs, her dress still covering her cunt, encouraging me to touch her in front of Hell, to witness what she means to me.

I take absolute care in kissing her thighs and shifting my hands and face so no one sees her beautiful pussy. They can watch me in devotion, but they can't see what's mine. Deep down, I will always be a possessive asshole, and I will protect her with every fiber of my being, but at this moment, the statement is clear and undeniable.

I'm showing Lilith a respect I show no other creature, and the same respect is expected of others. I just so happen to get to taste her and fuck her.

She shivers as my hands glide up her thighs, my nose sliding up her slit. I use my teeth to move her dress and a finger to pull her panties to the side.

My tongue swipes against her wetness, and I hum my approval. My face is in her lap, pleasuring her as everyone watches what I'm willing to do for my queen. The respect, obedience, and submission I only offer to her. She tastes so fucking sweet against my tongue, and she gasps, her fingers tangling with my hair and crown.

My grip is tight on her thighs, and I can hear some voices carrying throughout the crowd. It's a mixture of shock, amazement, and sexual intrigue.

She grinds up toward my face, and I groan against her pussy.

"Leave us!" Lilith announces, and I hear a stirring of people leaving, but not all of them. She pats my face, and I cover her with her dress before we both stand up. I'm fully prepared to kill anyone who didn't listen, but Lilith handles it for me. "I said leave!" Her voice booms in a tone that insights fear, and the remaining bodies scatter.

She looks up at me, her thumb trailing down my chin, collecting her release before pushing it between my lips, which I take eagerly.

"That was some demonstration."

"Was it adequate?"

"Beyond," she confirms, looking up at me with loving eyes. She looks like a beautiful fallen goddess, and I don't think I'll ever tire of seeing her this way.

"What now?"

"Now, you tell me how you liked to be loved," she says softly and grabs my hand.

"Your affections are all I need to feel loved."

"Then let me show you just how much I love you," she says with a smirk.

"You love me?"

She nods her head and smiles. "Let me worship you." She shocks me by portalling both of us to my—our room. She's never done a ride-along portal with me, and I smile as we land.

"Have you been holding out on me?"

She looks over her shoulder, dropping her dress, exposing her beautiful body as she wears nothing but her crown and panties. "No, sir," she rasps, and if my cock wasn't already hard, it is now. "Sit in the chair."

This chair used to be just a piece of furniture in my room, but lately, it's become sentimental to me.

I expect her to straddle me or get on her knees in front of me, but she doesn't. She's a good two meters away from me on her knees as I sit on the chair, my legs spread and waiting.

She crawls toward me, and I have to rub my face, along with trying to subdue a groan. My queen is on her knees and crawling to me. Her breasts sway as she moves until she is in right front of me.

"You're not the only one who kneels."

"Love, you're going to destroy me."

She smirks. "Good."

"Fucking Hell." Her nimble hands unbutton my trousers, and her nails trail down my thighs. She looks up at me from her lashes as she places gentle kisses on the side of my cock, before kissing the head. Her tongue reaches out and licks up the pre-cum from the tip.

"You taste like mine," she says, and I can't help but shiver. "You taste like sin, salt, and so completely mine."

Her lips part as she takes me deep down her throat, never able to take all of me, but what she can't fit in her mouth, she uses her fist to stroke. Her crown doesn't falter on her head as she goes down on me, and it makes me feral.

Grabbing her from her underarms and tugging her onto my lap, she sinks down on my length. "You're going to make a mess on my cock, aren't you, love?"

She moans, and our lips crash together. I grip her luscious ass, moving her up and down on my cock as she grabs my shoulders. I can feel the bite of her nails through my shirt.

Her mouth is so plush and soft against mine, and I can't get enough of her. The way she feels wrapped around me, her scent, her soft noises. Eternity is forever, but I'm unsure if it will be enough.

One of her hands leaves my shoulders and grips my jaw, her nails digging into my cheeks as she kisses me roughly.

Her lips leave mine, and she looks into my eyes as she rides my cock slowly.

"You feel so good," she tells me. "Nothing will ever feel like this. You're so good for me."

I groan, not knowing how much I would enjoy her speaking to me like this. I squeeze her ass harder and thrust into her.

She's so wet that she slides easily down my length each time I thrust into her, and there's the wet slapping of our skin.

"My sweet, little demon is so fucking wet for me. Are you going to come for me too?"

She drops down low, taking more of me and grinding her clit against my pelvis as she takes my length deep inside her center. She moans against the side of my face, our crowns clinking together as she gets closer to finding her release.

"That's it, love, use me. I want to feel you come around my cock."

She whimpers, and I let go of her ass cheek to grip her face so she can't look away from me. Her eyes are hooded, and her lips are parted. There's a sheen of sweat on her forehead as she keeps moving up and down, my hand helping to guide her movements.

"That's it. Always such a good girl for your king, aren't you?"

The noise that leaves her throat will be ingrained in me forever. She doesn't break eye contact as she shatters around me, her thighs shaking and her cunt gripping me tightly. I thrust my hips from the chair, fucking her through her orgasm. She whimpers and grabs my shoulders tightly, but I don't relent, holding eye contact and filling her with my cum. Her eyes soften as she watches me reach my climax.

It's a slow crescendo with both of us staring at each other. Both of our hands not leaving one another as we pant heavily. The weight of the words shared tonight, along with the overwhelming sensations of being together so wholly, is overwhelming.

Suddenly there's a sharp shattering of glass on the ground. When I look over to my left I see that the fucking cat has knocked over a goblet of wine.

"Doom, that's a bad kitty," she scolds.

"Fucking cat."

"He just needs attention," Lilith says, and I mock pout.

"I also need attention."

"I think I just gave you plenty of attention."

"Not nearly enough."

She brushes my jaw with the backs of her fingers. "What about a little honeymoon?"

I furrow my brows and look at her. "What do you mean?"

"Like a little trip away from Hell. Just you and me." I must give her a look that says it's impossible because she retorts with, "You have Mara here now, and Toth is here to protect her. I think after the showing this evening, no demons are going to try anything. Now is the perfect time to go."

"I can't be away from Hell long."

"How long?"

"Probably three mortal days."

"Then we take three mortal days. Just you and me. I think we deserve it."

I push her hair off her shoulders, tossing it behind her back. "And where would you like to go, my queen?"

She blushes and shakes her head. "You know I was being serious, I just wanted to be your girlfriend in public."

I shake my head and kiss her bare shoulder. "I promised I'd give you everything. This is everything. If you want to take a trip. We'll take a trip."

She glides her hands to the back of my neck, kneading out some tension. "And this is our room now?"

"Love, this is our room, our mansion. Fuck, this entire realm is ours."

She sighs and looks at me in such a reverent way, one I never thought she would ever direct at me. "I do really love you, you know."

"I know," I smirk, and she pushes against my shoulder. Shifting her weight against my already semi-hard again cock.

"Again?" she whispers. I nod my head and bring her in for a searing kiss.

LILITH

EPILOGUE

"You're sure you can handle this?" Lucifer asks Mara.

"A few days lurking around the manor without stumbling upon you two fucking like rabbits? Yeah, I can handle it." Lucifer crosses his arms as he looks down at his daughter. She rolls her eyes and starts counting down on her fingers. "Rule one, do not leave the manor unless accompanied by none other than the fearless warrior Toth. Number two, feed the cat, and number three, try not to kill anyone."

Lucifer nods his head and sighs, giving Toth a look that says he needs to keep Mara in line, which, to be honest, I don't see that being a possibility.

"If you need us, summon me immediately."

"So dramatic, it'll be fine. It won't be like any of the coming-of-age teen movies I've watched recently while being trapped in this extremely gothic, yet somehow cozy, creepy mansion."

Lucifer sighs and leans forward, giving his daughter a hug. She doesn't resist as she wraps her arms around him.

"Seriously, have a good time. I've got it covered," I hear her whisper, and I can't hide my smile. She pulls away from Lucifer and hugs me too, whispering in my ear. "I'll give you ten bucks if you can remove the stick up his ass during vacation." I can't help but laugh as I pull away, and Lucifer gives us both an irritated look.

"Come on, Satan. We're going on vacation," I say, holding out my hand to him, which he takes.

"I still think this was too soon."

"Oh, hush. Have you been on vacation before?"

"No," he says plainly.

"You're supposed to relax. I can't believe you wore a suit for our honeymoon."

"What was I supposed to wear?"

"I don't know, shorts? A linen top?"

He looks down at me and glares. "The king of Hell doesn't wear fucking shorts. Now shut up, and let's do your honeymoon. I'm wearing my suit."

"Our honeymoon," I correct him.

"Fine, our honeymoon."

He spins me so we're facing each other, and I have to crane my neck back to look up at him. I'm extremely thankful for my demon body, or my neck would hurt like a bitch from always having to look up at his perfect, irritated face.

"Where to?" he asks.

"The realm of the fated," I reply. He pets my hair down and cups my jaw.

"You're sure?"

I nod, and he leans down to kiss me before portalling us back to the lake, where he told me everything.

There's a small cottage on the lake, a simple space with a single bed and a small kitchen. It has everything that we need to just enjoy each other. He places our shared bag on the floor.

"What now?"

"We relax."

His shoulders are stiff, and I shake my head at him. "How about a swim?"

"Is the lake sanitary?"

"Only one way to find out," I reply, ripping my dress off and heading out the back door to jump in the lake. The water is clear and cool but not so cold that I shiver. I see a still fully dressed Lucifer standing at the bank's edge. "Are you coming?"

"Fine," he groans, taking off his clothes and neatly folding them on the grass before walking into the water. He doesn't make a face of discomfort as he wades into the water to where I'm floating. He stands before me, his collarbone and face above the water.

I easily wrap my legs around his waist and my hands behind his neck. "Did you and Lily ever come here?"

He looks at me cautiously; I haven't brought her—or I guess my past life up—since the last time we came here.

"My time with Lily was short-lived. I knew we were fated; she was beautiful, and I enjoyed our visits, but no, we never did anything like this."

"Was she fun?"

He smirks. "No one is as fun as you."

"Mmm... he avoids the question."

He pushes my wet hair back off of my face. "This is the only variation of you I want. The past is irrelevant. Loving you in this life and sharing our future is all that matters to me."

"There's nothing you would change."

"Nothing," he confirms while looking at me.

"Not even the cat."

"Not even him."

"What about my smart mouth?" I ask, and he shakes his head.

"I like filling that smart mouth." His thumb trails down my bottom lip before leaning in and kissing me.

"Not even my penchant for violence?"

"I quite like that part. As I told you before, my darkness calls to yours."

I kiss him back. The water cools down my skin, but his touch heats it right back up. I wonder if this feeling will ever get old; how all-consuming it feels to be loved by such a powerful man, one that only laughs and smiles for me. Who loves my smart mouth and the way I push him to try new things. A part of me knows that even though we have eternity, a connection like this will never be stagnant.

Lucifer—the Devil—is my soulmate, and I don't care what anyone thinks about that. I don't care if it makes me evil or a monster. Something this pure and cosmic could never be wrong.

Our lips part, and he looks at me softly. "What else are we supposed to do on this honeymoon?"

"Eat delicious food, drink wine, dance, swim, relax, whatever we want."

"What about tying you up to the bedframe and making you come so many times that you beg me to stop."

My breath hitches, and I nod. "Yeah, we can do that."

"Perhaps later," he says with that smirk on his lips.

I splash his chest, letting go of my hold on him as I swim away. He starts swimming after me, and I shriek as I try to swim as fast as possible. With him being so much taller, he catches me quickly. His long arms wrap around my stomach as he kisses the side of my head.

"What does my little Hellfire want?"

"Just this," I say, squeezing his arms. This is truly all I want, and for the first time since I can remember, I feel truly happy. I'm finally my true self, and not only that, I'm loved by a man who accepts and loves me for who exactly I am. The path here wasn't easy and was covered in bloodshed, but I'm finally who I'm supposed to be, and I'm with the man who was always meant to be mine. A man who would burn the universe for me, as I would for him.

It might have taken dying and losing everything I thought mattered to me to get this perspective, but I'm happy for it.

"I think I'm ready to tie you up now."

"Oh, are you now?" I reply, like I'm not totally excited to be tied up.

"Be my good girl, and I won't make you wait for your first orgasm."

"How chivalrous."

"I thought so," he jokes back, and I spin in his arms, cupping his face, kissing his lips as he carries me out of the water and drops my wet body on the bed. "Fuck, you're beautiful."

His kisses trail up my leg, and I can't help the shiver that overtakes me. His shadows come out to play as he ties my wrists, and the rest of me, to the bed.

"Are you going to be good?" he asks.

I smile with a nod. "Yes, sir."

He groans and does as he promises, worshiping me like the good lord intended.

A LOOK AT CHARMING AS HELL

Toth is preoccupied in the banquet area with some demon that has an issue, and it finally gives me an opportunity to leave the manor. Not that I don't enjoy Toth's company, the hot-as-hell demon just won't give in to any of my advances. I know for a fact that he's holding back, I feel how hard his dick is every time we spar. He's totally and completely into me, which he should be. My corporeal body is pretty. Insanely hot, actually. I couldn't be more pleased with the turn of events.

There are a few things that are bothering me, though. I'm not sure how I can tell, but I know my father is lying about Beelzebub, and I'm ready to get to the bottom of it. Plus, I'm so fucking bored of being cooped up in this house. I need an adventure.

Toth has been teaching me how to portal... at least, that's what he thinks. I've been portalling for years when I didn't even have a physical form. The only issue is I don't know my way around Hell. I can visualize the front gates, at least. I can see those from the window in my bedroom.

I portal to just outside of the gates and start walking, portalling as far as my eyes can see. It takes me a while until I reach the city. Toth and Lilith gave me a run down about souls and blah, blah, blah. This town is boring, and all these 'people' look creepy as fuck. I want the good stuff.

It takes more walking than I would like, but I'm finally on the outskirts of where the souls live, and I see the massive, creepy-as-fuck building in front of me.

Bingo.

My boots hit the pavement as I walk right into the pit of Hell and begin exploring the halls. It's very sketchy here, in the best way. Blood splatter is found on some patches of the walls and the floor. There are a plethora of weapons in each room that I poke my head in while others are filled with lifeless bodies. I can't help but be drawn deeper and deeper into the pit. It's like something or someone is beckoning me, and my confident steps take me down some stairs. The temperature gets hotter the further down I go, and the lights dimmer. I can see my hand in front of my face, but that's all. There's a flicker of a light about ten feet ahead, and when I take another step, I hear a deep, delicious voice.

"You don't belong here, little princess."

"I think I do," I say into the void with complete confidence.

"Leave," he grunts.

"Mmm... I think not."

There's loud, heavy footsteps that come closer and closer to me. When the owner of the voice reaches me, I have to tilt my head all the way back to see him. His strong body is smeared with blood, and his masculine face is handsome in a brutal way. His white-blond hair is in a bun and speckled with blood.

"You shouldn't be here, princess," he reiterates, and his dark, deep voice does something to me. Something similar to the way Toth cutely tries to boss me around. But this one... he's deadly, and I like it.

"I've got a better idea," I suggest, putting a finger on his rock-hard abdomen.

"I'm going to run through these halls. If you catch me I'll do what you say."

He grunts, and I think he's going to tell me to fuck off, but the only thing he says in his deep timbre is. "Run then, little princess."

A wild giggle escapes me as I start running down the halls. It doesn't take long to hear footfalls behind me.

Hell just got ten times more fun.

ALSO BY

Pucked Up Omegaverse

One Pucked Up Pack
Coming soon:

Don't Puck With My Heart
Why Choose Omegaverse Hockey Romance coming Summer 2023
Piper was supposed to become a surgeon, not fall in love with an Omega with a bad heart.

Heat Haven Universe

Heat Haven

Omega's Obsession

Protector's Promise

Too Tempting

Heat Haven Holidays

Want to take a walk on the paranormal side?

Charming Your Dad

Charming the Devil

Charming As Hell coming October 2023
"Hell just got a hell of a lot more fun."

ACKNOWLEDGMENTS

Nikki - Thank you for beta reading and letting me pick your brain multiple times on this book.

Leisha – Thank you for loving these characters and your constant feedback.

Jessica- My editor, it was so fun to work with you on this book. You really helped me take it to the next level.

Lindsay- Thanks for hopping in and your feedback on this story. You've been amazing to me and I appreciate you so much.

Sandra- Thank you for all the love on this book and for assuring me that it was the right direction!

Stephanie – You always help me with any last-minute fixes and I appreciate you so much!

Laura – Thank you for jumping in last minute for formatting.

Content Creators – To anyone who posts an image, a comment, or a video about any of my books just know I absolutely adore you. The work that goes into creating content is one of passion and it really warms my heart that you liked my book enough to post about it. Thank you for your hard work and effort.

About the Author

Sarah Blue writes contemporary sweet omegaverse, erotic, why choose romances. She loves romance in nearly any genre. When she isn't writing you can find her nose buried in a book or lit up from her kindle. She loves the sweeter side of romance and creating interesting characters while adding adventure and spice. Writing strong female characters and male characters willing to show weakness is something that makes her gooey on the inside.

Sarah lives in Maryland with her husband, two sons, and two annoying cats. If she isn't reading or writing she is probably working on a craft project or scrolling on Tik Tok.

For more information visit authorsarahblue.com